I0685470

NO SMOKE
WITHOUT FIRE

by
Robert Coulsdon

Front cover photo by Anita Morton

Copyright © Robert Coulsdon 2022

First Edition. Published by Robert Coulsdon 2022

This is a work of fiction. Names, characters, places
and incidents are either the product of the author's
imagination or are used fictitiously. Any resemblance
to actual events or locales or persons, living or dead, is
entirely coincidental.

Robert Coulsdon asserts his right to be identified as the
author of this work under the Copyright, Designs and
Patents Act 1988.

All rights reserved. No part of this publication may be
reproduced, stored in a retrieval system or transmitted,
in any form or by any means, without the prior consent
of the author, nor be otherwise circulated in any form
of binding or cover other than that with which it is
published and without a similar condition being imposed
on the subsequent purchaser.

ISBN: 978-1-7391727-1-8 Paperback
ISBN: 978-1-7391727-3-2 eBook

Printed using paper from sustainable managed forests
by Printed Word Publishing
www.printedwordpublishing.com

To Wendy, for her patience, advice and encouragement.

Acknowledgments

I would like to thank Anita Morton, a talented photographer and friend, for allowing me to use one of her excellent photos for the front cover, and Wendy, my wife, who helped to proof-read and edit the manuscript.

About Jonah

So, how did Jonah come to wander his way into this second story?

Again, he just happened to be there, although on this occasion he's a more passive player, there in the background, rather than taking a central role. But in one important way, he's more than that. He has no family, no money (except for the money he begs on the street), no home, nothing most of us take for granted. But he does have a friend, his booze. And that gives him a reason for living at the same time as it's killing him.

Any of us who live in a city or larger town have met Jonah, or avoided him, as he stumbles along the pavement. He'll usually have a few days stubble, making you wonder why he shaves some days instead of growing a beard? But that's not the type of question Jonah wastes time on, he's a man with a mission, to get enough money for the next drink and, if he's lucky, for a night in a hostel.

He's grateful, when someone gives him money, afraid of being beaten-up much of the time, and always alone, even when he's with the other street people with whom he hangs out. He has vague memories of a better, earlier life, and sometimes he feels tears welling-up as the images appear and he recalls what he's lost.

The problem is that passers-by see only the outstretched hand and shabby clothes, they don't see Jonah. And that's a pity, Jonah deserves to be seen, even if he doesn't usually choose to reveal much about himself, other than his addiction. Get to know him and he'll tell you more. I'm glad he wandered into the story – otherwise it may never have been written.

1

The mistake, looking back, had been to believe in being happy. Everything was temporary and, ultimately, meaningless.

People blooming like flowers and dying, and being replaced by new people, who bloomed and died in their turn. People who remained said kind things, then looked at their watches and found they had to go.

And, like people, emotions flowered and died. Elating and then draining, promising new opportunities and then denying them. He stood there, still for a moment, shaking his head and feeling the tears welling-up inside him.

He was too tired to start again, shut his eyes and kicked the steps beneath him away.

2

"Oh, God," Sam reached out to turn off the alarm. "Another bloody day squeezing behind pipes and water cylinders." He pushed back the duvet, staggered slightly as he swung his legs out of bed and stood up, and then reached for his bathrobe on the back of the door. The arm was twisted, and he struggled to put it on.

"Do you have to make such a row?" Ros pulled the duvet back around her.

"Sorry, time to get out of bed, the world awaits you." He drew back the curtains, allowing the light in.

"The world can wait a little longer." She turned onto her back, her arm over her face shielding her eyes, her blonde hair strewn across the pillow. "Put the kettle on, my mouth's parched, I could kill for a cup of tea."

Sam opened the bedroom door and climbed down the narrow stairs of the old, terraced house, leaning on the bannister for support. He turned through the small dining room into the kitchen, filled the kettle and placed the mugs on the counter. And then, out of habit, he switched-on the TV to listen to the News. It was the usual story, arguments about government spending, political spats and a war somewhere he needed an atlas to find.

"Don't know why you listen to that every morning," Ros ran her fingers through her hair, trying to tidy it as she walked into the kitchen, "It's all about things we can't do anything about."

"God, you've woken-up in a happy mood," Sam poured the tea and passed her a mug, then took a sip from his own. "That's hot," he shook his head, "Maybe there'll be something interesting on the local news."

> *"A man's body has been found in Lark Avenue.' A woman reporter was pointing at a house in the road behind her. "The man, described as middle-aged, is believed to have been dead for several days. Police have named him as John Morrison and are not treating the circumstances as suspicious."*

Ros put her mug down and pointed at the tv screen, "Did she say John Morrison?"

Sam shook his head, "Sorry, I wasn't listening that closely, just heard a guy was found dead."

"Where's the remote," Ros found it on the counter and turned the volume up in time to hear the reporter begin an interview with another woman who she described as one of the dead man's neighbours.

"I understand you became suspicious after being asked to accept a parcel on Mr. Morrison's behalf."

"I thought she said Morrison, it must be John they've found." Ros looked shocked. "Poor John, he worked in our sales team until a few months ago, he was one of the guys they made redundant."

"Yes, we hadn't seen him for several days and, when we looked, his curtains were closed. It didn't feel right, so we tried knocking on the door, but there was no answer."

"What did you do then?"

"Well, we couldn't see through the windows, so we pushed the letterbox open and shouted through that. That was when we realised something was wrong. So, we called the police and they found him hanging from the loft hatch. He'd had a tough time recently. His wife and daughter were killed in an accident, and then he lost his job a couple of months later."

"That must have been tough," the reporter nodded, agreeing with the woman, "Where did he work, before he was made redundant?"

"I think he was a salesman for a local textile company, or something, down on the Saddle Hill Industrial Estate."

The reporter thanked the woman as she signed-off and returned the audience to the studio.

3

"That's awful, he was such a terrific guy," Ros started crying and grabbed a tissue from a nearby box. "It hit him hard when his wife and daughter were killed, but we thought he was beginning to come to terms with it all. He came back in the office recently to see Alison and me and seemed much more like his old self. He took Alison out to lunch afterwards."

"Poor sod," Sam said, "Fancy dying alone like that. Why do you think he did it?"

"I don't know, I guess he just couldn't face the future," Ros blew her nose, then picked-up her mug again. "Losing your family like that, it must have seemed like the whole of his life had been destroyed in one awful moment."

Sam walked over and put his arm round her "Come on, you need to get ready to go into work and you can't do that if you're eyes are all red and puffy."

Ros shook her head as she turned away from the tv, "I need to call Alison first." She wiped her eyes again, "She's known John for years, she'll be devastated. And Jack, poor Jack, he was the one who had to tell John he was redundant, he's bound to feel guilty when he hears about it."

3

Jack put his cup of coffee down on his desk and was checking his calendar for the day when the 'phone rang.

"Morning, Jack," he recognised the MD's voice. "Did you see the local news on TV before you left home?"

"Morning, Roger. No, why? What's happened?"

"I'll brief you when we meet-up. There may be a local issue we need to deal with. I've asked Geoff and Max to come to my office in twenty minutes. Need you to do the same. Cancel anything else you have in your diary."

Twenty minutes later Jack found the other managers sitting round Roger's office table and nodded to them as he sat down.

"Right," Roger walked over from his desk opened his notebook, drew a line across the previous notes and dated the entry. "We might be picking up some flak from the media and we need to get our story together. Geoff," he turned to the HR Director, "That last round of redundancies, how many people did we let go?"

"Around a dozen, overall. Mainly in the Marketing and the Sales areas," he looked down at his notes, "We let some admin people go as well."

"Did we look into any of their individual circumstances before we reached a final decision?"

"No," Geoff shook his head, "The decisions were based on their performances. We don't really know about personal circumstances, and if we tried to take them into account people could claim we were biased."

"So, how did we decide on who to let go from the Sales area, Jack?"

"We did a rationalisation exercise on existing sales areas, reduced them and then let the poorest performers go. Why, has someone made a complaint?"

"No, it's worse than that, a lot worse," Roger paused for effect, "What can you tell me about a guy called Jim Morrison?"

"Jim Morrison was a musician," Max, the PR Director, interrupted before Jack could answer, "Sang with a group called The Doors. But what's he got to do with us Roger?"

"Very witty, Max," Roger shook his head, "Just the sort of superficial crap we might expect from PR."

"His name was John Morrison," Jack smiled, amused by Max's interruption. "He'd been with us nearly thirty years, but he was past his best. It was a simple choice between him and the younger guy on the adjoining patch."

"Did we know about the deaths of his wife and daughter?"

"Yes, he needed compassionate leave to make the arrangements for the funeral," Jack indicated the HR

Director, "Geoff and I discussed whether we should take it into account, but decided we had to follow the agreed process to be seen to be fair to everyone."

"What about Morrison's mental state? Did we know anything about that?"

"Well, obviously the deaths struck him pretty hard," Jack paused, "But as far as I know he was handling things ok."

"Well, he clearly wasn't because he's topped himself," Roger sat back in his chair and stared at Jack, "And the local TV News includes a mention of him losing his job shortly after his family was killed.".

"That's not going to do much for our reputation if our name comes out." Max looked up from the pad he was doodling on.

"Well, that's why we've got you here, Max, to limit the damage, make us look more caring than we might otherwise appear."

"What did he do? Take pills or what?"

"Does it really matter how he did it, Max?" Roger threw his pen down on the table, "It's the fact he did it after being made bloody redundant that makes it likely the media are going to have a field day with us. But, in case you think how he did it is important, he hanged himself."

"We did treat everyone the same and we were more generous than we were required to be." Jack turned to Geoff for support.

"Jack's right," Geoff nodded, "Although it's true that Morrison was the oldest to go and his recent sales record and age would have made it more difficult for him to find another comparable job. We did offer to send him on a course to help him with job interviews – we did as much as we could with all the guys we let go."

"Still sounds like we kicked a guy when he was down." Max shook his head, "It's not a great story."

"We're a bloody company, for Christ's sake. If we don't take care of the business, everyone employed here loses." Roger picked his pen up again and pointed round the table. "And that includes us, besides all the guys outside."

"Look, we'll spin it as well as we can," Max finished shading-in a new doodle he'd been playing with on his notepad, "But we need to recognise the media is likely to have an agenda and, if so, it's going to be difficult to divert them."

"That's why we employ you, Max," Roger leaned forward, "It's bloody easy for the media to sit there and criticise, but the fact is, we never promised to employ people for life – none of us round this table have that bloody luxury."

"I hear what you say, Roger, but it's not an argument that's going to win us a lot of friends."

"What about saying nothing and avoid giving the media anything to feed on?" Jack asked.

"'No comment', isn't a great option in these circumstances, Jack," Max started to doodle again, "The public can read a lot into 'no-one was available for comment', it's almost like an admittance of guilt."

"Look, why don't we just say we were very sad to hear about Morrison's death, but the redundancies were necessary for the continued well-being of the company and to protect jobs in an increasingly competitive market?" Roger looked round the table for a response.

"And we can say that we wouldn't have fulfilled our legal obligations, if we hadn't treated everyone equally," Geoff added.

"With respect," Max put his pen down, "People aren't interested in any of that, they just enjoy poking the moral finger."

"What would they have done," Roger was feeling increasingly irritated. "Damage the whole company for one man?"

"That's the beauty of being a member of the media or public, Roger, you can take a view or make a comment without any responsibility or comeback. What was Morrison like as a person, Jack?"

"Quite charismatic when I first met him but seemed distracted as the years went on. I got to know him quite well at one time – we used to play snooker together each week." Jack shook his head as he remembered. "But then he seemed to lose interest in snooker, and we became less close."

Roger closed his note folder, indicating the meeting was finished, "Maybe we should just say we don't feel it's appropriate to comment on an individual employee in such tragic circumstances. Get something on my desk in the next hour or so, please, Max. We need to be ready if the media come calling."

"I think that's 'when' rather than 'if' they come calling," Max said as he got up to leave.

4

The pub was noisy when Sam arrived, crowded with people enjoying a drink after work. He looked round for Mike and saw him sitting at the end of the bar. He was wearing the usual smartly pressed suit, but with his tie pulled loose and a pint in his hand he looked relaxed. Sam made his way across, pulling out the stool Mike had saved for him.

"Hi, glad you could make it," Mike stood up and caught the barman's attention, "Usual?"

"Thanks," Sam nodded, "I've spent the whole day replacing someone's boiler, I could really do with this." He held up the glass, and savoured the first mouthful, "Cheers, that tastes good! So, how's things with you and my favourite would-be entrepreneur?"

"Well, I'm feeling a lot better now I'm sitting in front of a bar instead of a potential customer. And Gill's ok, still trying to get new clients and come up with new ideas for corporate events – it's hard when it's your own business. Sends her regards – I told her we were having a drink after work. How's Ros?"

"Ros is fine, but she had a bit of a shock this morning, a guy she worked with, used to be a rep in their sales team, committed suicide. It's upset her and a lot of the other staff apparently. She called me before we met-up."

"You're talking about the guy whose wife and daughter were killed in a crash a few months back; I saw it on the news." Mike shook his head, "I'm surprised the company didn't make a special case and keep him on for a while, the routine and interaction at work would have been important to him after they died."

"According to Ros some of the staff are saying it's almost like corporate manslaughter." Sam nodded at Mike's empty glass, "Do you want another one?"

Mike nodded, finished his lager and put the glass down. "I wonder how the bloke who fired the guy feels?"

"Ros says he's a nice guy, but you know how it is." Sam ordered more drinks "Someone says 'we've got to save money' and everyone goes away and comes up with a plan. Everyone hides behind everyone else – it's never one person who's responsible."

Mike shook his head and took another gulp of his beer, "It's scary. When that bastard sacked me twelve months back, after I fell out with his mistress, I realised how easy it is to end up on the street – and how impossible it might be to find my way back."

"What, like our friend Jonah," Sam had a sudden flashback to a ragged figure in a charcoal-coloured overcoat, carrying his red vinyl bag with cans of strong cider as he staggered along." Haven't seen him around recently. Wonder if he's still with us."

"God, people like him always make me think what a tragedy their lives represent. Mum has new baby, parents full of hope and then it all goes sour – be interesting to know what Jonah's story is one day."

5

Jack parked his car in the drive and walked across to the front door. He turned his key in the lock and called out he was home as he stepped inside.

"You're late," Charlotte looked up as he came into the lounge.

"Sorry, it's been a bit of a nightmare day; John Morrison's suicide has hyped Roger up. He's worried it might get in the national news and affect the firm's reputation."

"Do you think it will?"

"No, I don't think so. Max has been working on it and whilst he behaves like a bit of an idiot sometimes, he's good at pouring PR oil on potentially troubled waters." He turned to leave the room, "I'm going to get some wine, do you want a glass?"

"Some white please," She heard the clink of the glasses on the kitchen counter, the rattle of the bottles in the door as the fridge was opened and then a second rattle and the thud of the door as it closed again. "And don't be too long, the local news is coming-up on the TV."

He walked back into the lounge, handed her a glass, and sat down in his usual chair.

> 'More news now about the death of local man John Morrison, who took his own life after being made redundant. Our reporter is with Max Gregory, Communications Director at Mr. Morrison's former employers.

"This seems to have been an avoidable death, doesn't it? Mr. Morrison's wife and daughter were killed in a road accident recently. Why didn't you take his bereavement into account when you made him redundant? You must have recognised the potential impact on him?" The reporter held the microphone out for Max to talk.

"As you'll appreciate, we're not in a position to comment on individual situations but, sometimes, companies have to take difficult decisions, to remain competitive and protect the jobs of all their employees." Max paused to emphasise the point. *"And in any redundancy programme we must treat everyone fairly. If we don't, it just shifts the impact from one person or family onto another."*

"Surely, though, the special circumstances of this situation should have made the company re-think its programme, it needn't have meant selecting someone else for redundancy, just making one less person redundant."

"But that wouldn't have achieved the savings the company needed." There was another, practiced pause, before Max continued. *"And, whilst we regret Mr. Morrison's death, it couldn't have been foreseen and may not have been due to his redundancy."*

"Well, how do you think he did?" Jack turned to his wife.

"It all sounded a bit 'corporate', and a lot of people are still going to feel the company acted coldly. But memories are short, most people will have forgotten about it in a few days. It must have hit John hard though."

"Well, that's what you might think, but it wasn't quite like that. I said I was sorry his redundancy came such a short time after the death of his family, but he told me not to worry. I got the impression he thought it would give him the opportunity to do something new; he'd been with us a long time and his payout was particularly good."

"Maybe he was just putting a good face on it," Charlotte shook her head, "We all get sad from time-to-time, but most of us know we'll feel better later on. Sometimes, though, a person can't see things getting any better, they just see things going on down and down, and can't bear it any longer."

Jack nodded. "By the way, it's very quiet, where are the lads tonight?"

"Oh, they're up in their rooms; I think they were a bit worried about how you'd be when you got home. Some of the Mums were talking about the suicide outside the school gates, and most of them felt the company should have been more sympathetic. The boys know you work there, and it was difficult for them to hear what people were saying."

"That's bad, they shouldn't be involved in something like this." He got up from his chair. "I'll pop-up and see them."

6

Roger opened his office cupboard, pulled out a bottle and poured himself a whisky. He walked over to the window and stood looking down at the world below. It was one of the advantages of being top man, having a large office on a higher floor, with panoramic views over the town and surrounding green hills. It provided a sense of serenity when he needed to think strategically about the business. He could close the office door, look out over everything around him, and detach himself from the ordinary day-to-day decisions.

Still, it was dangerous to take his eye off the ball. The guy that had hung himself was receiving too much media coverage for comfort. Jack and Geoff had admitted knowing about the guy's wife and daughter being killed and it wouldn't have taken much imagination to anticipate the possible consequences if they made him redundant. They could still have fired the guy, but maybe delayed him leaving – given him some contract work for a few months. The guy may not have topped himself then. He made a mental note to take a closer look at the members of his team over the coming months – maybe he needed to consider some changes?

The light was beginning to fade. He checked his watch. The early evening news would be on in a minute or two and Max was being interviewed. He turned on his office TV and watched the interview; Max pissed him off a lot of the time, but he handled the media well, did an ok job. It was followed by an interview with the local MP. The guy was a pain in the arse and Roger was going to have to endure a dinner with him and listen to him droning on about politics and asking for donations, but at least he'd repeated what Max had said about the firm being a major local employer and the business needing to thrive if the remaining jobs were to be protected.

He turned-off the tv, took a last look at his computer screen and opened the latest sales figures. Despite being slimmed down the sales team was doing well. Satisfied, he switched the screen off, put his empty glass on the corner of his desk for the cleaner to clear, took one last look around the office and turned-off the light.

7

The car slowed as it approached the house, the driver pulling-in to park opposite for a brief look. The front door had been boarded over, where the police had broken in to recover the body the neighbours had found. The house, which had once been a home, looked as empty as she felt, sitting still, staring at it. A dead, cold building, devoid of the lives that had once filled it; bustling, arguing, working lives. And now, nothing, just a shell, waiting for the next people to bring it back to life, to energise it, change it, and, hopefully, be happier than its former occupants.

She caught sight of someone walking along the pavement and bowed her head as they passed the gate, closed now, with no one needing to use it. She'd never been inside, knew nothing about how the rooms looked, the way it was furnished and decorated, and was tempted to walk across and peer in through the window. But she didn't want to be seen, or, even worse, accused of being some sort of macabre voyeur by neighbours who wouldn't understand why she was there. She put the car into gear, checked it was clear to pull away and drove off – feeling a sense of guilt for what had happened and wishing she hadn't come.

8

Sam had got home in time to catch the evening news, and after he'd listened to Max, he turned off the tv and went into the dining room to set out the placings for dinner. "A man dies, and they can't discuss individual cases." He called out to Ros as she carried their meals in from the kitchen. "Actually, that's the issue, if they'd treated him like an individual the guy might not have died. And I'm not sure whether that guy in your PR department should be ashamed of himself for selling his integrity or proud because he did such a smooth job."

"Max? He's only doing what he's paid to do. Roger Grimshaw's a hard man, not someone you'd want to cross." Ros put their plates on the table and sat down. "And how do you know John wouldn't have committed suicide anyway, even if he'd kept his job? He changed after his wife and daughter died. I know I said he'd seemed better the last time I saw him, but Alison, who knew him best at work, said he'd still been having mood swings, euphoric one time and withdrawn another."

"So, do you think the managers, directors, or whoever else was involved, are able to go home at night with clear consciences?"

"I'm sure that Jack Docherty will be feeling bad about what happened – but less sure about Grimshaw, I don't think he cares about anyone except himself. And Geoff, the HR guy, is just a Grimshaw puppet, he'll say and do anything Grimshaw wants him to." Ros stopped eating and pointed with her fork at Sam's plate, "Come on, eat your dinner, I put a lot of effort into preparing and cooking it whilst you and Mike were out enjoying yourselves at the pub."

9

Jonah sat drinking a coffee in the breakfast kitchen, enjoying being able to sit safely indoors, instead of being out on the streets where he couldn't relax. He'd eaten his breakfast, the plate was still on the table in front of him, and he was ready for a drink, but, this morning, he fancied staying a little longer.

"Come on, mate, time to move out." One of the volunteers was cleaning the tables and picked-up Jonah's dirty plate. "Sorry, but we've finished serving breakfast and need to start getting the place clean and ready for the next meal."

"Still not finished me drink," Jonah said.

"Five more minutes then," the man smiled and took Jonah's plate across to the trolley, to take to the kitchen. "But then you have to go. Your mates all left earlier; time to join them."

Jonah finished the coffee and placed the mug back on the table. He put on his charcoal-coloured coat and fastened it with some string tied around his waist, then he collected his red vinyl bag with his cans of extra strong cider from the reception area and raised his arm in a 'goodbye' gesture as he walked out the door.

"Poor old sod," one of the volunteers said as the door closed behind him, "Been living rough for a long time now. Must be hard."

"He's not going to change; it's gone too far." The other volunteer stared after Jonah as he locked the door. "I'm not sure he's got anyone left, except Mary and the others, and they're just like him. Such a waste."

"Makes you wonder what keeps him going, what makes his life worth living?"

"The booze, I guess. He stays alive because he enjoys his addiction – even if it's killing him."

"Such a fucking waste of a life. "The first volunteer shook his head as he turned away.

10

Richie was outraged by the inhumanity and unfairness of what he'd heard on the tv news. His voice was raised, and he jumped up from his chair and brought his fist down hard on the small table in Jim's living room.

"Capitalist bastards." The bottles on the table rocked as he hit the surface. "They get away with fucking murder. They should be taken outside and bloody shot."

"Calm down," Jim picked his bottle up in case Richie smashed his fist down again, "I'd rather drink my beer than wipe it up with a bloody towel. Anyway, nothing's going to happen until people understand enough about the benefits of a socialist society to vote for one."

"It's all the fucking capitalist propaganda they get thrown at them. It's incessant, all the ads urging them to aspire to fucking brands to give them a sense of self-worth. They won't need to compete to feel their worth once we get a fair wage system and an effective state schooling with equal opportunity. We won't have this fucking great divide we've got now between the rich bastards who steal all the wealth and the working class who create it."

"And we won't have guys going round killing themselves because they've been thrown out of their jobs when they've just lost their bloody family." Jim nodded in agreement with what Richie was saying.

"Too right, we've got to keep fighting," Richie raised his fist in a salute to brotherhood, "One day my friend, one day."

"But maybe this guy's suicide gives us another opportunity to get our message out there." Jim paused, "It could give us a bit of a platform, some real publicity. Maybe we could tip off our contact in the local tv news team, let them know something interesting's going to take place, get the tv cameras there."

"Get the message round and organise a bit of a demo, you mean."

"Exactly. We can organise some banners: 'Capitalism Kills', 'People not Profit', 'Martyred for Money', 'Shame on you'. You know the normal type of thing." Jim tossed the last of his beer back, took two more bottles out of the fridge and gave one to Richie. "And we could block the gates in the morning, stop cars or deliveries going in."

"Won't be long before the pigs start trying to move us away. Cheers," Richie raised his bottle.

"Then we'll just have to try to keep it peaceful, mate. Claim the right to peaceful protest. Better start ringing round, put something up on social media. We need to seize the moment, before it fades from the news."

11

When Roger drove towards the company gates the following morning, he was confronted by a crowd of people blocking the road. A TV crew was filming them as they walked backwards and forwards shouting slogans, and the fence was plastered with banners about capitalism putting profits before people. The security guard stood inside, ready to stop anyone who might try to get in but unable to clear the entrance.

Roger put his hand hard on the horn, kept it there and edged forward. The demonstrators retreated until they were trapped between the gate and his car, and he couldn't edge forward any further. "Where are the fucking police when you need them?" he shouted, banging his hands on the steering wheel in frustration before reaching for his phone and calling the local station. "Grimshaw, Roger Grimshaw, I'm the MD of Middlefield Textiles on Factory Lane and I'm being prevented from entering my property by some loony left agitators. There's twenty or thirty of them and they're blocking the public highway and stopping me and my work force entering the premises – I want a police presence immediately to clear them and give me and my employees access."

"We'll get a squad car there as soon as possible," the person at the other end of the line said.

"This isn't good enough; we pay our taxes, and we expect to be able to go about our lawful business without some lunatic demonstrators preventing us. We need someone to clear these idiots away."

Someone wearing a mask tapped on his window, but Roger ignored them and sat staring ahead. Someone motioned him to turn the window down, so they could talk and, when he didn't the first egg hit his window and then more eggs hit the windscreen and the other windows. He called the police again and reported what was happening and asked when he could expect the gate to be cleared.

"We've got a car on its way now," the call handler said, "Should be with you in about ten minutes."

Roger stayed sitting there, his doors and windows locked, and called Max. "Hi, Max, we've got a bloody demo outside our premises, I can't even get into the office. And there's a TV crew here. For God's sake call your contacts and make sure they're covering this from our point of view. This is insane."

"I'll get on to it right away, Roger, but I can't promise they'll cover it as we'd like them to."

Other cars began to queue up behind Roger's and he heard people shouting. Looking in his mirror he saw that some of his employees had got out of their cars and were remonstrating with the demonstrators. More eggs started flying and suddenly there were scuffles. Infuriated by his inability to move, he jumped out of his car and shouted at the people standing in front of the gate. "Move or I'll cut your bloody legs off."

"You wouldn't dare, that's illegal," one of them shouted back.

"So's stopping us going into work and obstructing the fucking highway," he shouted back. "And I fucking mean it, you've been fucking warned," he stabbed his fingers at the demonstrators, "Open the bloody gate," he shouted at the security guard, "We're coming through."

The security guard did as he was told and Roger got back in his car, started the engine, revved-up hard and moved forward. With nothing now blocking the roadway the demonstrators parted and Roger drove in, followed by the cars that had begun to form a queue behind him. The demonstrators didn't follow, and other cars started to arrive, greeted by a new hail of eggs and screams of 'shame'.

Roger stood and watched grimly as he waited for the promised squad car. When it arrived, the officers got out and asked for the organisers of the protest. There appeared to be two, one with distinctive red hair, and the other taller, but with less identifiable features. Roger guessed that both men were in their twenties and could see them and the police talking and nodding together. After a few minutes they seemed to have reached an agreement and the police walked into the car park and approached Roger.

"Are you one of the managers here?" the first policeman asked.

"I'm the bloody MD," Roger said, "And I want these idiots away from my gates."

"I appreciate your concern," the officer said, "But it's not quite as simple as that. These people do have a right to protest peacefully."

"So, throwing eggs at vehicles and starting scuffles with people who are trying to go to work are peaceful are they? And what about covering our fence with their ridiculous banners? I want them down and the demonstrators dispersed."

"Well, as my colleague has told you," the second officer took over, "There is a right to peaceful protest and we have gained assurances that no more eggs will be thrown, there'll be no more prevention of access to your premises and the demonstration will remain peaceful from here on. If those assurances are observed, we can't really move the demonstrators on."

"What about the bloody banners tied to our fence? I want those removed or I'll bloody take them down myself. They've put them there for the bloody TV film crews."

"We'll talk to the leaders about that," the first officer pointed to the crowd, "But we would advise against any precipitate action on your part, Sir, it will only be seen as provocative."

"What, and standing outside my premises, shouting and hanging up slogans on my fence isn't?"

"I appreciate you're angry, Sir, but we're just trying to minimise any tension."

The first officer walked away and approached the two men he had spoken to previously. He pointed at the banners tied to the fence and Roger saw them shake their heads. The second officer walked across to support his colleague, but there still appeared to be no agreement.

Roger pointed at one of the banners and shouted at the security guard to take it off the fence. The guard hesitated. "If you value your job, take that banner down now – you can do it without going outside. Oh, for God's sake man, I'll do it with you." He walked across and they started to take the banner down.

A cry from one of the protesters alerted others in the group and they rushed to put the banner back up, hitting the fence and trying to force Roger and the security guard to back off. The TV crew, alerted by the disturbance pushed through to get pictures of the tussle.

"Right, let's put a stop to this now," the first officer shouted pointing at the protesters, "You, move away. And you too, please sir, you're only provoking them."

"Fascist pigs!" The cry came from the back of the group and started other cries. The crowd pressed forward again, pushing the officers back. The TV crew, spotting an opportunity for more footage, got into position and started filming.

"Right, if you don't move away, we're calling for back-up." The officer was shouting now. More cars were arriving and trying to get into the premises, and a lorry with a delivery backed the traffic up further. Some of the protestors ran over and tried to speak to the driver, but he remained in his cab, avoiding eye contact. A protester jumped onto the running board and banged on the window, but the driver ignored him, still staring ahead.

Other cars and vans were trying to drive down the street and found their way blocked by the traffic; and arguments started with individual protesters. A siren could be heard a street away, but the police van couldn't get through. The officers arrived on foot and started to push the protesters away from the gate.

With more support the original officers approached Richie and Jim again. "Look, back off, take your banners off the fence, you've got other banners here you can carry about to make your point. And make sure things stay peaceful, then you can stay and protest. Otherwise, I'm afraid we're going to have to start arresting people."

"What you going to bloody arrest them for?" The red-haired man was fired-up now and wanting to take the police on.

"Back-off, mate. Calm down." Jim pushed Richie away. "Ok, Officer, my friend is just riled-up because of what these bastards did to that poor guy who committed suicide when they fired him." He grabbed his friend's arm and took him across to some of the other protesters. Then they moved everyone off the road and watched as the banners were taken down from the fence but continued to shout and hold individual banners up for the TV camera.

12

The protest had stayed peaceful when Max arrived, people in small groups on either side of the gates, holding-up placards and chanting slogans. The TV crew was still there and some of the police remained to ensure there was no repetition of the earlier violence. He parked his car and went inside, calling Roger when he got to his office to brief him.

"Ok, the downside is that the tv people don't seem that interested in our side of the story," Max started, "They said they'd be happy for us to make a statement or give a short interview down at the gate – but that would only spark more shouting and slogans. It would be chaotic; we couldn't exercise any control."

"What about interviewing me here?" Roger asked.

"It wouldn't make good TV," Max shrugged, "They want activity, noise, a bit of drama; they're not here to present a positive image of us, believe me. News has to be exciting nowadays, campaigning headlines, like the tabloids."

"So, what the hell happens from here?"

"Not a lot, I guess, unless something new stirs it all up again. But let's look on the positive side, a lot of viewers will dismiss the protests as agitators causing problems and costing the police money and resources. All we have to do is keep our heads and be seen to behave like good citizens – unlike them."

"But how long will it go on, Max? How long are we going to have to put up with this harassment?"

"Not long, I suspect," Max closed his note pad, ready to leave, "A few days, maybe and then they'll move onto the next cause. The guys who organise these things aren't stupid, they'll milk the situation to get the exposure they want, and then divert their resources elsewhere. Ok, some of the protesters will genuinely care about what happened to John Morrison, but for the organisers it's just a way of achieving their political objectives."

"A socialist state's never going to happen," Roger threw his pen down onto the table.

"Maybe, Roger, but they believe it will," Max stood up, pushed his chair back and, when Roger nodded, left the room.

13

A few days later, Jim was sitting in his flat enjoying a cup of coffee and a book about the reasons for the future failure of capitalism when he heard the front doorbell ring. He got up from the sofa marked the page and walked to the door. Looking through the peephole, he could see Richie standing there and opened the door to let him in.

"Well, the protest's still going strong outside that bastard's premises; I've been there for the past couple of hours."

"But nobody's listening anymore," Jim said, "It's all gone a bit stale – yesterday's news. I think we need to find a new platform for the cause."

They walked back into the living room.

"So, what've you got in mind?"

"I don't know," Jim shook his head, "There's nothing we can use. The local TV team's gone cold on the issue and the company aren't saying anything, just laying low."

"When's the guy's funeral?"

"No idea, but we'd have to be careful how we approach that – we don't want people thinking we're just taking advantage of the guy's death. It would make us look as bad as the bloody capitalists."

"You know what they say, Jim, 'the end justifies the means' and I've had an idea; what about a memorial demo outside the town hall? We can count on some of the Councillors coming out in support?"

"That's not a bad idea, we'll get some of the group together and plan things properly – you know, showing sympathy and respect in support of a brother. And we can tip-off the TV guys so they're ready to cover it. We need to find out when the funeral's planned for, I'll get onto it later."

14

Her eyes kept filling with tears. She wiped them away, but new tears appeared, a mixture of anguish and anger sweeping through her. She'd said she felt unwell, needed to go home. They'd offered to call her a taxi, but she said she was fit to drive and needed to collect her car from the car park, and she'd left immediately. Now she was out of the city and the traffic was lighter, making it easier to drive. Soon she'd be turning off into a narrower road that led to a small collection of houses, with a church and a pub that sat on opposite sides of a bridge over the river. Her previous visits had been undertaken for pleasure, but this time she was seeking solace.

She parked on a small area of gravel outside the church, grabbed her bag and locked her car; standing still for a moment and looking up at the tall church tower before starting to climb the few steps into the churchyard. Once inside, she hurried past the graves, intent on reaching the twin timber doors that led into the small porch with its notice board and parish messages. She lifted the heavy antique latch, pushed the door open and walked through, stepping into the church itself. The air felt cooler, and the space was huge and silent. She shut her eyes and breathed deeply, then opened her eyes again, turned into the nave and went into one of the old wooden pews, sitting down and staring up at the large stained-glass window behind the altar. The window pictured the ascension, with Christ rising into the heavens and his apostles below, looking up as he left them.

She looked around, taking-in the rest of the church in more detail; the choir stalls, the memorials on the walls and the ancient timber pulpit, used in previous times to deliver thunderous sermons with dire warnings about sin and its consequences, and instructions about how to lead a better life. She hadn't attended church since her teenage years, some thirty years previously, and no longer believed that God existed, looking down on her and her fellow beings and judging them on their actions. She'd gone to the church to think, away from the bustle of her normal life. To be on her own, apart from other people, particularly those closest to her – their presence disturbed her more than anyone's.

She wasn't sure how long she'd been sitting there before she heard the door latch being raised again and the church door opening. She turned to see who was entering and saw the priest. He looked across and smiled, acknowledging her presence but not intruding on whatever thoughts had brought her there. She watched as he tidied a small pile of leaflets, looked at the visitors' book to check if there were any new entries and then crossed himself as he faced the altar before disappearing into a small room in the base of the tower. Then, she got up and left, not wanting to be there when he came back into the church itself.

15

Roger picked his note folder up, carried it over to the large table he used for meetings and waited for the team to arrive. Max was the last in and closed the door behind him.

"OK, everyone. Well, thank God we've got rid of most of the protesters outside the gates, but now we've got another possible issue, and I've asked Geoff to brief us on developments in his area."

"Thanks, Roger," Geoff opened his file, "After the death of his wife and daughter, Morrison named a brother and a sister as his next of kin and they've been in touch and set a date for his funeral. Which raises the question of how we, as a company, respond? It places us in a difficult situation, caught between appearing cold and indifferent if we don't attend or insincere if we do."

"I wouldn't feel comfortable attending," Jack said, "Not because I think the firm is responsible for John's suicide, but because it was me that actually told him he was redundant."

"But you were his line manager," Geoff said, "And not going could be seen as an admittance of responsibility."

"To be honest, I think I'm the very last person who should attend on the company's behalf. I'm not sure any of the management team should go." Jack put his pen down on his notepad and sat back in his chair, shaking his head.

"What do you think, Max?" Roger looked across, "How do you think we should play things?"

"I think Jack's right when he says he shouldn't attend, it could be seen as provocative. And I don't think Geoff or I, should go either – a PR man is hardly an appropriate representative in the circumstances. But there will be some members of staff who'd like to show their respect for John, so we could circulate the time and date of the funeral and say anyone who wants to attend can do so. And we could ensure transport is provided to and from the funeral, to enhance the 'caring company' message."

Roger looked round at Jack and Geoff.

"I'd go along with that," Jack nodded in agreement.

Geoff paused before answering, hoping Roger would give his own reaction to the idea; but when it became apparent Roger was waiting for his opinion, decided on a compromise position. "I see where you're coming from, Max, but why provide transport as well as time off?"

"Well, it might cost us a bit more, but it's got a practical advantage, allowing us to control how long staff are away from their jobs. It's a 'win, win' solution as far as I can see. I think it's neat."

Roger nodded and Max smiled to himself as he left the meeting, pleased with both the idea itself and the knowledge he'd embarrassed Geoff.

16

"So, how was work today?" Gill asked.

"Same old, same old," Mike walked over and kissed her. "What about you?"

"About the same, I suppose. Got a text from Ros to say the funeral of that guy who committed suicide is taking place in a couple of weeks. Apparently, staff are being given time off to attend."

"Big deal," Mike shrugged his shoulders.

"For God's sake Mike, we've been through all this before; you can't be sure the guy committed suicide because of losing his job. And there isn't any suicide note – at least I haven't heard of one and neither had Ros when I spoke to her."

"I agree that's strange, because I thought people usually left something." Mike shook his head, "But it's obvious, isn't it? I mean, he didn't kill himself after his wife and daughter died, he killed himself after he was made redundant."

"A lot of things look obvious from one angle but very different if they're looked at from another one, Mike." She hesitated, then softened her voice as she continued. "And I can understand why you feel like you do, you've been paranoid about redundancy since it happened to you, but you found a way back."

"I've been afraid of ending up on the street ever since."

"Some people live on the street," Gill said, "Look at that alcoholic you and Sam go on about."

"Jonah," Mike smiled, "Bit of a coincidence; I saw him today, Sam and I were only talking about him when we went out for that drink and saying we hadn't seen him recently. And today, there he was, large as life, dancing in the street."

"Dancing? What like Fred Astaire?"

"No, not like Fred Astaire, more like a dancing bear. You couldn't make it up. There were two young women playing

Irish reels on violins, in that small area in front of those old gravestones opposite the shopping centre; they were really good and attracted quite a crowd. Jonah must have been sleeping on the bench under the tree behind them. Anyway, I saw him sit up and watch as the crowd were throwing money into the girl's instrument cases – they were collecting quite a bit. You could almost see Jonah having one of those lightbulb moments and realising how much booze he could buy if people started throwing a similar amount of money at him!

"So, he leaves his old grey coat on the bench, together with the bag he carries his booze in, and takes up a position in front of the girls. I think everyone was a bit bemused at first and then he starts doing a very poor imitation of an Irish step dance, you know tapping his feet and turning round with his arms above his head. Well, stumbling round, if I'm honest – he nearly spun over at one point, someone had to catch him to stop him falling! It turned into a bit of a party, people began to laugh and clap, and stamp their feet, encouraging him to keep going.

"But the drink has obviously impaired Jonah's athleticism, if he ever had any, and it wasn't long before he was finished. One bloke went up and gave him a fiver – looked like he was feeling sorry for the violinists and paying Jonah to move away and stop spoiling their pitch. And, when he walked round, holding out his hand afterwards, several other people gave him money. Unbelievable."

"What did he do then?"

"Well, he took the money, made one or two theatrical bows to his audience, then picked-up his coat and bag and staggered away. Actually, I reckon he did the women a favour, he'd attracted an even bigger crowd than before and some of them stayed and put money in the women's violin cases afterwards."

"I'd love to have been there."

"Well, looked at in one way, you didn't miss much; he wouldn't have won a talent show as a dancer – but as a comedy act it was inspired. Pure Jonah. Only he could have got away with it; it's that mischievous smile of his, I think, a bit like a naughty monkey! I wish I'd filmed it on my mobile, he's a real character."

"I wonder how he became an alcoholic?" Gill thought for a moment, "What his background is? There must be a story there somewhere."

17

After his dance debut. Jonah took the money he'd received and bought some more booze. He decided to go down to one of his favourite places, the riverbank. It was away from the town centre, over one of the several bridges across the river and, when he got there, he wandered along until he felt he was far enough away not to attract any attention. Sitting down beneath a willow, he folded his overcoat into a pillow and rolled-up the sleeves of his red-check shirt. He opened a can of strong cider and soon there were two empty cans thrown down by his feet.

Initially, the drink relaxed him. But as he drank more, he began to feel an increasingly pervasive panic that displaced any other mental pictures he tried to view. His innate dread of the winter ahead blanketed his mind, destroying his casual enjoyment of the warmth and stillness of the afternoon. He hated the winter with its dark, cold days, filled with depression and fit only to sleep through. Winter was a time of survival until the next summer when, God-willing, he would still be alive. Some friends would be gone, their places in the hostel queues taken by newer, younger bodies who pushed and shoved more vigorously.

Jonah smelt the air, anxious to enjoy it to the full. It was subtly scented after the gross summer perfumes, and delicately dry now the oppressive humidity had gone. But he could not enjoy it for long; the winter haunted him. The warm afternoon and gentle ampleness of the grassy bank no longer existed. He looked inwardly and felt the loneliness welling up from his stomach, until it reached his throat and forced tears from his eyes by the strength of its pressure.

Even if there had been someone to put their arms around him, it was not enough. It would be a temporary comfort but not a timely one. His distress was from another time. Inside him there was a memory that kept breaking into his present, a memory from which he might temporarily distract himself but to which he continually returned.

The third can was empty, and his head was beginning to spin. He heard the voice of the woman he had known and concentrated upon her. She emerged from out of the darkness; onto the stage his mind was creating. He felt her touch him, her body softly close upon his.

"I was bloody in love with you," he mumbled.

"No, you just needed me." Her voice was soft, reminiscing.

"But you didn't bloody love me," he accused.

"Perhaps," she turned her head away.

"You didn't. Look at me." His fingers gently turned her cheek. "I knew you didn't. That time when we were in bed together."

"No, I was not in love with you. But I wanted you to be satisfied and, if you had asked me to, I would have stayed with you."

"But you left me." He lay across the old sofa and watched her walk away. She passed into the hall, and he heard the front door of the flat close behind her. "I didn't feel alone when we were together," he called after the image.

"You were always alone, particularly when you'd been drinking. The words would come tumbling out, sodden with resentment or self-pity. But I still didn't know whether it was the real you. And anyway, you weren't in love with me."

Her voice was firm, and he could not break through the barrier and touch her.

"If I had been I would have felt more vulnerable, more alone. I wasn't in love, but I was contented – and I wasn't afraid."

"That was only because you were younger." She swept her brown hair from her face. "You would have been afraid eventually. There was nothing that could distract you from yourself. Nothing that could keep you from looking inwards."

"I wanted to satisfy you, to make you love me." The tears rolled down Jonah's cheeks and he shuddered.

"It sounds as though it was yourself you were satisfying." Her voice was crisper.

"I was lonely. All I wanted was some company, somebody who would cuddle me as I fell asleep and who I could wake in the night without angering."

"I wasn't angry." Her voice softened.

"Did you have me just because I wanted you?" He asked.

"No, because I wanted to. Because you were close and warm. And because I had my own reasons for wanting someone."

"Why did you go?"

"Ssh," she put her finger against his lips, and he could smell the light sweetness of her perfume. "Don't, it was a different time."

"It was a golden generation; I saw it in the papers. They wrote about it all the time. We asked questions."

"But they weren't new questions." She was always so sensible. "And we didn't find any new answers. Everybody rushed around, inventing new dances, wearing new fashions, persuading themselves they were doing something that previous generations hadn't. Everybody but you."

"What did I do wrong?" he asked.

"You didn't do anything wrong. You turned against the flamboyance and tried to douse it with the cynical flood that burst through the walls which you erected against the world." She shook her head sadly.

"I didn't build walls; they were there already."

"Only because you couldn't stop questioning your existence. You couldn't forget your logic and join in the irrational fun." Now she sounded bitter as though their meetings had deprived her of something irreplaceable. "I needed to go out, to dance and scream at the music, but you wouldn't let me. You couldn't stand in a crowd without contempt for its enjoyment. To you it was all hollow."

"I enjoyed our evenings together. As for the music and the clothes, they were just drugs, things that made you feel high. But it was all meaningless."

"But nobody wanted to hear about that. They wanted to be happy."

"They were fools."

"No more foolish than you." Her voice was cold. "You found your own drug to hide behind. It made you feel good for a while. And sometimes, when it depressed you, you would drink more until you fell asleep. It was the sleep you really wanted, an anaesthetic to protect your sensitive soul."

"You didn't even like me."

"Oh yes, I liked you. And I would have stayed with you. Your vulnerability was attractive. But each time I came back you put your arm around me and submerged yourself in a temporary comfort which ignores passing seasons and pretends that, finally, we won't be alone."

She ran her finger against his cheek and his reverie was broken as he felt it catch against the unshaven bristles.

"Then why did you leave me?"

He felt cold as the afternoon began to merge with the evening and he recalled the cosiness of the small flat to which he had gone home after work. In the summer, the windows had been thrown open and he had listened to the sound of traffic in the street below as he sat and drank. In the winter, the windows stayed closed, and he drew the curtains early to keep in the warmth.

She used to come up and cook for him. And sometimes, afterwards, they would go to bed. As his drinking got heavier, he had started to miss work, sporadically at first, but then more regularly. They had warned him. And then they fired him. Afterwards, he sat inside and drank more heavily. Until, one day, his money was gone. But, by then, she had left him.

"Why did you leave me?" he asked again.

"Because I couldn't satisfy you. Because I couldn't reach inside and cuddle you. You were always there, beyond me, beyond help. It was useless. We could never have been together."

"You made me feel better."

"But only for a moment. And anyway," she frowned, "I was never sure who you were."

"I was me," Jonah whispered. "I was me."

"And who is me?" she asked. "I felt you, slept with you, and still couldn't break through. You were like a shell, which I held to my ear to listen to the sound of the sea. But there was nothing inside. It was my own senses that made you alive."

Jonah curled up tightly, aware only of the coolness of the late afternoon and the brittle bones that housed the void in which he existed. Ahead was the winter, cold and sparse, until the next brief summer and the autumn that followed.

"Do you know who you are?" She prompted him.

"No, because of this memory that is inside me. I don't believe in any afterlife and yet the memories crowd in.

Fields I never knew, and people, important people, whose names I can't hear. It's as if they came from a previous life."

"But you don't believe. It's impossible." She stopped. "It's like a graveyard with yew hedges that frightens you at midday. You're afraid of what you will see in the next lane between the hedges. But you know there can't be anything there."

"We ran," Jonah muttered, "both of us."

"There was nothing there." She sounded betrayed.

"Not that day," he said defensively.

"And if we had gone back every day, would there have been something? Would there ever have been anything?"

"Probably not." He felt tired. "The time has passed."

"So, how are you now?" She bent over him, as he lay there, curled on the bank.

"Alone."

"It was always that way," and she ran her fingers through his hair.

"No, at one time I did belong. There were old aunts and uncles and long summer days. I can't remember when the loneliness began. There was a time when it wasn't there."

"But is it true?" She stood up and stared down at him.

"Why would I feel it so strongly?"

"I don't understand how you became as you are." She seemed concerned. "How did you become alone and no longer part of what went before?"

"What went before is gone. It can't be recovered. Even the memory is fading."

He tried desperately to stay awake.

"And what will happen now?" She shook him. "What will happen?"

"Let me sleep. It will just carry on until, one-day, it's over. One day, under a tree, on a cold bench, or on a bloody, soiled hostel mattress, it will be over and forgotten. Nobody will remember."

"I will remember."

Her voice was seductive, but he knew she was only a dream. She would forget. She'd already forgotten. And, ahead, there was only the winter to endure.

When he awoke, the sun was much lower in the sky. He felt better; refreshed by the sleep, and it was a long walk back into town. He put his coat on and belted it tight around his waist with the coarse string he always used. Grasping his precious red vinyl bag, he set off along the bank. They served dinner in the evenings at the hostel, hot dinners that warmed your bones. And Jonah was feeling the cold. The days would get colder still but being alive was better than nothing. And today, he had money in his pocket.

18

Alison followed John's coffin into the chapel, filing-in after his brother and sister and their partners, his only remaining family. There were some neighbours present and a couple of friends, but most of the people attending she recognised from work. She sat on her own deliberately, several rows back, and wished that Jack could have been there. She guessed that she and Jack were the two closest colleagues John had had, the nearest to being friends.

When she saw the coffin, standing there in the chapel she started to cry. It looked so small, so alone, nothing like the man she had known, whose laughter and personality had filled the office and made work fun. A joker, but a man with a big heart, always ready to help or comfort the people around him. And she felt a sense of guilt at his death, sorry that she'd been unable to offer him the same comfort that he'd offered her and others when they needed it. Such a small, lonely coffin, such an insignificant end to a person who'd had such significance for her during his life.

The eulogies from his brother and sister seemed inadequate, as though they hadn't really known him, detached from the present and focusing mostly on the past, when they'd all been young. And, come to that, she'd never heard him talk much about his natural family, the only people he talked about had been his daughter and wife. When the time for reflection came, she found it impossible not to cry again, memories of him flooding back.

Outside, after the ceremony, she stood in a small line of people offering their condolences to his family. She waited until the person in front had moved on and found herself in front of the woman she'd assumed to be John's sister

"Thank you for coming. I'm Susan." The woman held out her hand and gripped Alison's briefly, "How did you know John?"

"I'm Alison and I worked with John for some years, I was his sales coordinator. Myself and my assistant, Ros, look after everyone in the sales team, handle calls to the office, make sure orders go out on time – try to make things run as smoothly as possible for the guys. By-the-way, Ros sends her condolences, she wanted to attend as well, but one of us had to stay behind in the office." Alison paused, feeling her voice begin to break and wanting to control it. "I'm so sorry, John was a good man. I'll miss him."

"I will, too," Susan looked down for a moment, "My only regret is my brother and I didn't see more of him in recent years." She turned to the man standing next to her, "Allan, this is Alison, she worked with John."

The man next to her was tall, taller than John had been but, close-up, Alison was struck by the similarities between them, although there was a tautness in the brother's bearing that she'd never seen in John whose casual attitude and quiet humour had made it so easy to like him.

"Hi, thank you for coming." He turned and introduced the woman next to him. "This is my wife, Heather."

The woman held out her hand and shook Alison's. Unlike her husband she had a friendly face, ready to smile

Alison thought, and her hair had been coloured and styled professionally, blond streaks hiding any greyness in a sleek wavy bob. Although she was much shorter than her husband, the firmness of her small handshake suggested a determination that belied her appearance.

"Maybe you'll join us afterwards," Allan said, "We're hosting a small gathering of friends and neighbours at 'The Chequers', and it would be good to talk to someone who knew and worked with John."

"I'd like to stay, but I'm not sure if I can," Alison hesitated, "I'll call my boss and ask him. Some of the sales team are here as well, I'm sure one of them will give me a lift to 'The Chequers' if it's ok."

"It would mean a lot if you could," the man said, "You see, John moved away from the rest of the family when he came to work here and Susan and I didn't see him very often, except at family events, like the funerals of our parents and his wife and daughter – and then only for a short time. We never got on with his wife that well, she seemed to want to separate him off from us somehow."

Alison nodded and moved away, whilst the remaining few people in the line offered their condolences. She searched in her bag for her mobile, found it and called Jack. He agreed immediately and one of the sales team gave her a lift to the hotel. A sign directed her to a small room upstairs with three or four tables and a buffet lunch – but there were only a few neighbours and the brother and sister with their partners, and the place looked cold and empty. Alison walked over to the buffet, picked-up a plate and selected a few items of food.

"It was ok for you to come, then," Allan had walked across and was standing behind her. "Would you like a glass of wine?"

"White, please." She took the glass he poured for her. "Yes, Jack Docherty, he's the sales manager, was fine about it, totally understood."

"So, this Jack Docherty was also John's boss, I suppose."

Alison nodded "Yes."

"Did he know John long?"

"Yes, Jack's worked there for years, like John had. They used to be quite close, play snooker together every week at the local hall in Tower Street. In fact, Jack still goes there on a Tuesday night – he loves the game."

"I never knew John was a snooker player," Allan took another sip of his wine, "I knew he used to watch it on television, but I didn't know he played."

"Yes, but he stopped playing regularly a couple of years after I joined the company."

"Speaking of the company, we were a little disappointed that none of the management attended the funeral."

The statement caught Alison off-balance. She realised it was really a question, implying criticism about the company's motives, and putting her on the spot about how to answer. She decided the truth was the best response, that the man standing opposite her would recognise any attempt at dissemblance immediately.

"I've heard they wanted to avoid embarrassing anyone as John had been made redundant – whether or not that was the reason for his suicide."

"I'm sure it contributed," Allan said, "I don't understand why he would have waited for so long after his family's deaths otherwise. Was Jack the person who actually made him redundant?"

"I think so," Alison felt the conversation was becoming more uncomfortable as it continued, "But, ultimately, everything comes down from Roger Grimshaw, the MD. Jack would have had little choice but to do as he was instructed – Roger's a very aggressive boss."

"Well, I'm not really up to speed with all of this, but surely they could have taken the family's deaths into account?"

"I'm sorry," Alison shook her head, "I don't know exactly what the situation was, but I do know they felt it was necessary to make some people redundant to ensure the firm was viable, going forward."

"And what's Jack like?"

"He's a nice guy and he's a good boss, takes care of his people as far as he can."

"He didn't take care of John." The statement was direct, stark even, and Alison began to recognise how very different the two brothers' characters were. John had never been a hard man, it was part of his charm and part of his downfall, but his brother was showing a tough, unforgiving side to his character, a steeliness she'd never seen in John.

"I'm not sure he was allowed to," Alison shook her head, "He's always been very reasonable in my dealings with him."

"So, why didn't he try more to help John – show more sympathy after his family were killed?"

"I'm sorry, I can't help you." Alison was feeling increasingly pressured, "I really don't know what went on – all I do know was that I liked John, he was great."

"Has this Jack Docherty got a family of his own?"

"Yes, he's got a wife and two young boys – I've met them on a couple of occasions, they're a nice family."

"Then, surely, he must have understood the emotional toll that losing his family would have placed on John."

Alison hesitated but was saved from having to continue the conversation by Susan's intervention. "I'm sorry, I'm afraid John's death has upset Allan more than he admits. I think both of us feel cheated because we had so little time with him over the past few years." She put her hand on Alison's arm and started to guide her away from her brother. "Allan, you ought to go over and talk to John's neighbours, it was good of them to come today."

Allan did as she suggested and Susan picked-up the bottle of wine and offered Alison some more. When she hesitated, Susan poured some into her own glass and held up the bottle, "Come on, there's not much left, help me out." Alison smiled and held up her glass, feeling slightly pressured again, but relaxed when the other woman began to ask her about her brother.

"He was always generous," Alison thought back, for examples to give Susan. "I mean, he never got angry or bad-tempered – even when things didn't go to plan sometimes."

"That's how I remember him being, as a brother. Allan's different, harder, quicker to judge, but I guess some of that is down to his time in the military. John was always softer; I sometimes wish he'd been more assertive for his own sake – and for ours. Perhaps, if he'd stood up to Faith, we'd have seen more of him. I suppose he must have been happy enough with her though, particularly if her death and that of my niece had such a devastating effect on him."

19

The report on the 'mourning day' outside the town hall finished. The coverage had been appropriately subdued; the protesters standing still, holding their banners aloft, heads bowed and joined by Councillors who'd emerged from the Town Hall and Union officials who'd accompanied them. 'Capitalism kills', 'Money murders' and similar banners had been displayed prominently, and the coverage had ended with the reporter saying the company had been approached for a comment but had declined to make one.

"Roger's not going to be happy about this." Jack got up from the sofa. "Would you like another glass of wine?"

Charlotte nodded. "I'm not sure it was any better or worse than Max's interview the other night. The mourning was just as detached in a way: very little about the man and an awful lot about the political views of the participants. The placards and the people said it all."

Jack walked back in with a refilled glass and gave it to her. "The only saving grace is there were fewer protesters than we might have expected, I guess they wanted to use the funeral as a fresh trigger for their campaign."

"Are you alright, though?" Charlotte stared across at him. "After all, it was you who had to make him redundant."

"Obviously, I feel bad about it. I'd known John for years – he was a great guy – but what could I do? It was him or somebody else, and the rules had already been agreed."

"I know," Charlotte smiled, "You wouldn't willingly hurt anybody, you're too kind for that. I'm just afraid that people who don't know you as well as I do will start attacking you, because you're the obvious person to target."

"Ultimately, it was Roger's decision. He set the whole cost-saving programme in motion."

"But I don't think that's something he's going to admit in the current climate."

"No, Roger's a survivor, his fallback position will be that his instructions were misinterpreted, hadn't been carried out as he intended."

"Which puts you right back into the firing line – in all senses of the words." Charlotte frowned. "I think I'll go and start dinner; are you going to come and help me prepare it?"

Jack nodded and followed her into the kitchen. "I do feel bad though – it's impossible not to."

"And would the outcome have been any different if you hadn't done what you had to?" Charlotte passed a chopping board to him.

"Thanks," Jack picked out his favourite knife from the block on the counter. "I get the impression that some of the people in the office think it would have been."

"Who are you talking about, they must know it's Roger who ultimately dictates what happens."

"Well, Alison who works for me in the sales office, for example. John's death seems to have upset her particularly; mind you, she'd worked with him for years."

"Are you sure you're not imagining things?" Charlotte took another sip of her wine. "Not being over-sensitive?"

"Maybe, but the whole atmosphere has changed. It seems to have created a schism between the management and staff that wasn't there before."

"Is that just in your department?"

"I don't know, although my guys are bound to be more directly involved. None of the other members of the management team have said anything."

"Probably because it's not a team really." Charlotte turned round and faced him, to give emphasis to what she was saying, "I wouldn't trust Roger or Geoff, they'll both want to cover their backsides if it all blows-up, and they'll be looking for a fall-guy."

"Geoff can be trusted to say what he thinks Roger wants to hear. What about Max?"

"Strangely enough, although he's a PR man and paid to put a spin on things, I think he's more honest than the others – I like Max, he seemed different when I met him. More thoughtful, and less brutal."

"He sits and doodles in management meetings, drives Roger crazy," Jack smiled as he visualised Max sitting there, playing with his pad and pencil. "But he's good at what he does, and much as Roger dislikes his casual attitude, I reckon he's secure. He approaches issues rationally, doesn't allow emotion to cloud his judgment, whereas Roger charges in like a bull in a china shop. Roger's drive and

Max's calmness make them a strong pairing." Jack shook his head, "Do you know, I'm not cut out for all this. I'm not a politician, I just want to do my job and manage the sales."

"I know," Charlotte reached up and kissed him on the cheek. "And don't ever think that the kids and I aren't grateful. You know how much we appreciate what you do." She held out her glass for a re-fill, "And I'll appreciate you even more after you've prepared the vegetables and poured me some more wine."

20

Alison took a sip of the coffee she'd made earlier, but it was still too hot to drink, and she placed it back on her desk. She'd started preparing the monthly sales figures, but recollections of the previous day's funeral interrupted her concentration. In particular, she kept recalling how uncomfortable she'd felt whilst talking to John's brother and returning to the disparity between their personalities, despite the similarities in their appearance. It seemed strange that two brothers could grow up so differently, one so approachable, the other so forbidding. She sat musing for a moment and then found she'd missed some figures whilst she'd been distracted and dragged her attention back to her work, re-checking her calculations. Then the 'phone rang, she swore quietly to herself and answered it.

"Hi, Alison, it's Meghan in reception, I've got Allan Morrison, John Morrison's brother, down here. He's asking to see Jack."

"Great, that's all I need," Alison pushed her hand through her hair in frustration. The figures had to be ready by the end of the afternoon and she needed some quiet time to finish them. She was also wary of meeting Allan Morrison again, after the aggression she'd detected the day before, and decided to avoid the situation. "Look, Meghan, I met

Allan at John's funeral yesterday; he's a bit intense and obviously upset by John's death. Besides, Jack's got a dental appointment and he's not in yet. Any chance you can put him off? Ask him to call another time?"

"I'll see what I can do." Meghan ended the call and Alison started re-checking her figures but was interrupted when her phone rang again.

"Hi, Alison, I told him Jack's not here, but he'd like to know how long it will be before he's back. Apparently, he's driving home today and wants to talk to Jack before he goes."

"I'll come down – I don't think it's a good idea for him to see Jack if he's still feeling the same as he did at the funeral. The last thing we need is a scene in reception. Tell him I'll be there in a minute."

Allan smiled politely when he saw her. "I take it Jack Docherty's not prepared to see me?"

"No, as I think Meghan has told you, he's got a dental appointment and he isn't in yet."

"What time are you expecting him?"

"I really don't know, and that's not a put-you-off, Allan, it's the truth. Alison looked him directly in the eye, challenging him to disbelieve what she was saying. He's got an off-site meeting afterwards and I'm not sure whether he's coming back here beforehand or going directly there – he could be out all morning."

" Well, I can wait to see him, before setting off." Allan stared back, meeting her challenge with one of his own. "I'll give you my mobile number, please call me when he gets in and I'll come over."

Alison took down the number. "I can't guarantee he'll be able to meet you, I need to talk to him first. Couldn't he just phone you?"

"No, I prefer to talk to people face-to-face, it's easier to communicate that way."

As they were speaking the reception doors opened, and Jack rushed through, saw Alison with a visitor and interrupted before either of them could respond. "I'm sorry," he smiled apologetically at the other man, "But I need to talk to Alison for a moment." He started to draw Alison aside, but the other man stepped forward and asked whether he was Jack Docherty? Jack nodded he was.

When the man stepped towards Jack, Alison backed away and started shaking her head agitatedly and mouthing 'No'.

"Let me introduce myself," the man didn't offer his hand, just stood there, staring at Jack. "I'm Allan Morrison, John Morrison's brother. I met Alison at the funeral yesterday and called-in to arrange a meeting with you. Is it possible to fit me in later today?"

Jack thought rapidly, "I'm sorry, but that's not possible," he saw the relief in Alison's face. "I'm running late and I'm going to be out for the rest of the day. I'm sorry to rush off like this but this meeting's very important and I need to check through a few things with Alison before I leave." He reached in his pocket and took out a business card; "Here's my number, Alison manages my diary, so she'll be able to arrange something, although it can't be for a week or so."

The man took the card, looked down at it, and was about to say something when Jack spoke instead, "I am sorry about John," Jack hesitated before saying anything more, but felt he had to, "I liked him, and we were colleagues for years. He was a good guy." He reached out to touch the man's arm in sympathy, but Allan moved away. "I'm sorry, I must go." Jack motioned to Alison to come with him and moved off through the reception doors into the office.

"God, thanks for warning me," Jack let a long breath out in relief, "I thought he looked familiar, but I hadn't worked out he was John's brother. There was something different about him."

"He's difficult, John was never like that." Alison shook her head, "I'm not sure it's a good idea for you to meet him at all, he's not in a good place. We spoke at the funeral yesterday and he clearly blames the company and you for John's suicide. He and his sister both live a couple of hours drive from here and I'll feel much better when they leave. I think they're going back this afternoon."

When he got in his car some fifteen minutes later, Jack looked across the car park at the visitors' spaces and saw Allan still sitting there. As he drove away, he raised his hand in acknowledgement, but the other man just stared back.

21

Roger checked his watch impatiently, anxious to start the meeting. "Either of you seen Jack?" he looked at Geoff and Max for an answer.

"I saw him talking to Alison in his office a couple of minutes ago," Max said. "I think he'd just got back from a meeting somewhere."

"Sorry, I'm late," Jack closed the door behind him as he walked into the office and took his seat at the table, "Something came up this morning and I needed a briefing from Alison before this meeting."

"Right, let's get started," Roger sounded irritable. "Did any of you watch the local TV coverage of that so-called tribute to Morrison outside the town hall last night?" The men round the table nodded. "So, what did you think?"

"Not much," Jack said, "And if I hadn't known John Morrison, I wouldn't have known who he worked for. Plus, while I think people may feel sympathy for John, I think they may also start to see events like the funeral tribute as somewhat staged, politically inspired."

"What about you, Geoff, what's your opinion?"

"Well, it's not my area, Roger, but I just wonder whether Max might feel some balancing coverage would have been helpful."

"What sort of coverage did you have in mind, Geoff?" Max addressed his colleague directly. "What is there we might have said that would have been newsworthy."

Geoff shrugged.

"Exactly," Max continued, "What is there we can say that wouldn't drag discussion back to his redundancy and this firm? And, I agree with Jack, people aren't stupid, they understand posturing when they see it. My take on the situation is that, to all intents and purposes, it's over. We just need to ensure that we don't do anything to place it back under public scrutiny."

"Let's hope you're right, Max," Roger opened his notepad, "Next item on the agenda."

"I'm sorry Roger but I would like to raise one further connected issue; it's why I was late." Jack interrupted Roger's flow.

"Go on then Jack, but let's make it brief, we need to discuss the trade exhibition, it's just over a month away now and it's the biggest potential showcase we have all year. I'd like reassurance that we're all geared-up for it."

"Yesterday, when Alison went to the funeral, she met John's sister and brother, and she said the brother was asking some accusatory questions about the company's role in John's death and seemed annoyed that no one from management had attended. And this morning he turned-up in reception asking to see me; I couldn't stop to talk to him, so I asked Alison to put a meeting in my diary, although obviously I wish I hadn't now. Anyway, she's arranged a meeting for just over three weeks' time and the question is what you and Max think I should do about it?"

"Get Alison to cancel the bloody meeting," Roger said, "She can tell him the Exhibition is on and the last-minute arrangements we're involved in make it impossible to see him now."

Max nodded, "I'm inclined to agree with Roger. Postpone it as long as you can, the emotion he feels currently is likely to reduce the longer it's left – and so will any potential public interest; it'll be yesterday's news by then."

"Right, I think that's decided, get Alison to diary a cancellation a few days before the meeting is scheduled." Roger looked round the table. "OK, let's move on to the arrangements for the Exhibition."

22

Ros had started to prepare their evening meal when Sam got in; he put his bag down, changed out of his working clothes and went back to the kitchen for a chat. He smiled as he looked at her, five foot two of blonde hustle and bustle as she chopped the food, got out the pans and placed them on the hob. 'Small and tall', Mike had called them after a few drinks one evening and he guessed it wasn't a bad description.

"Can I help?"

"You can lay the table and get me a drink." She turned round for a moment as he bent down and kissed her cheek, "I'll have one of those ciders, please, they're nice and light."

Sam poured her drink, placed her glass on the worktop and then poured himself a beer. "How did things go at work today?"

She stopped chopping the carrots and took a sip of the cider, "Actually, it was a bit difficult. You remember John Morrison, the guy who committed suicide," Sam nodded, "Well his brother turned-up in reception and wanted to speak to Jack. Fortunately, Alison went down and managed to warn Jack, who bumped into them as he was coming in."

"Lucky Jack. I can't imagine it would have been a very comfortable conversation. How's everyone else taking it after the funeral?"

"OK, I think, although Alison was crying in the loo when I went in before leaving work – she'd worked with John for years. I asked her what the matter was, but she just shook her head, so I didn't push things. When I first started working there, I sometimes wondered if Alison and John had something going on between them, they were always joking about, flirting a bit."

"And did they – have anything going on?"

"No, I don't think so. At least, I never found out if they did. Eventually I decided they were just messing around, just liked each other and shared the same sense of humour."

23

"Well, wish me luck," Gill picked up her bag, walked across and gave Mike a kiss as he lay in bed."

"Bit bloody early to be going to work." He pushed back the duvet and grabbed his dressing gown, wanting to see her off.

"Big day, I need to be there a couple of hours before it all kicks off, make sure everything is ready and the technology is working. I can't afford anything to go wrong."

"I thought you'd set it all up yesterday afternoon?"

"We did, but we need to run it through again this morning – can't take any chances. If this goes well it might lead to more new business."

"I'll keep my fingers crossed."

"How do I look?" she flicked a speck off her suit skirt, smoothed the lapels of the jacket and did a quick spin in front of the long bedroom mirror. Her hair was brushed immaculately, a dark inverted bob framing her face, and her suit looked perfectly styled – and expensive.

"Terrific," Mike stifled a yawn as he took in her slim figure, accentuated by the high heels she was wearing and the cut of the suit.

"So, that's a yawn of approval, is it? You really know how to make a girl feel good."

He grinned. "I haven't seen that suit before. It's impressive – svelte even."

"It's new, I bought it as an investment in the business."

"So, was it as expensive as it looks?"

"It was, but it makes me feel better than a yawn, gives me more confidence. But you recovered slightly with svelte – so early in the morning! I can see now why you chose to be a salesman. And what are your plans for today?"

"Oh, usual round of fascinating sales calls, monthly sales review meeting in the office this afternoon – you know, push, push, push."

"Do you remember that first conference I organised after we met – the one I took you to, to stop you moping around on your own all day after you'd lost your job?"

"How could I forget going to that hotel and catching the bastard who'd fired me with his mistress. I'll always treasure seeing the panic on her face when I saw them there together."

"And look how well it's turned out. He helped you get a new job to keep you quiet, and you haven't looked back since."

"Yes, but let's not kid ourselves, sales are over the moment they're logged, and they just raise the bar higher when the next year's targets are fixed. It's bloody brutal."

"Imagine how I feel, running my own business." She kissed him again, took another look at herself in the mirror and opened the front door, turning and waving as she went down the stairs.

24

Jonah fancied a cigarette and walked round to the small tobacconist shop by the car park, where he cadged cigarettes from the woman who worked there. He could always rely on her for a fag or two, but, today, she shook her head and told him she'd given-up smoking.

"My kids have been on at me to stop, and my chest has been tight recently, so sorry Jonah, I can't help you."

Jonah shook his head in disbelief. "'Ow long since you given up?"

"Just a couple of days now. And don't give me that soppy look," the woman wagged her finger at him, "It wouldn't hurt you to give up smoking."

Jonah shook his head and picked-up his bag. As he did so a young man walked into the shop.

"Hi, Mum, how are things? I see you've got a visitor." He looked at Jonah.

"Yes, but I don't think Jonah here is impressed by me giving up smoking. It's been a couple of days without fags now."

Mike took out his wallet, asked his mother for a small packet of cigarettes and, when she handed him one from the shelf behind her, gave the packet to Jonah. "OK, Jonah, have these on me."

Jonah nodded, took the cigarettes, touched his forehead in thanks and shuffled out of the shop.

"Never changes, does he?"

"No, poor old sod," his mother said, "He never gives up. He'll be happy now, thanks."

"You're a bit soft on the old bugger, aren't you? What's it about him that gets to you?"

"I don't know. I guess I've just got to know him; he's part of my life; comfortable, predictable, and never threatening. I just like him." His mother smiled, "Anyway, how are things with you?"

"Fine, it's good at the moment. And Gill's business appears to be doing well."

"It's only a year back you were in so much trouble – no job, nothing. Things have improved."

"It was scary at the time; meeting Gill was a life-saver. I don't think I've ever met anyone quite like her."

"What would she think about you buying Jonah cigarettes?"

"She'd tell me not to be so stupid and then feel guilty and buy him some herself. Contrary, or what?"

"You're a lucky man, take care of her." She reached up and kissed him, "You need a woman like her behind you."

25

Mike was making a mug of tea when Gill arrived back. He put a tea bag in a second mug, poured the water over it and, when the tea was made, handed the mug to her and asked how her day had gone.

"It went well, thanks. The clients were really pleased with the feedback. I must sit down though; these shoes are killing me." She carried the mug into the lounge, hung her jacket over the back of a chair and kicked off her high heels; then sat down on the sofa and sipped her tea. "God, that tastes good. The only issue was a small group of protestors demonstrating about that guy's suicide again. Ros' company were holding an offsite meeting at the venue in the morning, and someone had obviously tipped them off."

"That's a bit of a coincidence, was Ros there?"

"No, it was a meeting of the managers from the manufacturing area. I called Ros and she reckons that someone from the factory is liaising with the protest group. Some of the workers must still be angry."

"You've got to give it to the protesters, they're persistent."

"That's true, but the hotel soon had them cleared away from the entrance. There was one thing that was interesting, though," Gill took another mouthful of tea, "I got talking to Louise, she's worked at the hotel for years and liaises with organisers of events to make sure they're happy with the arrangements. She was a bit pissed-off about the protest, worried it might affect the chances of any repeat business. Anyway, she told me the wife of the guy from Ros' office, the one who committed suicide, used to work there and, in Louise's opinion, the only surprise was that the guy waited until she was dead to kill himself!"

"That sounds a bit harsh!" Mike looked surprised, "What was wrong with the woman?"

"Most things, according to Louise. It doesn't sound as though she was very popular. Apparently, she was what Louise described as 'one of those people whose assessment of their own value is far higher than their real worth'. Even though Louise had to admit she was a good-looking, well-presented woman, she described her as tight, unable to let herself go, and cold. It sounds as though she married the guy Ros knew because she thought he was ambitious and began to resent him when she realised that he preferred an easy life and was quite contented staying as he was. She used to complain continually about him to the other women."

"So, why did she stay with him?" Mike was confused, "They were together for years had a grown-up daughter."

"Who knows why people do things?" Gill finished her tea and put her cup down on the counter, "Probably because of the daughter. The girl and her father were very close, and Louise reckons the mother was jealous. She heard the guy and the woman arguing one day and says the wife, her name was Faith I think, was extremely rude and dismissive, treated him like a piece of dirt. And there was more, a bit of gossip! Louise reckons Faith was having a fling with the hotel manager at the time – trying to establish a better place in the pecking order. She says it carried on for a couple of years and Faith was often seen emerging from one of the bedrooms with him. But it sounds as though it all went wrong when Faith got pregnant; the guy was sacked whilst she was on maternity leave, when one of the chambermaids complained he'd come into the room she was cleaning and attempted to grope her. He'd gone by the time Faith returned to work."

"That must have been a bit humiliating," Mike shook his head imagining how Faith must have felt. "I don't suppose that made things any better at home for the guy Ros worked with – his woman scorned by another man! Life must have been hell for a while; I wonder whether he ever knew what had happened? So, perhaps the guy wasn't that upset when his wife was killed, maybe it was just his daughter's death that would have affected him?"

"That's how Louise made it sound, although, who knows? He might still have had feelings for her."

"I guess so, but it kind of changes one's perception of things. The distraught husband and father, killing himself because he'd lost his whole family. One thing's certain, we're not going to find out anything more now."

"Anyway, whatever the truth is about Faith and the guy Ros worked with, the important thing from my point of view is that the day went well and the agency I use came up trumps. They've got a new marketing consultant with some fabulous ideas. A woman called Misty."

"Sounds a bit way out, 'Misty'?"

"She is a bit left field, but there was nothing misty about her approach, the designs were very focused and got the messages across beautifully. The client has already mentioned giving me more business. And it's good to have some forward bookings, makes me feel more secure.

Besides it might enable me to invest in another new suit!"
She brushed her skirt appreciatively.

"Well, we've always got my job as a fallback. And that's
more than we had when we first met. At least I know it was
my charisma and not my riches that first attracted you."

"I'm sorry, I don't recall the charisma bit." She giggled.
"I think I just felt sorry for you! What's for dinner tonight?"

"Right, there you are, glamorous job, directing the show
and constructing the drama, and here I am, generating the
sales and money that pays for it all! And you still expect me
to cook the dinner!"

"But you're so good at it, and, anyway, I need a bath."

"Asses milk or water?"

"Water unfortunately, unless you're lactating, in which
case asses' milk will be great!" She grabbed her cup and
jumped up from the sofa, before he could catch her. "Oh,
and by the way, there's a bottle of Prosecco in the fridge, a
bath always feels so much better with some bubbly."

"So, tripe and onions?" he called after her.

"I think I'd prefer those prawns we bought with pasta,"
she reappeared in her bathrobe. "And don't forget the
Prosecco – if the business takes off, we could be drinking
Champagne one day. And you know how good Champagne
makes me feel." She posed dramatically, pouted and blew
him a kiss, before disappearing into the bathroom.

26

When he entered the Church, the woman was sitting in
the same pew as before, staring ahead, completely still,
her dark hair hanging thick and glossy down onto her
shoulders. She turned as she heard the door, smiled briefly
as she recognised him and then turned back and faced the
altar. Despite such a short glimpse of her face, he could see
she'd been crying. He thought back, trying to remember
how long it was since he'd first seen her and decided it must

have been almost a month. So, whatever was causing her to seek the peace of the church must be a continuing and deeper issue. If she'd attended any of the usual services he'd have asked if there was something he could help with, but he'd been a priest long enough to recognise when a person still needed time and space to think, to come to terms with whatever had happened to upset them.

He checked the entries in the visitor's book, as he always did, bowed and crossed himself as he faced the altar and then went into the vestry at the rear of the church to plan the service for the following Sunday. As he re-entered the Church some twenty minutes later, he heard the latch of the large timber door opening and caught sight of the woman's back as she stepped through and shut the door behind her. This time, he made a mental note to speak if he saw her again.

27

The two men sat down across the table from each other. Allan played with his ring, twisting it round his finger repeatedly. His whole being seemed concentrated on the twisting motion, his eyes fixed on the ring as it turned. Finally, he looked up and stared at the other man.

"Look, Stuart, we've been through some difficult times together and I need to know you're with me on this. This man killed my brother; somebody else may have loaded the pistol but this guy pulled the trigger."

"I'm in, but only because of what you did for me back then, when we were in the desert. I'd never have got back to the helicopters on my own. I still get pain somedays from that bloody bullet wound in my leg. I'm in, but I'm worried about Heather being involved and I don't want us all to end up in jail."

Allan put his hand across the table and held his friend's wrist briefly, "Well, I could hardly leave my fiancé's brother behind, Heather would never have forgiven me if I had; besides I'd have missed having you around, we grew up together." He paused, smiled at his friend and took his hand back across the table. "OK, so now we have to plan where we go from here; it's all dying down, the media have moved on and people are forgetting that a man named John Morrison died."

"What are you thinking of doing?"

"We need to punish the person who's most obviously responsible, hold them up for scrutiny and make them feel what John felt. Get them to experience the emptiness, the loss of all hope. Get them to the stage where they decide it's not worth going on – and give them the means of ending everything."

"No, that's going too far, we'll get done for murder if we're caught."

"Well number one, we'll plan not to get caught. And number two; we don't need the guy to die, just for him to take the decision that he wants to. Then, if we release him, he can tell everyone how he felt when it no longer seemed worth living. To apologise for his part in what happened."

"And how do you intend to do that?"

"Put the guy in a similar situation to John's. Take away his normality, place him in isolation, disorientate him."

"But how are we going to pick him up? And, most importantly, where are we going to keep him?"

"It shouldn't be too difficult; we can watch him for a while and grab him when he's in a place where he won't cause a fuss and we won't be seen. As for holding the guy, we need a place where there's no sound, no light, no way of knowing the time or knowing how long they've been there."

"Have you got somewhere in mind?"

"Yes, it's in an old industrial building in that estate over in Wrighton. The tenants have moved out and the whole area's scheduled for re-development. So, it's ideal. All the evidence will be destroyed when the demolition gang moves in. And, for the time being, there's still power down there so we can fit up some cameras and some low lighting and there's a kitchen space where we can put a microwave."

"But how can we be sure we've got enough time? And how can we monitor and feed someone and still live our normal lives without attracting attention?"

"It needn't take that long; a couple of weeks should be enough. Silence and solitude are powerful stimuli. But we've got to get the place ready. We both know a guy who can be trusted to keep his mouth shut and set-up some security cameras and lighting. And we'll need to make sure the door is strong enough so it can't be broken down from inside and still allow us to pass food and messages in without being seen. A mattress, sleeping bag and pillow, and a table and chair and we're ready – we're not providing 5-star accommodation."

"How are we going to feed the guy?"

"That's where the microwave comes in, it'll be simple to give him microwave meals. We can use disposable plates, water bottles and plastic cutlery."

"But the power company will realise we're using electricity, that someone has been there."

"Not if we don't send meter readings to them – and we're not going to be doing that."

"It sounds bloody risky to me."

"Not if we plan it properly. He need never see us, and we can monitor him 24/7 through the security cameras."

"Picking him up's the easy part, the tricky bit's going to be getting him out when it's all over – without showing ourselves."

"We'll drug him, put something in his food and when he's asleep we can go in, hood and secure him and take him out. Are you in on it, or not?"

"Who else is going to be involved?"

"The guy who's doing the electrics and Heather. Four of us should be enough – we need to keep things as close as we can. So, are you in?"

Stuart paused before responding, "Yes, as I said earlier, I owe you, Allan, but this is the final payback."

Great, I need someone I can rely on." Allan reached across and clasped Stuart's hand. "We'll need to get working on the space as soon as possible; take the door off the loo, so he can't hide away in there and put a reinforced door on the entrance with a hatch at the bottom to pass food through – we can't allow him to see any of us. Then we can put the original door back afterwards"

"But supposing he won't co-operate?"

"What choice does he have? We'll be feeding and watering him, and we provide the only way out of his prison. We'll control everything, he'll have nothing to bargain with."

28

Ros' 'phone rang. She checked the screen, saw it was Gill calling, and accepted the call.

"Hi, Ros, do you fancy a quick drink after work? After all, we can't let the lads have all the fun."

"Fine, where do you want to meet?"

"How about the wine bar in the High Street?"

"Great, but I'll need a little time to get into town."

"I'll have a bottle ready."

Gill ordered the wine and sat down at one of the lower tables near the window to wait. She sat back in the chair, poured herself a glass and put the bottle back in the chiller. The wine was cool and citrussy and she took a second longer sip, appreciating its elegance, before opening her business case and taking out the responses from the recent corporate event she'd arranged. They were flattering, and she felt a flush of satisfaction as she read them. The door opened, disturbing her concentration, and she looked-up and waved to Ros as she saw her come in.

"Hi, great location, I love meeting-up here," Ros looked around the bar, the shelves of wine bottles, the furniture and the décor, "Makes a change from the pubs the guys like, so crowded and dark." she sat down opposite Gill, put her bag down beside her and held out the spare glass. "Pour me a large one, please, it's been a long day."

Gill poured some wine into her glass and saluted her. "Cheers."

"Cheers, so what are we celebrating?" Ros asked.

"Nothing, really, I just fancied getting out of the flat for a while. It gets a bit claustrophobic working from home. And, that last event went well, so I thought I'd earned a bit of a reward."

"So, what exactly was the event?"

"A thought leadership conference; you know, show off the company's expertise, invite their clients along and impress them with the company's knowledge and products."

Ros took another sip of her wine, "Sounds a lot more exciting than my job, sitting there, nurse-maiding customers and the sales team. Some of them can be so unreasonable – and that's not just the customers I'm talking about!"

"It's great when it goes well, but there's always a bit of insecurity, working for yourself. I'm beginning to build a good client base, but I could always do with some more."

"So, what did you actually have to do?"

"You know the sort of things you need for an event, arranging the sound system and videos, getting the invites and programmes designed and printed. It's not very different from what you're going to be doing for that big trade show that's coming up."

"Fingers and everything else crossed that that goes ok," Ros held a hand up to show her crossed fingers, "Jack Docherty, our sales manager, has been arranging it all, but, of course, that guy's suicide has been demanding some attention, there's been a lot of local exposure."

"Yes, I realised that the other day, when I saw the demonstrators outside the hotel where some of your managers were meeting. It must be difficult with such a negative spotlight on the company."

Ros nodded. "When the guys got back and told the big boss, a guy named Grimshaw, about the protesters it's rumoured that he did a very passable imitation of Queen Victoria – he wasn't amused and has started trying to find whoever tipped off the protesters. He's the guy who's really behind what happened – grim by name and nature."

"What did you know about the guy who committed suicide?"

"He's been with the company for years, much more laid back than some of the other sales guys. I liked him; I think everyone did."

"But what did you know about his home life?"

"Nothing, except what most people know, that his wife and daughter were killed in a car crash. Why?"

"Well, bit of a coincidence, but apparently his wife used to work at the hotel where I bumped into your guys, and after the protesters had been moved off the hotel grounds one of the staff started talking about it all. From the sound of it, the marriage wasn't one made in heaven." Gill repeated what she had told Mike the previous night.

"Really," Ros looked surprised, "I'll talk to Alison at work, see what she says. She was closer to John than anyone else in the office and she'll know what was going on if anyone does."

29

Jack looked up at the kitchen clock as he carried the plates in after dinner. It had just gone seven and he needed to get moving and drive to the snooker hall for his usual Tuesday night session. He put the plates in the dishwasher and went back into the lounge to say goodnight to the boys. He bent down, kissed each of them and told Charlotte he'd be back at the usual time, then picked-up his cue and went to his car.

The weather wasn't good, wet and miserable, and there were fewer vehicles around than usual as he approached the small multi-storey car park, along from the hall. Concentrating on turning into the entrance and with the rain interfering with his wider view, he didn't notice the two men, sitting in a white van, parked across the road from the snooker hall entrance. He drove past obliviously, and up the ramps onto the second floor, grabbed his phone and his cue from the back seat and hurried down to the street towards the hall entrance.

And he didn't see the van driver pointing him out as his slim, just under six-foot figure walked past, frame slightly bent, his free arm shielding his dark, grey streaked hair from the rain. Or hear the driver as he said to his passenger, "Make sure you can recognise him when you get inside," and the passenger respond by asking whether it wouldn't be easier to knock him down and hood him as he went back to the car park. Or hear about the drug they planned to use so he couldn't recall what happened, experiencing a period of amnesia for a few hours after they abducted him.

Once inside the hall Jack felt more relaxed, it was like a separate world, secure and dark, with lines of green baize tables lying stretched out beneath the long, low lighting hanging above them. And men gathered around each table, concentrating fixedly on the white ball in front of them and quietly eyeing-up potential shots. It was a small weekly haven, in which he could enjoy a couple of hours away from the pressures of work and the noise of the boys and home. He looked around and saw his two friends standing by their usual table, each holding a glass of beer.

He waved, pointed to the bar and went and bought himself a drink before joining them.

They started as always, tossing coins together to see who would play first, and continuing until one of them came down the opposite side to the others. This evening, Jack was one of the first pair to play, chalked his cue and broke for the frame. He played well, better than he'd played in a while, and in a final rewarding stroke, sent the black ball into the pocket. His form continued into the second match against his other opponent, and he won that as well, leaving his two friends to play a final frame together.

Jack watched them break and stayed for the first few shots. Then he walked across to the bar and ordered and paid for a second pint. Whilst it was being poured, he decided to visit the 'gents'. He missed the new man who'd entered the bar and ordered the same drink for himself. And he missed the man as he turned his back on the barman and poured a small phial into the glass, before swapping the two glasses and starting to drink the one poured for Jack. Jack came back in, picked-up his glass and carried it back across to the table to watch his friends.

After fifteen or twenty minutes, Jack began to feel more drunk than he thought he ought to. His head felt dizzy and slightly confused. He decided he'd had enough beer and indicated to his companions that he was leaving, but he found it awkward forming the words. He'd hoped that going outside would clear his head; instead, as he left the hall, he started to find it increasingly difficult to control his muscles and leant against the wall for a moment, clenching his cue in his fist, afraid of dropping it. He didn't notice the hall door open and shut behind him.

30

Outside, in the van opposite, Allan had finished his sandwiches, drank the remains of his tea, put the cup in his lunch box and stowed them both neatly behind the seat. It was nearly nine thirty as he put his mask and gloves on, ready to use. He heard the hall door bang open and saw Jack emerge and lean against the wall, and immediately got out and checked the street both ways, to see if there was anyone there. But the street was quiet. Then he saw the door open again, and Stuart step out, put on his own mask and gloves, and call out to ask if Jack needed help. Jack tried to wave Stuart away, stumbling along the pavement as he tried to get back to the safety of his car.

"Who the hell'r you? Jack's speech was slurred, as he looked up and saw a man in a mask in front of him. For a moment he stared, trying to make sense of what he was seeing, before turning back in a hopeless attempt to escape. He found a second masked man behind him, and his knees began to buckle. The two men caught Jack's arms and supported him across to the van. They opened the back doors, hooded him and lifted him in, lying him down on a mattress.

"Hold him still," Allan said, "We need his 'phone, watch, wallet and keys. We'll leave them in his car. I'll put his cue there, as well."

They found the items they wanted, and Allan held Jack's finger against the 'phone pad and made sure the 'phone stayed switched on whilst Stuart locked the van doors. They took off their masks and started searching through Jack's contacts for his home number, and, when they'd found it, Allan began typing a message. Muffled shouts and some initial banging were audible from the back of the van but stopped after a few minutes and they guessed Jack had gone to sleep.

"Worked like a dream," Allan patted Stuart on the back, "Are you sure no-one saw you spike his drink?"

Stuart shook his head. "It was easy, he was with two other guys, and they took it in turns to play. Our guy," he indicated the back of the van, "Finished playing, went to the bar to get another drink and popped into the gents whilst the barman poured it; I did it then and when he returned, he picked-up what he thought was his drink and went back to the table with his mates. He drank most of it, then realised he was feeling a bit drunk and left. He started to weave a bit as he got to the door – it went exactly as you said it would."

"Right, you get in the van, and I'll find his car and leave his things in it." Anxious to get away, Allan put on his mask again to avoid any CCTV, hurried over to the car park, and went inside, reappearing after a few minutes and getting into the van.

Stuart looked across. "What did you do with his 'phone?"

"Sent the message to say what we've done and left it with the other things on the passenger seat. He turned the ignition key and his face visibly relaxed as the engine started – now, we need to get out of here fast, the longer we hang around, the more chance we have of being seen."

31

Charlotte took another look at the clock. Jack should have been home by now. She picked up her phone and called him, but the message went to answerphone. She was surprised – it was unlike Jack; he hadn't said anything about being late. The lads had finished their evening meal and were getting ready for bed, so she went upstairs and said 'goodnight', reassuring them their father would be home later; but when she got back downstairs there was still no message on her 'phone. She'd been expecting to hear the car come into the drive, the driver's door slam shut and Jack shout out as he entered the house; but there'd been nothing. She felt confused and tried calling him again, but the phone went to answerphone, like it had previously, and she put it down, becoming more concerned that something must have happened. To try and take her mind off Jack's lateness, she decided to give the kitchen a final tidy and, as she did so, heard her phone buzz indicating she'd received a message. She went back into the hall, picked it up and was relieved to see Jack's number. The message read:

'Your husband has been abducted to give him time to consider his part in the death of John Morrison. He'll be held until he admits the evil he's done.'

Charlotte read the message several times, first in disbelief and then trying to make sense of what it was saying. Her first thought was how the lads would react. She re-read the message and felt an overwhelming anxiety about whether she would see Jack again. One side of her brain kept telling her it must be some sort of a hoax, that, maybe, Jack had lost his 'phone and somebody had found it and thought it would be amusing to send the message. But the other side told her she had to act quickly, that what was happening was real and she walked back into the lounge, knowing it was less likely either of the lads would hear her call 999 from there. When the call was answered she asked for the police, gave her name and address and repeated what had happened: her husband had not arrived home as usual after playing snooker, his phone was on answerphone and then she'd received a message suggesting he'd been abducted and was being held prisoner.

"And you're sure this is not someone's idea of a joke?" the Operator asked, "Why would anyone do this?"

"It seems it's some sort of punishment, to make an example of Jack because his company fired a man a few weeks back and the man subsequently committed suicide – it was on the local news a short while ago, you might have seen it. But my husband didn't order the redundancy, he said it was part of a company-wide programme he had to implement."

"And you're sure this isn't all some kind of a prank?"

"My husband hasn't returned home or contacted me – it's totally out of character. He always makes a point of trying to get back to talk to our sons before they go to sleep."

"Where is your husband's car?"

"I don't know. I have two young sons to look after – I can't go out searching the streets. He normally leaves it in the car park on Trafford Street near the snooker hall."

"What's the registration number?"

Charlotte couldn't remember immediately and called upstairs to the boys. "Do either of you know your father's car number?"

The younger lad, Tony, shouted the number down and confirmed he was sure when Charlotte asked him. She read the number back to the police operative.

"Ok, Mrs. Docherty, we'll send a car to look round the carpark and we'll get back to you when we've completed our investigation. In the meantime, we're allocating a case number." The Operator repeated the number for Charlotte to write down.

Charlotte thanked her, put the phone down and stood helplessly in the hall.

"Why did you need to know Dad's car number?" Daniel, the elder boy had got out of bed and was standing at the top of the stairs, "Has he had an accident? He's normally back by now."

"Yes, when is Daddy going to be back," Tony had joined his elder brother and was standing beside him, rubbing his eyes. "I want to see Daddy before I go to sleep."

"I'm not sure, I think he might have gone for a drink after his game of snooker," Charlotte walked back up the stairs, trying to remain calm as she shooed them both back into their rooms. "I'm sure he'll be back by the time you wake up in the morning. Come on, try to go to sleep, you've got school tomorrow." When they were settled, she gave each of them a kiss, gently tousled their hair to reassure them and then went back downstairs, walked into the kitchen, supported herself on the counter, and started to cry.

32

The police car drove along the different levels of the car park, looking for Jack's car. They found it on the second floor. It was unlocked, his keys, wallet, watch and mobile on the driver's seat, his cue in the back – and no sign of a struggle.

"Why would someone leave their car unlocked in a carpark?" the first policeman asked his partner, "It doesn't feel right."

"It isn't," his partner said, looking round the car-park floor. "I reckon the caller was right and something's happened here. He picked-up his radio, radioed the call-centre and confirmed what they'd found.

"I think we've got a new case on our hands," the Operator told her manager, "We need to get forensics to take a look at the car and then start searching for this guy immediately."

33

Charlotte heard the front doorbell and looked through the hall window before opening the door. There were two policemen outside.

"Mrs. Docherty?" the first policeman said, and when she nodded, asked if they could come in and talk.

She stood aside and motioned them into the lounge, then followed them in and stood there, expectantly, not wanting to ask what they'd found because she was afraid of the potential answer.

"Please sit down, Mrs. Docherty, we've got a number of things to go through with you."

Charlotte did as she was told and sat down. "Have you found my husband's car?" she asked.

"We have, it's in the carpark, where you say he normally parked. It was unlocked, so we assume he may have been about to enter it when the abductors took him. We're sorry not to have better news."

"But what about his phone? I received a message earlier, just before I called you."

"His phone was in the front of the car, along with his wallet, watch and keys. They must have sent the message before taking him to wherever they're going. It was lucky no one had found the car was unlocked before we got there and taken any of the items, or the car itself for that matter."

"So, are there any clues as to who was involved and where he may have been taken?"

"Sorry, Mrs. Docherty, but we've only been able to conduct an initial search of the car, forensics are taking a more detailed look as we speak. And as soon as we hear anything more, we'll let you know."

"So, what am I going to do in the meantime? What do I tell the boys?"

"There's nothing any of us can do, except wait until we find a clue about what actually happened and more information about the possible whereabouts of your husband. As for the boys, we do have officers trained in dealing with such situations; we'll have one here in the morning and we wouldn't advise telling the boys anything until we know more."

"So, what do I say if they wake-up and ask again tonight? They're already unsettled because he isn't home." Charlotte heard her voice rising and tried to control the helplessness and frustration she was feeling.

"The only thing you can say is that their father won't be back until later – no point in stopping them sleeping. We'll get you some help round in the morning, to talk to them in more detail – perhaps keep them at home for the day, just in case the news surfaces tomorrow. It's better they have you here for support and a Counsellor to help you all through this first stage in what's happened."

"But how do we know they won't hurt Jack? What happens if he doesn't admit responsibility for John Morrison's death?"

"We don't know; It doesn't sound like ordinary, run-of-the-mill criminal activity – more as though there's a moral or political dimension and there's no suggestion of a ransom. For my part, I've never come across anything like this before." The officer shrugged his shoulders and stood up to leave. "Have you got anyone you can call, a friend or family member, to come over and stay the night?"

Charlotte shook her head. "It's too late to call a friend and I don't want to worry my parents at this time of night. I'll call them, first thing, tomorrow."

34

The first thing Jack was conscious of was a thumping headache. He tried to make sense of what had happened to him but couldn't remember anything after his game of snooker finished. He was aware of a hood over his head and both his hands and feet being bound, and then heard a metal door opening. The next sensation was of being picked-up, carried for some distance and then placed down on a hard surface. Then there were footsteps, moving away from him and returning, and something being dropped down beside him. He was lifted again and placed onto a more comfortable surface, which he assumed was a mattress. It didn't help that he couldn't see anything; the hood was made from a heavy material and gathered like a shoe bag around his neck. He felt his shoes being removed, his hands untied, and he heard footsteps moving away. Then a door slammed and there was nothing.

He still couldn't make sense of anything that was happening, but realised he must have been abducted – it was the only plausible reason for the situation he found himself in. And he guessed it must be some sort of a mistake, that he'd been abducted in error, that someone else must have been the target and the abductors had messed up. His head continued pounding and, unsure whether he was being guarded and afraid of inviting punishment by moving, he lay still, where he'd been put down, the bag still over his head. He waited for what seemed a long time, but could sense nothing around him – no noise, no movement, no presence – and decided to risk taking the hood off. He moved his hands slowly, seeing if there was any reaction, but there was nothing.

When he lifted off the hood, he saw he was in a bare, rectangular room with concrete walls and floor and a high ceiling. At the end of the room was a door with a metal skin. There were no windows or other openings, and it looked as though he was in some kind of storage facility. He'd been placed, as he'd guessed, on a mattress on the floor with a sleeping bag and pillow neatly stacked by the side. There was a table and chair along one wall and the chair had what appeared to be a towel hung over its back. In the far corner, there was a cubicle, which he assumed contained a toilet, and he decided to investigate. He leant forward and untied the rope about his ankles, massaged his calf muscles and stood up, shaking his feet to relieve the stiffness he felt after being confined. Once his legs felt looser, he walked across and found the cubicle contained a toilet with a WC and an accompanying washbasin on the wall, but the door to the cubicle appeared to have been removed. A plastic bottle containing hand or body wash had been placed on the washbasin but, apart from a packet of toilet rolls, the cubicle was empty.

'So, what happens next? And why am I here?' The obvious questions competed for attention with his pounding headache, but there was no one to ask. He checked his wrist to look at the time, but his watch had been removed. He was alone, in a hidden space, with no way of connecting to the outside world, no idea of the time or where he'd been taken. He listened for sounds of activity, to try to place where he was, but he couldn't hear anything. Confused by his situation he looked for clues around the room. The light was low, four bulbs, one in each corner of the ceiling, and four security cameras, one on the wall facing the cubicle and the others on each of the remaining walls. It meant he could be seen wherever he was, and he assumed he was being kept under surveillance.

On the table, there was a pad, placed under a water bottle, and a pen and he could see something written on the top sheet. He picked it up and read the message.

> *'I was hungry, and you didn't feed me.*
> *I was thirsty and you didn't give me a*
> *drink. I was sick and you didn't care for*
> *me. Now it's judgment day.'*

He knew it was a paraphrase of a biblical verse but couldn't see immediately how or why it applied to him. What judgment was being made and by whom? And what had he done that was so bad it justified the treatment he was receiving? He thought back over the past few months and wondered again if they had mistaken him for someone else? He could see no reason why anyone would want to abduct and imprison him.

Confused, he started to worry about what was happening at home. Charlotte would be wondering where he was, trying to call him. His 'phone had been in his pocket, but it wasn't there now – he wondered what his abductors had done with it and guessed they must have disposed of it somewhere to avoid it being tracked – in which case it might just have been switched off. He could imagine Charlotte ringing round to see if anyone knew where he was, but she'd be hampered by having Daniel and Tony to look after. And he worried about the lads, the sense of insecurity and fear his absence would cause.

He decided to look more closely at the entry door and noticed a gap in the metal skin, towards the bottom edge. There was a small panel and he pushed against it with his foot, wondering if it would fold back. But it was bolted from the other side and didn't budge. He walked back to the chair and table and sat down, considering the message again.

"So, why have you brought me here and who's going to be my judge?" He shouted out loudly and winced as the effort produced more pain waves in his head. There was no response, just continued silence. He wondered what happened next and waited, but nothing happened. So, he picked-up the pen and began to doodle on the pad for something to do.

After what seemed like an hour or so, a bell rang and the panel at the bottom of the door swung open, then swung closed again; he heard the sound of the bolts being pushed across. There was a tray on the floor with what looked like a meal on a plastic plate. He walked over to retrieve it. Alongside the meal there was a new water bottle with two pieces of paper underneath. The first contained a new message: *'You will be your own judge'*. The second was more mundane and straightforward: *'Put your used plate back on the tray by the panel in the foot of the door when you've finished and move away.'*

Clearly, whoever they were, they'd heard his shouted message and must be listening to him. But now, again, there was silence, a nothingness he'd never experienced before. He began to feel unsure. What were they expecting him to do? What would be the result of any judgment he reached? And what was happening back at home?

In the meantime, he was hungry, and he started to eat the meal. It was a microwaved shepherd's pie, but it tasted good. When he'd finished, he remained seated on the chair, savouring the taste. He guessed it must be late evening, a time when he'd normally be reading to the lads, talking with Charlotte or watching TV, but tonight there was nothing. The uncertainty and nothingness were becoming mentally draining, difficult to deal with, and he got up and walked round, trying to relieve the tenseness. He told himself they would be able to see him, and he mustn't show the anxiety he was feeling. So, partially to hide his anxiety, he opened the bottle and drank some of the water, being careful to conserve it, not knowing when the next bottle would arrive. It helped him feel slightly calmer.

"So, what am I judging myself for?" he shouted, "What am I meant to have done?"

But there was no response, just silence.

35

Max turned away from his computer screen, picked up his note pad and tore off the front page with its doodles of branches spreading their way around the sides. He left his office and made his way to the obligatory weekly briefing in Roger's room. He smiled and nodded at Margaret, Roger's PA, on the way in and then looked round the table at which Geoff and Roger were already sitting. "Where's Jack?"

"We don't know," Roger said, "Margaret's trying to contact his wife. He hasn't called in and there's nothing in his diary."

Roger's 'phone rang, and he got up to answer it. They saw his face change. "What do they want?" The voice at the other end of the 'phone spoke, and Roger listened. "Ok, show them up," he put the handset down. "I'm sorry, but we're going to have to postpone this meeting, apparently there are two police officers downstairs who want to speak to me."

"Do you want either of us to stay?" Max asked.

"No thanks Max, I'll brief you later," Roger picked-up his folder and pen and stood-up. "It's about Jack."

36

Margaret brought the officers up to Roger's room. He invited them to sit down as they came in, pointing to the chairs round the office table. When they were seated, he walked across to join them.

"Good morning, Sir," the first officer started. We'd like to talk to you about Jack Docherty, he's your Sales Director we believe."

"He's not appeared this morning," Roger replied, "And I don't think he's been in touch."

"Probably not, sir. We believe he's been abducted. We received a call from his wife last night to say he hadn't arrived home. So, we checked where he normally parked his car and found it unlocked, with his phone, keys and personal items inside. And there's still been no contact this morning."

"Well, thank you for letting me know Officer," Roger sat back in his chair, "So how can I help you?"

"His wife was also sent a message from Mr. Docherty's phone, saying he'd been abducted because of the part he played in John Morrison's redundancy and subsequent suicide. We wondered if you could help us understand what happened?"

"There's nothing to understand," Roger said, "We had to cut costs and undertook a redundancy programme. The sales department was the most affected and Morrison was one of those made redundant."

"And has the firm received any threats to any of its staff since Mr. Morrison's suicide?"

"Not to my knowledge. There was some TV coverage initially, particularly whilst we had the loony left demonstrating outside the gates, but since then things have quietened down, as they inevitably do."

"So, were you aware of Mr. Morrison's mental condition, before the decision to make him redundant was taken?"

"I don't think we were aware that he might be suicidal, if that's what you mean. Jack Docherty and our human resources people were aware he'd lost his wife and only daughter some months previously, but the pay-off we gave the affected people was generous and designed to make the whole experience of losing their jobs less painful. Personally, I felt it was too generous. And, if Jack has been abducted, I'm not sure how he was identified; no names have appeared in the media except Max Gregory's, when he was interviewed on local television news."

"Unless, of course, Sir, someone inside the firm identified Mr. Docherty and colluded in his abduction. Do you know of any particular personal tensions, or can you think of someone who may have been particularly affected by Mr. Morrison's death?"

"No, Officer, I don't believe for one moment it would be one of my senior team and below that level we employ over a hundred people. We've already suffered disruption to our business by the protests and I don't want further disruption by police interviewing every single employee."

"I don't think it will be necessary to interview everyone," the second officer intervened, "But it might be helpful in finding more about the abduction if we can identify any members of staff who have been especially vocal about Mr. Morrison's suicide."

"But how long is all this likely to take? This whole thing started because we had to make cost savings amongst the workforce – carry on like this and we may need to make more!"

"I'm very sorry Sir, but abduction is a crime; people can't be allowed to just go round picking-up people forcibly on the streets – whatever the reason. And you are, if I may say so, Sir, overlooking the effect of the abduction on Mr. Docherty's family. They're already suffering mentally, worried about him and what's happening to him whilst he's imprisoned."

"They'll be suffering a damn sight more if there's no job for Docherty to come back to, as will the families of the rest of the workforce."

"It will only be necessary to interview members of your immediate team, Sir, and maybe the managers below them, to pick-up on any undercurrents amongst the main body of employees. It needn't disrupt your business whilst we do so."

"It's already disrupting the business, Officer," Roger was beginning to feel angry, "It's not just the questioning that will be intrusive, there's all the speculation it's likely to cause. It's distracting, stops staff working properly – you know how people love to gossip."

"I'm sorry, Sir, but one of your senior staff has been abducted, probably because of a work-associated activity, and we need to find him and the people who undertook the abduction."

Roger held up his hands to shut down the conversation. "Alright Officer, carry out your interviews, but try to do so with the least impact on the business. I'll introduce you to my PA, Margaret, and, if you tell her who you want to talk to, she'll arrange everything and have a room placed at your disposal."

"Thank you, Sir." The policeman paused before leaving, "Please ensure that Mr. Docherty's abduction remains confidential until we've had the opportunity of talking to the staff. We don't want our investigations to be compromised."

"We can't say nothing." Roger shook his head doubtfully as he considered what the officers were saying. "His colleagues aren't blind; they'll see he's not at work and they're bound to start asking questions – you must know what the workplace grapevine is like. What do you suggest we tell the staff?"

"Why not let the grapevine do its own work, Sir? Let it leak out that Docherty's feeling the pressure of the recent protests after the suicide and recognises that some people are angry about his role in it, so he's been given some time away from work?"

"That may work for the workforce generally, but I'll need to let my senior management team and my PA know what's going on. However, I'm sure we can rely on them remaining silent. More importantly, though, the sooner you find Docherty, the better." Roger looked at each of the officers in turn, "I assume you're throwing all available resources at locating him?"

"We're doing everything we can, Sir," the first officer said, "But in the meantime, the fewer people who know he's been abducted, the better. If you feel your senior managers need to be informed, please emphasise how important it is they don't confide in anyone else – including their families. It's vital that nothing leaks out at this stage."

37

Roger called the managers back in as soon as the officers had left and briefed them about Jack's abduction and the need for absolute confidentiality.

"Well, I hope this doesn't mean the rest of us are going to be targets," Geoff looked round the table anxiously, "We haven't done anything that other managers in other companies haven't done."

"Exactly, Geoff," Roger nodded, affirming Geoff's reaction. "But it does raise the issue of whether we might have been in a better place if we'd taken the loss of Morrison's family into account and offered him a stay of execution until he'd had more time to come to terms with it all."

A brief frown crossed Max's face.

"Is there a problem, Max?" Roger's tone was sharper than it had been.

"No," Max looked-up, "It was just an unfortunate phraseology – 'stay of execution'."

"Well, that was down to Jack," Geoff interjected, wanting to get his point across, "Jack knew Morrison better than any of us and he didn't see fit to suggest we delayed making him redundant. If he had, we'd have consulted with you immediately, Roger. Besides, how did the abductors get Jack's name, I wasn't aware we'd released any names." He looked pointedly at Max.

"We didn't," Max said, "But that doesn't mean any of us shouldn't be more careful over the next few weeks, the staff all know who we are, and the most probable source is one of them. Which is, presumably, why the police want to conduct some interviews." He turned back to his pad and started a new doodle, this time more complex geometric shapes, the perspective varying according to which way they were looked at.

"But can we use Jack's abduction to our advantage, when the news finally comes out, as inevitably it will. Won't the majority of people be outraged by Jack's treatment?" Roger was searching for some upside in the situation after the public condemnation the company had received.

"Sorry, Roger, but I can't see any advantage for the company. When news of the abduction emerges, any sympathy is likely to be for Jack and his family. And, of course, it just reminds the public about the original issue and John Morrison's suicide." Max shook his head as he considered the situation and continued doodling on his pad.

"For Christ's sake, Max, can't you stop bloody doodling for a moment?" Roger slammed his hand down on the table, frustrated by the increasing impotence he was feeling.

"There are times when not doing anything is the best course of action, Roger." Max stopped doodling and put his pad down. "The way I see things, anything we do now may just exacerbate the situation. Things are developing as we sit here, and we can't predict what's going to happen next. The safest message, when we're allowed to say anything, is to repeat what we've said already, that the firm's future prosperity and the jobs of all its employees might have been at risk unless we reduced costs. And, much as we regret John Morrison's death, his redundancy may not have caused his suicide and it's difficult to see how abducting Jack Docherty achieves anything other than causing his family unnecessary concern. Period. Boring, non-newsworthy, defensive maybe, but factual."

There was a pause as Roger considered what Max had said. He placed his hands together and held them against his lips trying to think things through. The issue was distracting him, making it difficult to concentrate on other issues that needed his attention. Inactivity felt unnatural and he was impatient for a solution – something that would allow him to tick a mental box and move forward. The company had played things by the book, been generous, and it irritated him that people were choosing to ignore that.

"I know Roger," Max spoke as though he was reading his boss' thoughts, "People are very quick to throw accusations and vilification is easy if you've never done anything, just let life carry you along. But there are an awful lot of people like that, particularly if it doesn't involve any risk for them. Just look at the way people act on social media."

Roger held his hands up, acknowledging the truth of what Max was saying. "Ok, let's say nothing outside this office for the time being. I'll get Margaret to talk to Jack's wife and make sure we're seen to have been treating her sympathetically when this all plays out. We don't want to provide the press with any more stories to throw at us. Besides, we need to work with the police, and we have to rely on them to tell us about any new developments."

"You need to warn Margaret that they'll probably allocate a female liaison officer to the family and her job's going to include fielding any incoming calls and controlling the release of information," Max paused for a moment, before continuing. "And tell her to tread softly, say you've instructed her to keep in touch and to ensure Jack's wife has anything she needs. There's more chance of keeping the lines of communication open using a sympathetic approach. And, by the way, Jack's wife's name is Charlotte, and they have two young sons, I thought it as well to check Jack's staff file before any contact was made."

"Good thinking, Max. I've met Charlotte a couple of times over the years, I liked her. Maybe we should arrange some flowers?"

"I'm not sure that's appropriate at this stage, after all it's not a celebration and we don't want to infer it might become a wake." Max shook his head, "Just get Margaret to let Charlotte know we're thinking of her and the lads and are hoping Jack is released soon. And tell her not to think twice about calling if there's anything she needs – establish as easy a relationship as possible and keep the line open for further conversations."

Roger nodded his agreement and then turned back to his notes.

"Right, before we close the meeting, we need to get back to business, So, let's talk about the Trade Show and what we do if Jack's not around to complete the arrangements.

As I've said previously, it's very important we do well." Roger looked across at Max. "I know you've already been working on the PR front, Max, but have you any idea where we are with setting-up and manning the Stand?"

"Sorry, Roger, I've not been involved in those areas, but I know Jack has commissioned the Stand and has been relying on Alison to ensure it's all properly set-up. I suggest we take her into our confidence, she's reliable, and we can get her to manage things for the time being. You'll need to talk to the sales guys at some point, but we've still got nearly two weeks to go and maybe something will change before then."

"I'll leave you to tell Alison, Max, and to keep an eye on everything. And stress to her that she mustn't talk to anyone else about what she knows."

"There's obviously going to be a lot of speculation amongst the staff, Roger, the sales team, in particular, is bound to wonder what's happened to Jack, though I think we can rely on Alison not to be drawn on the issue." Max picked up his pad and pen and prepared to leave, "But, obviously, when I tell her about Jack's abduction, I'll emphasise the importance of staying silent."

38

"OK, take me through the CCTV footage from the car park and let's see if that shows up anything." Detective Inspector Bracken pulled-up a chair and sat alongside her colleague in front of his computer screen.

"Think you're going to be disappointed, Ma'am," Sergeant George started running the footage, "Whoever carried out the abduction appears to have been well organised." He pointed at the screen, "They're coming into view in a moment."

The back of a man appeared on screen. He was wearing a balaclava and a boiler suit.

"Take a look at his hands, Ma'am, see what I mean? He's wearing surgical gloves. The whole thing was carried out with military precision."

They watched as the figure approached the car, held out the car key and opened the door. He then placed some items on the driver's seat, the snooker cue in the back, shut the door and started to walk away. As he turned, he bent his head and placed a gloved hand to cover the contours of his face. Then he exited the way he'd entered.

"I take it that the items he was placing in the car were the personal items we found belonging to Docherty?"

"We assume that's what they were," George nodded, "Nobody else went near the car again until our own guys arrived later that evening."

"Is there any other footage?" Bracken asked, "Were there any cameras outside?"

"No, sorry, Ma'am, this is all we have."

"Any witnesses see the guy leave the car park or notice any vehicles parked outside?"

"No, the weather wasn't good that evening and there weren't many people around, as you can tell from the empty spaces in the car park. Whoever it was who abducted Docherty couldn't have chosen a better day."

"Lucky as well as a good planner," Bracken shook her head, "Well, before we start seeing him as some superman, let's see how well he plays out the rest of the abduction. Make sure none of this leaks out for the time being, whoever's holding Docherty is looking to make an example of him, they'll want publicity and if we don't provide any they'll be forced to do something to generate it themselves."

"Docherty's boss knows about his abduction, we needed his agreement before we started making enquiries amongst his management team, but he's aware the abduction should be treated confidentially. The guys investigating at Docherty's workplace are trying to identify anyone who reacted adversely to the suicide and might be treated as possible suspects in our enquiries, but the unofficial line is that Docherty is feeling the pressure of the press coverage and is taking some time out."

"We'd better have a chat with Morrison's next of kin," Bracken stood up, ready to walk back to her own desk, "See if they have any idea about who may have kidnapped this Docherty guy. I guess we have their names and addresses on file following the suicide."

"We have, they live some distance from here, Ma'am, a brother and a sister. They were interviewed by the Coroner's Officer, because Morrison didn't leave a note, but they weren't able to shed any new light on why Morrison might have committed suicide – only the obvious, that his wife and daughter had been killed and then he'd lost his job. I can't see that we'll get anything further from them about the reasons for the abduction."

"It a long shot I know, Sergeant, left-wing activists are still the most obvious suspects, but we need to cover all potential bases."

39

Jack could hear a bell ringing; it interrupted his sleep and woke him. It only stopped ringing when he rolled over and sat up. He heard the panel open, the tray from his previous meal being withdrawn and a new tray being pushed through. Then the panel closed, and the bolts were slid across again. He got up and went to fetch the tray. His abductors had placed a plastic bowl of cereal, some milk and another bottle of water on it. And there was also a new note. It read simply *'John Morrison'*.

So now he knew why he was locked in the room, wherever that was. But what was he to judge? The redundancy programme had been a corporate decision, something he'd been required to do – not something he'd chosen to implement. And it had been decided before he'd spoken to John. So, why select him? Why not Grimshaw, the boss, the guy who'd ordered the redundancies? Besides, he couldn't recall his name being published in the media, Max had been very careful not to mention names. So, the only way he could think his identity might have leaked out was through someone in the firm, and it hurt that someone he knew would have blamed him sufficiently, disliked him enough, to have assisted his abductors.

As he thought about it more, he became angry, angry that Charlotte and the boys were being made to go through so much uncertainty. He found the anger useful, something he could concentrate on in the absence of other sensations. It was something he could feed off; make plans about when he escaped from his prison. Negative feelings that were alien to him, but which, nonetheless, helped him deal with what was happening. Anger was better than nothing, better than benign acceptance, better than being driven insane by nothingness.

"So, now you intend to punish the messenger," he shouted, "I had no choice but to make John redundant, you're punishing the wrong person! And you can't even be sure that John killed himself because of his redundancy."

There was no response, but he hadn't expected one, just the perpetual silence again. He'd shouted out more in frustration than any hope of changing his abductors' minds – things had gone too far for that to happen. He was where he was. There was no point in throwing the water bottle against the wall, or trashing the cereal, that would only harm himself, so he carried the tray back to the table and started eating, enjoying the taste of the food, but craving a cup of coffee instead of the water. He guessed it must be breakfast time – he'd been asleep, and the meal was a breakfast meal – but he didn't know when breakfast was served in his abductors' world, or whether they were just playing a new game to disorientate him. Just playing with his mind.

40

It had been a difficult night, Charlotte had been woken several times by vivid dreams from which she'd had to escape, waking in a panic and then finding it difficult to get back to sleep. And today she needed to talk to the boys who'd want to know why their father wasn't at home. She lay there thinking for a while, wondering whether to keep them away from school or to try to keep their lives as normal as possible – in case Jack was released quickly. But trying to maintain normality would involve some form of avoidance and she'd always tried to be honest with the boys. She decided to look at the news and if there were no reports of Jack's abduction send them to school as normal. The news didn't mention Jack and she put a call through to the family liaison officer. The officer confirmed the police had not issued any statements to the media and preferred the news to be controlled for the time being, whilst they waited to see who would claim responsibility for the abduction. So, when the boys came downstairs and asked for their father, she told them he'd had to leave early, gave them their packed lunches and drove them to the school.

Back at home she looked round the kitchen, wondering what to do to keep herself occupied. She filled the kettle and made a cup of tea, took it into the study and sat down at the computer, searching the news channels for any reports. There was nothing. She drank the rest of her tea and then stared hopelessly at the computer screen, not knowing what to do to relieve the anxiety that was dominating her thoughts. She spoke to the family liaison officer again and explained that she had to talk to someone and was going to talk to her parents. She rang them as soon as she put the phone down but started to sob when she heard her mother's voice.

By late afternoon there was still no announcement about Jack's abduction, and she decided to tell the boys he'd had to stay away on business. It had happened on occasions, and she felt comfortable in carrying-off the deception; but knew she might be forced to tell them the truth if the news of Jack's abduction came out before Jack was released. She checked the time, picked-up her car keys and drove to the school to collect them; the boys seemed happy and full of what had happened during their lessons that day. So, she heard them out and then told them their father wouldn't be home that night and, when they asked why, told them it was to do with his work. At least, she told herself, it wasn't a lie. At the same time, she cursed Grimshaw mentally for forcing Jack to go through with the redundancy programme. And then she felt remorse for all the times she'd shouted at Jack and berated him, and told herself how much she valued him, each morning when they woke-up together.

41

At first, after the initial shock and anxiety following his abduction, Jack had felt surprisingly relieved by his isolation. It gave him time to think, meditate almost. But the relief lasted only a short time, a few hours he guessed at most, and now the boredom that replaced it was beginning to agitate him and he found it difficult to control a rising feeling of panic. His heartbeat was increasing in speed and intensity, and his chest felt constricted when he breathed. He'd felt the symptoms before, when he'd been trapped in the toilet on an empty floor of an office block, after the door lock jammed. He'd known rationally he wasn't in danger and that he'd be found at some point, but the confines of the cubicle and the heavy floor to ceiling door freaked him out and he began attacking it, pulling the handle to generate friction between the lock plate and the bolt until the pressure resulted in the handle engaging again and allowing him to walk free.

This time he knew he couldn't open the door. He started to walk around the room, using each pace as a means of relaxing, of reducing the tension. Round and round, deliberately slowing the rate of his breathing and the speed of his heartbeat. Hands clenching and unclenching as he walked, pacing round until he began to regain control. There was still some water in the bottle on the table and he took a drink, carefully limiting the size of each mouthful and saving the remainder. He wanted something to eat, not because he was hungry, but because he wanted something comforting. It seemed hours since his last meal, but he couldn't be sure how long it actually was and realised he was losing track of time.

Being confined was difficult but he found the silence worse – the longer it continued the more insistent it became. He tried talking aloud, to hear the sound of a voice, even if it was his own, but it was difficult to find something to keep talking about, something superficial that didn't reveal too much about what he was thinking or feeling. So, instead, he started to sing, knowing the song lyrics by heart and not having to think about the words his abductors might hear. He chose popular songs, songs that gave nothing away about his mental state, but thoughts about Charlotte and his boys began to intrude and, when they did, his singing died away as he visualised them and wondered how they were coping. Then he stopped singing entirely and the sadness enveloped him. He felt the corners of his mouth turning down and clamped his lips together as he tried to control the tears he felt coming, aware of the cameras and determined not to allow the weakness to show. But he was only partially successful, shaking his head in denial of the emotion that was forcing its way out of him.

The boys would be ok; Charlotte would take care of that. She was always so organised, so capable. But there was the media; he wasn't sure how they could be protected from that – or from the unkind taunts of fellow pupils at their school.

He tried to think of something to exercise his mind – but there was nothing, just the writing pad and a bare room. He decided to invent something, a concept he could develop, or a game he could play. His mission, he decided, was to portray a calmness he didn't feel, and to remain rational; people would be looking for him, trying to find where he was. What he had to do was survive until they got there. But it still left him with the question of how to fill the time and avoid more panic attacks. He found himself doodling on the writing pad again and smiled as he remembered how Max always doodled in meetings and how much it irritated Grimshaw.

42

Grimshaw drove out through the gates and waved at the security guard who shut them after him. Jack's abduction had come at just the wrong time with the trade show imminent and the sales they'd anticipated now put at risk. He guessed he might have to attend the show himself, to gee along the sales team on the stand. Although he knew Max was extremely able, he worried about his application – and decided to arrange daily updates with Max and Alison He remembered Alison joining, an attractive woman, attractive enough to consider moving her into his own office as his PA, but when he'd put out feelers about how she'd react to the suggestion it appeared she preferred working with the sales team. Then Margaret had come along, and Margaret was easy going, despite the impression she gave everyone and, after a short time working together, they'd become close, very close. He smiled to himself as he remembered the first time they'd made love together, the excitement of having a different woman after being married to Hilary for so long. And even when she and her husband had divorced, Margaret hadn't made any demands on him, happy to meet-up whenever he suggested they did and always discreet at work – giving no indication of their relationship outside.

His attention was drawn back to the trade show and to the events that had preceded it. Morrison's suicide had made things extremely difficult; staff morale had been affected initially, and now the final arrangements for the show were being potentially compromised. And he couldn't absolve Jack of responsibility because of the way he'd handled his part in the process. The redundancies had been necessary to maintain profit levels, so the programme itself had been essential; the damage had occurred because of the way it had been implemented by his management team – Jack in particular and, to a lesser extent, Geoff. He sometimes felt he carried the whole business on his shoulders, so much of his time being taken in trying to ensure his managers performed their jobs satisfactorily. People talked about the big money he and people like him received, but they overlooked the contribution they made – ensuring that a lot of workers and their families had the means to feed their families. As for the protesters, he asked himself what they contributed to society? And then he stamped on the brake pedal as an unkempt figure staggered off the pavement and fell in the road.

"What the hell?" he felt his heart thumping, checked in the mirror to ensure the van behind had stopped and got out of the car. In front of him, pushing himself back up off the road was a ragged figure in a charcoal grey coat, a red vinyl bag with cans falling out of it, lying beside him. The figure had suddenly appeared from the pavement and fallen in front of the car and Roger congratulated himself on managing to stop.

"What the hell are you doing?" he shouted. "You could have killed yourself." Then taking a closer look at the man, he realised he was a wino and guessed he was drunk. "You're a bloody disgrace."

"Me cans," the figure was putting escaped cider cans back in his bag. One of them rolled further way as he tried to pick it up and, as it approached him, Roger kicked out, sending it along the street, where it hit the kerb and punctured, pumping out its contents onto the tarmac.

Roger walked back and opened the door of his car. The wino, his bag in his hand, lurched towards him shouting and, when Roger didn't respond, started to beat a hand on the bonnet of Roger's car. Roger sat in the driving seat and revved the engine, but the wino was not moving, just banging on the bonnet repeatedly.

Roger jumped back out of the car and shouted at the man. "Damage this car and I'll call the police."

"Me cider," the man was shouting, "You've spilled me cider."

"And you were so pissed you fell in the road and nearly caused a fucking accident," Roger shouted, "Piss off."

The man took no notice of what Roger was saying, just kept beating his hand on the car bonnet.

People on the street were beginning to stop and watch and there were a few shouts in support of the ragged figure. And behind him, cars began to queue, and drivers become impatient. Roger assessed the situation, took out his wallet and gave a five-pound note to the wino. "Right, piss-off, you're not getting any more." He got back in his car and the wino stepped aside, raising a finger to his forehead in acknowledgement of the money.

"Fuck off," Roger shouted, irritated by the unwarranted support the wino had received from onlookers. He revved up hard and moved away quickly, his tyres squealing as they gripped the road surface. When he got back home, he was still in a foul mood and poured himself a whisky.

"Bad day?" Hilary asked.

"Which day isn't when you're surrounded by idiots like some of the people I have around me?" He took a large slug of whisky, "I need to decide what to do about them."

43

"Are you ok?" a young man approached Jonah.

"I don't think the car actually touched him," a woman said, "I think he just lost his footing and fell in the road. Poor thing."

Jonah pocketed the five-pound note the driver had given him, picked-up his vinyl bag and nodded.

"But it looks like he's a bit shaken-up. Needs to sit down and recover. Have you got somewhere to go?" the young man was concerned, "Somewhere to sleep tonight."

"I don't suppose he's got his own place," the woman shook her head, "But there must be a hostel, somewhere they can all go for a meal and a bed."

Jonah shook his head at the woman. "Can't afford it, 'aven't got enough t'day for hostel."

"How much does the hostel cost?" The young man was feeling in his pocket, whilst the woman opened her bag and took out her purse.

"More'n I got," Jonah said unhelpfully.

"Here, take this and don't spend it on booze." The woman took ten pounds out of her purse and held it out for Jonah.

"Here's another ten," the young man matched what the woman had given him. "And do what she said, spend it on a night at the hostel."

Jonah thanked them both profusely, picked-up his bag and started off down the street.

"I wouldn't put any money on him doing what we told him to," the young man turned to walk back to the other side of the street.

"I'm afraid you're probably right," the woman put her purse back in her bag. "What do you reckon the odds are, hostel or booze?"

Jonah wasn't sure either as he shuffled along. There were still a couple of cans in his bag, and he fancied meeting-up with some of his mates at the hostel. But there was still some time left to decide and he might be able to beg a few more pounds in the town centre – in which case, he might be able to afford both.

44

"Where am I?" Jack shouted out loudly, hoping his captors would hear him and send an answer with his next meal.

"Nowhere," a voice said, startling him by its sudden intrusion into the silence. He paused, considering how to respond.

"That's ridiculous, I must be somewhere. I can see, feel – and now I can hear you. So, I must be somewhere."

"You think, so therefore you are? That is, if I may say so, a discredited proposition. Now, perhaps, you live only in a world of dreams, alive because somebody imagines you're alive, at least, until they wake up. A bit like Schrödinger's cat. I take it you've heard of Schrödinger's cat?"

"What the hell has Schrödinger's cat got to do with me?" Jack shook his head confused by what he was hearing.

"Well, if you remember, it was placed in a box with a fatal substance and is potentially alive and dead at the same time until somebody opens the box and finds out whether it's been killed by the substance or not."

"All very interesting, but I'll decide which state I'm in. After all, I'm in the box, so I know already."

"And presumably the cat knew – up to a point. But when the box was finally opened it might be found that the cat, like you, had been mistaken, believing it was alive when it wasn't."

"OK, let's try something a bit easier to answer. How long have I been here? What day is it?"

"If it's that easy, how is it you don't know the answer? And how would it help you if you did? Time is meaningless here. This is eternity; it just goes on – until it stops. And then the answer is irrelevant, because it can no longer be comprehended by the person to whom it was previously important."

"Oh, come on, this is ridiculous. I didn't enroll for some sort of quasi-university philosophy course; I'm here because you abducted me. You're my kidnapper, not my teacher. I'm here against my will."

"I prefer to look upon myself as a confessor, giving you the space and freedom to reflect upon your actions and motives, how they impacted on other people's lives, and to make your confession. And afterwards to perform the prescribed penance."

"I'm here, because of John Morrison, you made that clear in the notes you sent. And what's this about a penance?"

"You're here in an almost Messianic role, as an example to all those other people, like you, who put selfish interests before the health and well-being of their fellow men. And like other Messiahs before you, you must suffer for the sins of others. Away from here, you're news, there are protests on the streets and, hopefully, people in positions of power up and down the country reflecting on what could happen to them if they behave in the future as you did."

"Putting me in here isn't going to change the way the people at the top behave, they'll just choose another messenger."

"But the messenger must be willing to convey the message – and perhaps they won't do it as readily in the future. Perhaps the pressure from people to change the essential brutality of the situation will mean the type of risk assessment that wasn't made in John Morrison's case will be needed, before plans to make individuals redundant are implemented."

"I think you're living in a dream world."

"No look around. It's you who are living in a dream world and, the longer you're here the better you'll begin to understand."

"This is crazy," Jack shouted, but this time there was no response. He was alone again, in the silence of the room, cut off from everyone.

45

"Hi," Sam walked in, threw his bag down and gave Ros a kiss. "Did you have a good day?"

"Interesting," Ros paused, teasing him deliberately, knowing he would want to hear more.

"Why interesting?" Sam had been expecting one of the normal responses and 'interesting' was not one of them.

"I'll give you three guesses."

"I've no idea. Has one of the salesmen done something? Or Alison resigned?"

"Neither of those, at least I don't think so. One guess left."

"That's mean," Sam pulled a rueful face, "I was just thinking aloud. Give me a clue." he took a beer from the fridge and poured himself a glass.

"I'll give you a clue if you pour me a cider." She waited whilst he poured her a glass and handed it to her. "OK, cheers," she raised the glass, "Well, it wasn't Grimshaw suddenly offering everyone a huge bonus!"

"Now that would be interesting, but it didn't even begin to register on my believability scale. Ranks somewhere with pigs flying, so not much of a clue at all. Give me another one, a real clue this time." He took a mouthful of beer.

"Someone wasn't there!"

"Oh, great clue, Ros! I can think of hundreds of people who weren't there! The Pope for example. Or the Prime Minister. Or me."

"Well, you're right on all counts, but none of you three were supposed to be there – it would have been surprising if you had been! No, Jack Docherty didn't turn up at work today and the police have been interviewing some of the managers."

"So, what's the story about Docherty and why are the police interviewing people?" Sam put his beer down and looked in the cupboard for something to snack on. He opened a packet of crisps, but Ros shook her head when he offered her some.

"Well, nobody's really saying but the rumour is they're trying to find out whether anyone has been particularly vocal in their criticism of the firm or Jack. But why they're doing it is a bit of a mystery, and there's been no formal announcement at all about Jack not coming in. The suggestion seems to be that either he's been told to stay away for the time being or he's asked for time off because it was him who made John redundant."

"They must be pretty worried then," Sam shook his head, "I wonder whether Jack or the company has been threatened? Why else would the police be involved?",

"I don't know, but they're obviously taking this all very seriously." Ros took a sip of her cider, "I tried finding out more from Alison, she chats to Margaret, Grimshaw's PA, sometimes, but she says she hasn't heard anything either – just that Jack's not coming in for a while and we're not to get in contact with him."

"You've got that big Trade Show coming up shortly, haven't you? Surely Jack can't just take time out when that's on? No, I reckon there's more to it than you're being told."

"Who knows? In the meantime, Alison's taken over the arrangements for the Show; she's been working on it closely with Jack anyway. But it means me taking over some of her work, to cover for her. And, another thing, Gill says she was holding an event at a hotel where some of our guys were meeting, and there was a protest against John's death outside. Anyway, one of the staff was irritated by the protest and started to tell Gill about John Morrison's wife; a bit of a coincidence, but John's wife had worked there and, apparently, they weren't happy together. I'm going to mention it to Alison when I get a chance to talk to her alone and see what she knows. She was closer to John than anybody."

46

"Good morning, Sir, my name is Bracken, Inspector Bracken and this is Detective Sergeant George. May we come in, please?"

Allan stood aside and motioned the two policemen in, then shut the door behind them. "The lounge is the first door on the left," he indicated the door and motioned them forward, "Please go in, I'll call my wife, Heather."

The officers did as Allan suggested and waited until they were invited to sit down. Heather joined them and asked whether they would like some tea or coffee, but they declined and when everyone was seated began the interview addressing their questions to Allan.

"First of all, I realise that anything to do with your brother's death must be upsetting to you, Mr. Morrison, and I'm anxious not to cause you any more distress, but we're here because Jack Docherty, the man who made your brother redundant has been abducted." Bracken watched

Allan and his wife closely as she told them the purpose of her visit. Allan did not react, but Heather seemed nervous. "And I must emphasise the need to keep this information confidential, it isn't being released to the media for the time being."

"But why are you interviewing us?" Allan asked, "What possible interest do we have in Docherty being kidnapped?"

"Please don't think we're accusing you of any involvement," Bracken looked at Allan as she spoke, "It's just that we have to interview anyone with any connection to the case and eliminate them from our enquiries."

"Well, I think you can eliminate us," Allan looked at Heather for her confirmation and then back at the Inspector, "We may believe that what Docherty did was heartless and wrong, but this is the first we've heard about him being kidnapped. And I have to ask whether we really look like the sort of people who go round kidnapping other people? Besides, what would be the point?"

"It's not just a question of whether you abducted Mr. Docherty, but whether you know of any other people who might have a reason to do so?" Bracken turned and included Heather in her questioning.

"Why are you asking my wife and I a question like that?" Allan interrupted before Heather was able to respond, "I know you have a job to do but I rather object to you interviewing us in this way. Again, I have to ask you, what would be the point of us kidnapping this man?"

"Well," the sergeant interposed, "The kidnappers have contacted Mrs. Docherty to say that they have abducted her husband because of his involvement in your brother's redundancy and subsequent death and are going to hold him until he has admitted his responsibility for what happened."

"Look, we're already upset enough by my brother's death and, despite what you said about not distressing us further, I think both of us find this whole line of questioning somewhat callous and brutal." Allan looked at Heather again for support and she nodded her agreement. "And I find the whole idea that you believe two middle-aged people, without any previous criminal records, are capable of carrying out such an activity utterly fatuous."

"I'm sorry, Sir, but we have to carry out our enquiries," Bracken said.

"Well mightn't it be a good idea to carry them out with people who are more likely to have the capability and wherewithal to conduct a kidnapping and leave us to mourn my brother in peace?" Allan clutched the arm of the sofa as though he was ready to get up and escort them out.

Bracken recognised the body language and held her hand up to stop him standing, "Please Sir, bear with us for a few more minutes and, just to eliminate yourselves from our enquiries, tell us where you were last Tuesday night."

"Here," Heather said.

"And can anyone confirm that, Mrs. Morrison?"

"Only my husband,".

"And where were you, Sir?" Bracken asked.

"Here with my wife, we had our dinner and watched television together. Then went to bed."

"What did you watch?"

Heather told her what she and Allan had agreed, feeling more comfortable having prepared the answer, and proceeded to describe an episode of the serial she'd watched whilst the abduction had taken place.

"Have you ever met or spoken to Mr. Docherty, Sir? The sergeant addressed Allan directly.

"Yes, I have, I went to his office to see him the day after my brother's funeral. I wanted to speak to him."

"Why did you want to talk to him?" Bracken took over the questioning again.

"Because I was annoyed that none of the firm's management had attended the funeral, I thought that was disrespectful. And I wanted to ask Docherty how he'd found my brother when he fired him. We live a long way away, as you will have found when you drove here, and after the deaths of his wife and Keira we'd tried to be supportive, but we hadn't seen John since their funeral."

"So, you were angry with Mr. Docherty," Bracken begun, but Allan immediately cut across her.

"Don't try to put words in my mouth, Inspector. I was annoyed, not angry, I didn't go in there with the intention of hitting or shouting at Docherty; as I've just told you, I wanted to talk to him, to ask why the management hadn't been represented at the funeral and how he'd found my brother."

"And what did Mr. Docherty say?" the sergeant stepped in again.

"He didn't say anything," Allan paused and stared at the sergeant again, "He was in a rush and couldn't stop. He asked me to make an appointment with his assistant, which I did. However, that appointment was cancelled a few days ago, and now I understand why. At the time I just thought Docherty was taking the coward's way out and trying to avoid me."

"And may I ask you what you do?"

"I'm a retired army officer and work as a security consultant; I hire my services out when people need help with protecting their businesses."

"And do you work, Mrs. Morrison?" the sergeant asked.

"Yes, I'm a seamstress," Heather answered, "I've got a workroom at the back of the house."

"Look, I'm finding all this questioning somewhat unfeeling and intrusive," Allan turned back to the inspector, "And, quite frankly I would have thought there were other people who were far more likely suspects than we are. So, unless you have any more material questions to ask, I'd like you to leave."

The two officers looked at each other and Bracken nodded to her sergeant. They thanked the couple for their time and left. When they'd got back in their car, Bracken asked George what he thought of the couple's responses.

"He's hard," George shook his head, "She seemed nervous, but that's not unusual if people are being interviewed by police, particularly if they don't normally have contact with us."

"And do you think he's capable of undertaking an abduction, sergeant? Have we got any more background information about him, other than he used to be in the forces?"

"Yes, he's quite an interesting character, his military career was rather secretive, all I could establish was that he was involved in special operations and spent some time in military intelligence. Not the sort of person you'd want to cross. Be interesting to see what his sister's like."

Susan turned out to be charming and very relaxed, getting tearful only when she was reminded about her brother's death; and she had a verifiable alibi, having been at a local society meeting. Bracken ruled her out of any involvement in their investigations immediately, sure the alibi would check out.

"But I've still got concerns about the brother," she said on the way back, "Nothing to go on, but I reckon he'd be capable of planning and carrying out an abduction – his history shows that. But, if he is involved, where's he keeping Docherty? It's got to be somewhere Docherty can't be heard, or people see Allan Morrison going to and from. There's also the question of who would have helped him with the kidnapping; he can't have done it on his own, without attracting attention in the middle of a city."

"So, are you saying we should keep them on our list of suspects, ma'am?"

"Well, as he pointed out, there are more obvious suspects we can concentrate on, but I wouldn't forget him entirely if we draw a blank in our other enquiries. He has a possible motive and the opportunity, but there remains the question of whether he had the means to abduct Docherty."

47

"What did you make of the Inspector?" Heather asked when the officers had left.

"She's smart, I'll give her that," Allan watched as their car drove off, "We're going to need to be careful and make sure we're not being watched when we go to the industrial estate. We'd better get Stuart to take over feeding the guy for the next week or so, they don't seem to have identified him as a possible team member and won't be likely to be tracking him. And we need to be careful with the computers, in case they come back unannounced. I'll mention that to Stuart as well – we don't want them finding the video link to Docherty."

48

As he opened the church door, the Priest looked across at the pew where the woman had sat before, but it was empty. He'd come to trust in his intuition over the years and been expecting to see her, convinced her need for peace had not been satisfied on her previous visit; that she still needed to talk her concerns through to dissipate the burden placed on her. Perhaps he'd missed her the last time she'd come. Out of habit, he tidied the leaflets and looked in the visitor's book on the small table by the church door and then went into the vestry. It was quiet and he sat behind the desk, looking out at the sky, letting his mind wander over disparate events: a parishioner's grief after the death of her husband, the theme of his sermon the following Sunday, his parents and childhood. He thought about his childhood more as he grew older and it was easy to sit still and reflect in his present church; easier than it had been previously, with the constant sound of traffic in some of the urban parishes he'd served in. And there were trees and the river surrounding the church, instead of buildings. It reminded him of the quiet of the childhood woods, where he'd once played with friends, a less hectic time with fewer people, a time when the path ahead had seemed more straightforward than it had become later on. But it had still been a good life, a life he felt blessed to have had. He'd never been ambitious, never craved a higher office than the one he held, loving the simplicity of his role, celebrating his faith without trappings in the austere but atmospheric buildings in which he'd carried out his stewardship. Like this church, in which he hoped to end his priesthood.

His musing was interrupted by the latch opening on the church door and the sound of a woman's heels along the floor stones of the nave, stopping near the usual pew. He told himself his intuition hadn't been mistaken, checked his watch and continued sitting where he was, giving the woman more time to reflect. But his thoughts kept returning to her, driving out the earlier mental ramblings. Unable to concentrate on anything else, he forced himself to wait a few minutes more, and then got up and walked out of the vestry. The woman was sat where she always sat and seemed unaware of him at first. Then she turned and smiled, but it was a sad smile and lasted only momentarily. Unlike the previous occasions on which she'd been to the church, he walked towards her and sat in the pew on the opposite side of the aisle. When she turned again to look at him, he spoke to her, asking if there was any way he could help.

She shook her head. "Not now, but I will need to talk to someone later, when it's all over. Right now, I don't know what the outcome will be, and I don't want to compromise you, to put you in a difficult situation."

The priest stood up, reached for his wallet and gave her a card with his name and number printed on it. "Call me anytime, when you're ready."

"I think I will come here to see you when I'm ready and talk face-to-face. It's not something I can discuss over the 'phone."

"Well, I'll be here and, if I'm not in the church you can find me at the rectory; it's just down the road."

"Thank you."

"I hope things work out as you want them to." He turned away and walked back to lock the vestry before leaving the church. As he left, he took a quick look across; she was still sat in the pew, her face buried in her hands.

49

When he woke, Jack had no idea how long he'd been asleep; time seemed to go more slowly on his own and in the silence. The silence had been the most disturbing thing but now he began to be aware of shapes and flashes of light, seemingly just out of his line of sight, and wasn't sure whether he was awake or emerging from a dream. He looked at the table and chair and started, convinced that someone was sitting, watching him. But when he looked again, there was nobody there. Almost immediately he saw a movement over by the toilet cubicle. Again, he could see no one when he checked, so he waited, trying to concentrate on the cubicle entrance, readying himself for someone to emerge – but nothing happened. The frightening thing was his lack of control over the things he was seeing. He told himself they were just the result of being in a state where he was half awake and half asleep, but they carried on appearing, despite his efforts to blank them out. He told himself there was no-one there but reacted suddenly when he felt as though a person had touched his arm, spinning round and feeling just the hard concrete wall as his arm drove out to push whoever it was away. He began to feel anxious, the sensations surprising him as they occurred. The mattress seemed alive, and he thought he saw a rat run across the end, before disappearing somewhere in the room. He told himself that rats ran along walls, not across rooms, but then he saw another rat, following the first one – or, at least, the shadow of a rat.

He shut his eyes, but there were still flashes of light. Then he heard a buzzing and wondered how the fly had entered the room. He opened his eyes and the buzzing continued, but he couldn't see the fly. It seemed to come nearer, flying around his head and he waved it away, but it stayed just out of reach, the buzzing of its wings continuing to frustrate his flailing hands. His head felt as though it was exploding, and the room seemed to be moving. He tried to stop the hallucinations, hands over his ears to block out the sound of the fly, holding his head still in an effort to stop the room spinning. A sudden surge of fear overran him, engendering a feeling of helplessness and he heard himself shout out. The shout triggered something inside him, and Jack forced himself back onto the mattress and knelt down, head bent over, eyes closed tightly and his hands still covering his ears.

50

"Did you hear that? What's happening in there, Allan?" Heather pointed at the computer screen. "I thought you said he wouldn't be harmed by this."

"He's hallucinating," Allan seemed relaxed by what they'd seen, "It's common in people who're subjected to isolation and silence. It's nothing to get worried about."

"It's horrible to watch." She shook her head in disbelief.

"It may not look pretty, but in most people there's no continuing mental effects." Allan took another look at the screen, "I'm surprised he's lasted this long without any reaction, that this type of thing didn't happen earlier."

"He's only been in there a few days; I can't believe he's behaving so bizarrely."

"A few days can seem like a long time when you're deprived of company and of any sense of day or night; time seems to slow down in the isolation and silence." Allan continued to watch, studying what he was seeing.

"So, how much longer do we have to keep him like this? It doesn't feel right. It feels like we're torturing him."

"Well, perhaps we can move on now, give him the same option that John was left with and see at what point he decides it's no longer worth living."

"But how long is that going to take? And how long can we keep on like this, watching and feeding him. Someone's bound to notice us going in and out of that old building eventually and wonder what's going on."

"Not if we're careful, we need to do what we set out to do. To use this guy as an example of the system's inhumanity – promote change and remember John. Besides, there isn't that much footfall in the area now, so many of the factory units have been vacated."

"And why did the police want to see us? Do you think they suspect us?" Heather was beginning to feel panicky.

"I imagine they wanted to talk to us because of the message I sent his wife, connecting the abduction with John's death. They're just covering all the angles. Besides, they interviewed Susan as well, and she knows nothing about what we've done. There's nothing to worry about, you just need to relax."

"That's easier said than done," Heather looked up into her husband's face, clearly agitated. "This whole situation is making me very nervous."

51

Jack stayed on his knees, blocking out the room and the silence and regaining control of his senses. He practiced breathing and exhaling, letting the air out in long deliberate releases, taking control and calming himself down. He realised his captors, whoever they were, would have seen what happened and heard him shout and he was angry, both with himself for showing weakness and with them for imprisoning him. He imagined them smiling as they watched him lose control and the humiliation made him determined to prevent it happening again. The deep breathing was working, relaxing him and allowing him to think about ways of taking back control permanently. He needed stimulation to occupy his senses and stop them repeating the anarchic reaction he'd experienced. And he needed someone to share his imprisonment with him, a 'friend' to interact with, but that was impossible. He thought back to his childhood and remembered how he'd invented a friend to talk to. A private friend, someone he could carry around, talk to and bounce ideas off. Feeling calmer, he opened his eyes and raised himself up from his knees, stepping away from the softness of the mattress and onto the hard floor.

Over at the table he sat down and started doodling again, trying to think of ways that he could fight back against his captors, prevent them destroying him mentally. He realised they held all the cards and that made it difficult, but he was determined to resist and made a mental promise not to permit himself to do anything that Charlotte or his two lads might subsequently be ashamed of. He wondered how many captors there were and whether they were each committed in the same way to his punishment. So far, he'd heard only one voice, a man's voice, and he tried to recall it, to memorise it for when he was released – but he guessed there must be more than one person involved if they were maintaining a continuous watch on him. He thought of Max again and how his doodling irritated Roger Grimshaw and he reasoned that his resistance could start with something small, the problem was finding that thing.

52

"Did you know that Inuits used to engage in polygamy?" Misty looked comfortable, a glass in hand, relaxing on Jim's sofa.

"What the hell brought that up," Jim re-filled his glass and put the bottle back down, "Bit sexist isn't it?"

"Well, it wasn't always polyandry, sometimes the women had more than one partner and, on long hunting trips, the women weren't necessarily expected to abstain from sex – sounds quite sophisticated to me."

"Right," Jim held up his glass, "Do you want another one?"

"Why not?" Misty passed her glass across for a refill.

"Where's Richie this evening, I thought he was coming over."

"Said he'd meet me here, but he was going to some pub earlier to watch a soccer match on TV – probably had too many pints and got pissed."

"He tells me you're betraying the cause and working for some marketing agency, promoting capitalist companies and their products."

Misty shrugged, "A girl's got to earn a living, Richie's in and out of work all the time. Principles are good, but they won't keep us from being hungry or him in beer – not the way he's been drinking recently. I'm fed-up with him coming home pissed as often as he does – and rifling through my bag for money."

"From each, according to their ability …" Jim began.

"And you can put a sock in it," Misty picked up a cushion and threw it at him, "I'm as tired of the political slogans as I am having Richie coming home pissed. Talk about Inuits on long hunting trips; try living with a guy like Richie; the only trips he takes are over the front doorstep after too many drinks."

"What is this about Inuit's? Where did they come from?"

"North America, I think you'll find."

"Bloody idiot, that wasn't quite what I meant." Jim picked-up the cushion to throw back at her but Misty was too fast, raised her glass, pulled a face at him and took another sip of wine.

"I know that," she put the glass back down and giggled, "No, we were just chatting at work, and someone asked how Inuits used to wash themselves when it was so cold. So, we looked it up online."

"And how did they?"

"They used to have steam rooms, like saunas, to sweat the dirt away."

"And this is how capitalist lackeys spend their time is it? Playing on the internet?" Jim was smiling, "No wonder the country's in such a mess."

"Look, I don't like rich bastards creaming off all the wealth whilst so many people find things so difficult either. I'd like everyone to enjoy their lives, but I can't see any point in swapping one form of oppression for another."

"Dreams don't just come true like they say they do, you can't change things without organizing, you need to create a movement to achieve a revolution. Your way could take years to happen, decades, centuries even. That's no use to all those people starving out there." Jim pointed out the window too vigorously with the hand holding his glass and some of the wine slopped out onto the floor.

"Oh, thy cup truly doth floweth over," Misty disappeared down the hall and reappeared with a paper towel to wipe-up the spilled liquid. "You see, I don't want people to do something just because they're afraid of what will happen if they don't follow the party line, and I don't want to replace one big bad boss with another equally selfish bastard. I think you need to get people to do things because they want to, because they empathise with other people. That's the way to get active participation."

"You're dreaming again."

"The whole of my life is a bit like a dream. None of it lasts for very long. I look back on what I did last year and it's already history, the campaigns, the designs and the slogans. I help create pictures in people's minds, not societal monoliths."

"And this is the woman who was lecturing me about political slogans earlier."

"Oh, God, those never change. You'll be banging on about the same things years from now. At least things are always changing in my world."

"It doesn't look like Richie is going to get here."

"I take back what I just said, some things, like Richie, don't change." She put her glass down, sat still for a moment and then shook her head. "He's a fucking waste of space," the words exploded from her.

"Christ, where did that come from?" Jim was surprised by the sudden vehemence in Misty's voice.

"It's been coming for some time; I'm totally pissed off with him and the way he behaves." She was shouting now.

"Hey," Jim put his glass down, anxious about what was coming next. "Look I've known Richie for some time, his heart's in the right place – he's just a bit of an idiot sometimes."

"Exactly, it's where he keeps his brain that worries me – not his heart. His head's filled with revolution; everything's going to be wonderful afterwards. Believe that and you'll believe anything. And, in the meantime, he just goes on protests and gets pissed." She stood up from the sofa.

"You don't have to go, stay and have another glass."

"No thanks," she shook her head, "I've had enough."

"Look, don't give him too hard a time when you get back – I'll talk to him if you'd like me to."

"Don't worry, he won't get a hard time from me tonight, I'm not going back. I'll call into the store along the road and get some toothpaste and face wipes and then go and stay with a friend of mine – let bloody Richie rot on his own on the couch or wherever else he's fallen asleep."

"Let's talk about things a bit more, this isn't a great way to leave things. And you can stay here, if you want."

"What, like one of those Inuit women whose partner's away on a hunting trip." She paused a moment, picked-up her bag before leaving, and then turned and gave him a light kiss on the cheek, "I'm sorry, that was mean, it's a kind offer, but it'll be better if I stay at my friend's."

53

Richie found it difficult getting the key into the door and had to attempt it a couple of times before he felt it slide in. He turned the lock and fumbled for the light switch. The light should have been on and the flat felt empty. He guessed Misty had probably gone to bed and went into the kitchen to get himself a glass of water, trying to sober up before joining her. The water tasted good and when he'd finished, he put out the hall light and went through to the bedroom, but she wasn't there. "Christ she must still be at Jim's," he thought, pulled off his shoes, pulled back the cover and lay down.

He was cold when he woke, and his stomach felt uncomfortable. Rolling over he checked the clock; it was two in the morning and Misty was still not back. He got up, fetched his phone from the kitchen and called her – but her number was unavailable. His immediate reaction was to call Jim, to make sure nothing had happened and she was ok, but he guessed she might be angry with him and hesitated. But, if she was still at Jim's, he asked himself where she was sleeping – Jim had only one bedroom – and he hesitated about calling again. Jim was a mate, but Richie had felt Misty was increasingly distant over the past few weeks and they'd been seeing more of Jim as the protests had taken place. He told himself again that Jim was a mate but was still feeling agitated when he put through the call.

The number kept ringing, Jim wasn't picking up, but Richie knew Jim always had his 'phone by the side of his bed, used it as an alarm in the morning. And then he remembered it was Sunday, maybe Jim had turned the 'phone off and left it in another room – he generally stayed in bed on Sunday mornings. Richie's body still felt drained, his head aching, but instead of feeling drunk, he now felt apprehensive. He cursed himself for not meeting Misty at Jim's as they'd arranged and, for a moment, considered getting a taxi round there. But if Jim wasn't answering his 'phone he thought it even less likely that he'd answer the doorbell. For an even briefer moment he thought about calling the police but decided he didn't need help that badly. Instead, he got undressed, wrapped the duvet around him and tried to go to sleep.

54

The bell intruded into his dream and Jack realised he'd fallen asleep again. He looked across at the door and saw the usual tray. He'd expected breakfast, but the tray appeared to contain a lunch of sorts, with a burger and some chips. As he walked over to retrieve the tray, he could see a small bottle containing liquid and a note underneath. He took the tray back to the table and read the note.

'This doesn't have to continue. When you want it to end, like John Morrison wanted it to, drink the contents of the bottle.'

He looked at the contents of the bottle, opened the top and smelled it – but there was no odour. He screwed the top back on and placed the bottle back on the tray and sat staring at it. They could poison him at any time when they prepared his food, so why did they want him to drink the bottle himself? Did they really want him dead or was it all an exercise to destroy his spirit and relive the emptiness that John had felt – to teach him and the outside world a lesson? Was there really poison in the bottle, or was it some sort of drug? He was sure they'd drugged him somehow, before abducting him, although he didn't know how – he guessed it must have been in the snooker hall, he couldn't remember anything after he'd stopped playing. Maybe they wanted to drug him again, before setting him free? Or was the idea of freedom just hopeless optimism? If they wanted to drug him before releasing him, drinking the contents of the bottle was the quickest way out. But if their plan was for him to commit suicide it wasn't the way he intended to go. He reminded himself of his promise to do nothing that would make Charlotte or the lads ashamed and knew any attempt to drink his way out of his prison was too high a risk to take.

The longer he stared at the bottle, the more threatening it became. His mind became obsessed with it. He picked it up, turning it round in his fingers and deciding to throw the contents down the toilet, but then recognised how easily it could be replaced. And, if he continued to throw each bottle away, they might decide to punish him – perhaps by keeping him there longer, assuming they planned to release him. And that was something he preferred not to risk. So, he put the bottle back down on the table and tried to ignore it, but it sat there, malevolently, taunting him with its presence. He asked himself how he could get rid of the implicit invitation to suicide the bottle represented, and played with various ideas, and one began to capture his imagination. He needed a 'friend' in the room to help keep him safe and, maybe, he could befriend the bottle – tell himself it didn't want to be drunk, conspire with it to keep its liquid safe inside its glass shell. Give it a name, talk to it.

"I'll call you John," he said out loud, "In memory of John Morrison." He paused a moment, "What's that you say, John?" He pretended to listen to the bottle, leaning closer to hear it better, "Please don't drink you." He shook his head theatrically, "No, however hard they try to make me, I won't drink you, I promise. I'll empty you rather than drink you."

"Do you hear that," he shouted, hoping whoever was watching him was listening, "My friend, John the bottle, doesn't want to be drunk, he wants to stay here with me. And I've promised to empty him, rather than drink him!"

He waited, but there was no response. This time, though, it didn't bother him like it had previously; he and 'John' would have other conversations in the future and one of them was bound to be overheard. Befriending the bottle amused him and, at the same time, liberated him from the threat it implied. He picked up the pad, tore off a sheet and folded it. Then he wrote the single word 'John' on one half, placed the bottle on the corner of the table and stood the paper sheet in front of it – so his captors could see the name.

55

"He's gone mad," Heather pointed at the screen, "I thought you said isolating him wouldn't have any longer-term effect, but this isn't rational behaviour."

Allan looked at the screen and zoomed in on the bottle. "On the contrary, it's quite a clever move. He's turning a threat into a friend – having a friend will make him stronger."

"How can a bottle be a friend?"

"In the absence of any real person, it's smart to create an alternative entity to talk to. I'm impressed. But, at the same time, I'm irritated that he's chosen my brother's name as the name of his friend, the person he treated so unfeelingly. And there's a part of me that says it's deliberate, a sort of verbal fingers up to whoever he believes we are."

"So, what do we do from here?"

Allan thought for a moment. "Let's just wait and see how he copes over the next few days. He's started to show signs of weakness, maybe this is just a temporary fight back – don't underestimate the power of silence and isolation."

"Are you sure about this? Can we really justify what we're doing to this man? Have we even got the right man?"

"He's here, we've abducted him for Christ's sake! Do you want to release him after all the risks we've taken without achieving anything? It could be seen as an admission we were wrong; that what happened was acceptable. The media would have a field day, he might even be portrayed as a hero!"

"Can't we at least set a time limit on how long we're going to keep him locked up?" Heather placed her hand on her husband's arm and stared into his face, searching for some sign of softening in his features.

"Well, we can't keep him here too long, but let's just give it a week or so – if he hasn't cracked by then, we might have to start to think about where we go from there." Allan shook his head and turned away.

"He's holding something up now," Heather called after him, "Walking round the room and standing in front of each camera in turn, holding up a sheet of paper for us to read."

Allan turned back to the screen and focused-in on the paper. 'Now there's two of us – me and John.'

"Bastard," Allan thumped his fist down on the desk, "He needs to show more respect."

"Or what? What can we do that's any worse than we've done to him already?"

"If he wants to mess with our minds, maybe we'll start messing with his – after all, we control everything that goes into that room, including any news from outside."

"Like what?"

"Like what's important to him. His wife, kids, how people perceive him."

"But no-one except his immediate family and the police know he's been abducted, there's obviously an embargo on the news."

"But he doesn't know that, which gives us an advantage. And it also makes me begin to think it's time we let people know."

"How are you going to do that, the police are bound to try to silence the press – after all, nothing's leaked out so far? They'll just maintain it could endanger Docherty."

"Then we need to approach someone who's not prepared to work with the police, and I think I have just the people in mind."

56

When Richie awoke it was ten o'clock and Misty still wasn't home. He lay there wondering where she was and had just decided to ring her again when he heard a key in the lock. The door shut, he heard footsteps in the hall and called out, but there was no reply. He got out of bed and found Misty in the kitchen, making a cup of tea. She looked up and then turned away again.

"Hi, are you alright?" he asked.

"What do you think?"

"You're angry."

"Of course I'm fucking angry, what did you expect? I go round to Jim's place, to meet you as we arranged, and you don't turn up."

"So where did you stay?"

"What's that to you?"

"Jim's my mate."

"What's that meant to imply?"

"So, did you stay there?"

"Why not ask your mate that question? He was waiting for you too. We were both waiting. We just got fed-up wasting our time."

"So, you did stay there?"

"Is that a question or a statement?"

"Look, you go round to my best friend's flat and don't come home till the morning. I think I deserve an explanation."

"It's me that deserves an explanation. An explanation about why you sent me to Jim's flat but didn't turn up like you said you would. I don't think you *deserve* anything."

"All I want to know is whether my partner and best friend slept together. Because, if so, that's a pretty big deal."

"Ex-partner as of now. And if you reckon your best friend would sleep with your partner, then you haven't got much of a relationship with him either, have you?" She stopped for a moment and stared at him, but he looked so lost she decided to show some pity. "No, I didn't stay there, I stayed with a friend, and she's said I can move in with her until I find my own place."

Richie stood still, trying to take-in what she had just said. The enormity of it all frightened him. He shook his head in denial. "You can't just move out."

"Just watch me." She finished her tea and threw the residue down the sink.

"But how am I going to manage with the rent and everything?"

"Get yourself straight and hold down a job instead of jacking them in all the time. You'll thank me for this one day; treat it like a wake-up call. Smell the coffee or you'll end-up like those winos who hang around town." She took out her 'phone, started typing and, when she'd finished, put it back in her bag. "That's my contribution to next month's rent, I've transferred it to your account. Don't piss it up the wall."

"Don't go." He put his hand on her arm, but she shook it off and went into the bedroom. He watched as she grabbed some clothes and cosmetics, stuffed them into an overnight bag, zipped it up and moved him aside. "I'll pop round some other time and collect the rest of my things when you're not here."

57

"Well, John, I guess it's just the two of us this morning." Jack stroked the bottle with his fingers, then picked it up and examined the liquid inside. "Funny how fate has brought us together," he shook the bottle and watched the liquid move, "Your legacy in a bottle for me to consume when I experience the emptiness you felt. And, despite the situation I find myself in, I have no intention of consuming you without the certainty of getting out of here alive."

"Don't be so fucking disrespectful." The man's voice boomed out of the loudspeaker. "You help to finish a man's life and then you disrespect his memory by naming a bottle after him and talking to it as though he was your friend. You bastard."

"What do you know about it all? You clearly didn't know John. The last time I spoke to him he was optimistic, despite the redundancy, and full of plans about the future. And you, did you ever speak to him personally? Or is all this shit about some political point you want to make?"

"Bullshit! Total bullshit! Who the hell do you think you are?"

"I'm the guy you've chosen to make an example of for a 'crime'" Jack raised his index fingers and curled them repeatedly to resemble apostrophes, "A 'crime' you don't even know was committed. Against a person you certainly don't appear to have known. So, what authority does that give you? I'd say your credibility is non-existent, your morality bankrupt."

"Carry on like this and your food tray could be empty tomorrow."

"And that threat shows how bankrupt of morality and ideas you are. You're just trying to bully me into submission; using the same power play you accuse me of using with John. So, fucking starve me to death, because I'm not drinking John over there." Jack held his arm out, pointing at the bottle.

"And, what about your family?"

"What about my family? What have they got to do with this?"

"Aren't you concerned about them? How they'll feel if you condemn yourself because of your arrogance?"

"They'll never see my so-called arrogance, but they would feel my humiliation if I did what you wanted me to and committed suicide. All I have left is not to dishonour them, not to leave them feeling that I finally admitted responsibility for killing John – which, in any case I emphatically deny. Ok, starve me to death, whatever, but I will not be your witness, confirming your belief about what happened, because it's a lie. It didn't happen like you want to believe it did. You weren't there, you didn't know him. You've just rushed to judgment, and I've got news for you, you're no bloody substitute for a Solomon."

The loudspeaker went dead, and Jack waited, expecting a response. When it came, it was short and unsweet.

"Piss off, you know nothing about me and even less about your victim from the sound of it."

"Statements are easy to make, what proof have you got that I misread John's mood." Jack shouted back.

"I've got nothing to prove," the voice said, "It's you that have to prove something."

"And what's that?" Jack asked.

"That you're sorry for your part in his death."

"I liked John. I am sorry for his death, but I'm not sure that I played any real part in it."

"Then, perhaps you need more time to consider." The voice stopped and the loudspeaker went dead.

Jack turned to the bottle. "Well, John, seems like we're on our own again." But, inside, he was asking himself whether it wouldn't have been better to admit responsibility, even if he didn't feel it was justified, and try to negotiate his way out of the prison he was in. Act smarter.

He picked-up the pen and began doodling, relaxing as he played with the shapes on the paper. And he smiled as he remembered again how Max's doodling had upset Roger Grimshaw; the looks Roger kept giving Max who remained apparently oblivious of the displeasure he was creating. Or, maybe, it had just been a subtle sign of rejection on Max's part, displaying his disinterest in the discussions before rationalizing the content and presenting it in an acceptable manner to the company's audiences. He couldn't talk to the people who were holding him captive, but maybe he could write to them and release what he'd written when he returned his next food tray. He started to play with the messages he wanted to convey, ordering them in his head, searching for inconsistencies in what he planned to write down. And he considered how Max might have expressed the note, to put his message across.

58

"He left this note on the tray," Heather handed it to her husband. "He still seems adamant that the redundancy wasn't the cause of the suicide."

Allan took the note and began to read it.

> I worried about telling John he would be redundant so soon after the deaths of his

wife and daughter, but he said he had plans and it would give him a chance to move on with his life.

So, I was confused when I heard about his suicide.

He has a brother and sister; they're the people most likely to know what his plans were and why his mood changed so dramatically. I don't believe it was his redundancy – though some doubt will always remain with me.

Imprisoning me causes my wife and children, as well as me, pain. You claim to be compassionate, but what you're doing is cruel to them and unfair to me. It doesn't help whatever cause you represent – in fact it's more likely to alienate people.

Please let me go, it's in both of our interests

When Allan finished reading, he tore the note into small pieces and threw them in a large plastic bag, together with the empty food containers they'd collected.

"It's bullshit, the same old bullshit as previously. He seems to be in total denial."

"So, what do we do?" Heather asked. "What other means of making him admit his responsibility do we have? I'm sorry, but this isn't going as you thought it would, Allan. I think you may have under-estimated him – he seems stronger, more resilient than you thought he'd be."

"Yes, I'm more impressed than I thought," her husband nodded, "I reckoned he'd be like most bullies, weak inside, bullying because it makes him feel better about himself."

"The only thing that worries me is how long we're going to have to keep him locked-up. And, to date, there's been a distinct lack of publicity about his disappearance."

"We talked about that before," Allan said, "The police will be playing a waiting game, seeing if they can provoke a response that may give them a clue about where he is and who might have abducted him. We'll leave it another 24 hours to see if any news leaks out and, if it doesn't, we'll go ahead with the announcement. We need to make an example of our man."

"Even if he may not be the person who was ultimately responsible for the suicide?" Heather shook her head as she asked the question, indicating her doubt about the course they were taking.

"Yes, even if he wasn't the only person responsible, he still shares the responsibility – he admits to having a doubt in that bullshit note he just sent us."

59

Jim was reading, stretched out along his sofa, when the doorbell rang. He marked his place with the bookmark and put the book on the table. After the previous night he guessed it was probably Richie and wasn't looking forward to having a conversation with him. He shouted, 'hold on,' as he walked along the hall, paused to compose himself, and opened the door. Instead of rushing-in as he usually did, Richie stayed standing there and was clearly agitated. "Come on in," Jim held his arm out ushering him inside, "I'll make some coffee."

"What happened yesterday evening? What did you and Misty talk about?"

"It's what didn't happen yesterday evening that's important. And we talked about Inuits at first, until it became clear you weren't going to turn up as you'd arranged.

And then she kind of exploded, said she was going to stay with a friend and walked out."

"Inuits?" Richie was confused, "What the fuck have Inuits got to do with anything?"

"Nothing, but you getting pissed and not turning up certainly did. And she also mentioned you changing jobs so often."

"That's not fair, why should I have to put up with some of the capitalist shit that's been flung at me? If you believe in worker's rights, you have to stand-up and be counted."

"But she's a talented woman and ambitious. If you want to keep a woman like her, you have to offer her more than martyrdom for worker's rights – you need to find a way of exploiting the capitalist system in the same way it exploits you. Be smarter than the opposition. Look, where did you both leave things? Where is she now?"

"We didn't leave things anywhere, Richie emphasised the word 'things', "The only 'thing' that got left was me. She just walked out."

"Hey, that's heavy," Jim wasn't surprised, reached out and urged his friend to sit down on the sofa. "The kettle's just boiled, I'll get some coffee and we can talk about it all." He went to the kitchen and came back with two mugs. "That's going to make it difficult for you, isn't it? I mean how long's the lease on your flat?"

"It's only a couple of months until it ends, and she paid her share of next month's rent into my account before she left. But where do I live after that? I can't afford to stay there on my own."

"We'll ask around the group, maybe one of them will be able to help."

"Thanks, Jim. To be honest, I'm not sure the relationship would have lasted anyway – there were a lot of things we didn't agree on. I'm just feeling a bit insecure – it was a shock when she walked-out like that. I'll be alright in a couple of weeks."

"Makes you realise how that guy who killed himself must have felt when they chucked him out, the insecurity and isolation he would have experienced." Jim took a large gulp of his coffee, "It's a pity, but it's all gone quiet now. Guess we need to find a new cause, but, in the meantime, we need to concentrate on you – make sure you're ok."

60

"Congratulations to the pair of you." Roger looked up from the notes he'd been given and smiled at Max and Alison who were sat opposite him. "That was the most successful Trade Show we've had in several years. And a special 'well done' to you Alison for taking over the organization at such short notice – Jack couldn't have done a better job if he'd been there."

"I can't take all the credit," Alison felt herself flushing, embarrassed by Roger's comments, "Most of it's down to Jack, he laid the groundwork for the Show before he was abducted; it was just a matter of making sure things happened in the way he wanted."

"Don't be modest, take the compliment, it's deserved." Roger put the notes down and was about to move on when Alison started speaking again.

"Thank you, but the efforts made by the sales team also need to be recognised. They all put in a tremendous amount of work. They were terrific."

"Point taken, Alison." Roger nodded and made a note of what she'd said. "I'll write to the sales team later; the sales made at the Show are encouraging. And well done to you as well, Max, I thought that Morrison's suicide and the protests might have affected our reputation – and then, of course Jack's abduction wasn't helpful – but your PR strategy seems to have been successful."

"I don't imagine that Jack's abduction has been much fun for him," Max interjected, "I'm sure he would have preferred that it hadn't happened. I just hope he comes out of this ok."

"Well, I guess we all need to wait to find out about that." Roger closed his notebook and started to rise from his chair. "But, in the meantime, well done, again."

Taking their cue from him, Alison and Max picked up their files and got up to leave, but Alison held back. "Have you any more news about Jack, Mr. Grimshaw?"

"No, sorry, I haven't. I don't suppose you've heard any more from his wife, have you Max?"

Max shook his head.

"Well, thanks again, both of you, for making the show such a success. Now we need to build on that success." Roger nodded, dismissing them, and moved back to his desk.

Max looked across at Alison and noticed she still had something she wanted to say, but he shook his head and motioned her to leave with him. When they got outside, he signalled her to follow him to his office. He stood aside to let her in and then closed the door.

"What's so secret?" Alison asked.

"I was just concerned about you pressing Roger about Jack. It's not a good idea at the moment."

"Why not? Has something happened?"

"No, to your second question, but can I speak to you in confidence?"

Alison nodded.

"It's just that I wouldn't want this going any further. It's not the sort of thing I'd like to see spread round the firm."

"I'll keep whatever you say to myself. I promise."

"Ok. It's just that Roger seems to be blaming Jack for everything that happened after John Morrison was made redundant; the suicide and subsequent bad publicity, the demos outside the gates, becoming a kidnap victim even."

"But none of that was Jack's fault. It all started with Grimshaw deciding to save money by cutting the workforce. If he hadn't initiated the redundancy programme, none of this might have happened."

"You and I know that," Max said, "But Roger is beginning to re-write history. In his version of events, it was Jack's poor handling of the situation that was to blame for what happened to John, not the redundancy programme itself. He's saying privately that if Jack had raised the issue with him, he'd have kept John on for a while, in which case none of what followed would have happened. Instead, in his mind, it raises questions about Jack's competency as a manager."

"But that's ridiculous, Jack's a brilliant manager, "Alison shook her head unable to believe what she was hearing, "And I know that he did ask John about how he felt – whether he'd be ok. Jack's a really caring guy."

"So, now, perhaps, you can see why Roger was so keen to play down Jack's contribution to the success of the Trade Show, it doesn't fit into his new narrative. But don't get me wrong either, the work you did was superb – I really enjoyed working with you. At least Roger got that part right."

"What will happen if Jack comes back?"

"Who knows? Roger will either decide he can't fire him because it will bring the company further unfavourable coverage, or that firing him will show this is a caring company let down by one poor manager. I would counsel against the latter on PR, as well as moral, grounds, but wouldn't put my money on Roger listening."

"Poor Jack, it's not just Grimshaw who's gunning for him, Allan Morrison, John Morrison's brother isn't happy either."

"Why not?"

"Well, I called him to postpone the meeting I'd arranged with Jack and said I'd have to re-schedule it as Jack wasn't at work at present. I sort of inferred he might be off with stress. Anyway, he clearly didn't believe me, sounded angry and accused Jack of being unwilling to see him. Accused him of cowardice at one point, until he calmed down a bit. He's obviously upset at what happened to John and blames Jack."

"So how did you leave it?"

"I told him we'd rearrange a meeting when Jack was back at work – what else could I do?"

"And did he accept that?"

"Eventually, he had to, but he wasn't a happy man. At one point he was trying to get a meeting with Grimshaw instead!"

"That wouldn't have been very productive and certainly not a meeting of minds, I take it you said no."

"No, I'm afraid I dodged the issue and told him he'd have to talk to Grimshaw's PA to arrange one; and then I told him the line was engaged when he asked to be put through. Said he'd have to call back another time."

61

Ruthless Manager Kidnapped

Police have been suppressing news that Jack Docherty, the callous manager who sacked a grieving man and caused his subsequent suicide, has been abducted. Docherty fired John Morrison just months after his wife and daughter had been killed in a car accident and the abductors say they are holding him for re-education purposes.

The news was leaked to our offices by a member of the group who abducted

Docherty as a warning to other managers who may be planning similar ruthless moves against workers. Docherty was abducted several days ago, as he was leaving a snooker hall, and police found his car in a nearby car park. A message from the abductors was received by Docherty's family. Docherty is being held in an undisclosed location until he has admitted responsibility for his part in Mr. Morrison's death.

The Police have been approached for comment and to explain the news blackout but have declined to respond to our questions. In our opinion the people have a right to be told about this action, taken against the capitalist system and the people who perpetrate its inequality and unacceptable treatment of workers. Suppressing news, for whatever purported purpose, cannot hide the increasing support for a socialist agenda and the end of the inhumanity implicit in the capitalist system.

Richie read the Worker article in his inbox and immediately called Jim to ask whether he'd seen it, but Jim was still in bed.

"Hi, Jim, the Worker's come out with a scoop about the bastard who sacked the guy who committed suicide. You remember, the company we demo-ed outside for a couple of weeks. I reckon it's time to mobilise the members and go back there."

"Hey, it's good to hear you sounding so much better, Richie. Give me a minute to have a look and I'll call you back." Jim read the article and reached for his 'phone. "I reckon you're right Richie. This gives us a great platform to re-ignite the debate. Hey, do you remember that kid's game 'Where's Wally?' well I reckon we could use that as a theme. The article says the guy's name was Jack, so we can turn up with 'Where's Jack?' posters. We'll need to brief the local TV guys and get them there."

'Yeah, and maybe some 'Not alright now, Jack?' banners." Richie played with the image in his head, was pleased with what he saw and felt good for the first time since Misty had left. "If I get the members up to speed, will you call your mate at the TV station? We need to organise things bloody quickly, before the news gets round – show we're ahead of the game."

62

"Hey Ros, your company's in the local news again; seems like that guy you work for isn't taking time out at home, sounds like he's been kidnapped by someone."

"What?" Ros emerged from the bedroom carrying the mascara she'd been using and joined Sam in front of the TV. "This is awful, how could they do something like this to Jack, he's such a nice bloke? If they'd grabbed Grimshaw, I could understand it. People have been speculating about why Jack's been away, but I don't think anyone imagined anything like this. I wonder whether Alison's seen the news?" She reached for her 'phone and called Alison's mobile, but the number was unobtainable.

"You've got to give it to the guys in the demo, they've got a sense of humour," Sam pointed at the banners on the screen, some of which had a picture of a crowd and a text balloon asking, 'Where's Jack?' "Wonder if they have anything to do with any of this?"

"Who knows?" Ros grabbed a slice of toast from the toaster and took a bite from it, then rushed back to the bathroom to apply the last of her mascara. She grabbed another bite of her toast when she reappeared, stuffed her make-up into her bag and threw a jacket over her arm. "Sorry, better go, it's not the day to be late for work." She took a gulp of her coffee, a final bite of toast and gave Sam a quick peck on the cheek before rushing out the door.

Sam turned back to the television and continued watching. The interviewer walked across to one of the demonstrators and held out her microphone.

> "So, do you have any further information for our viewers about Mr. Docherty's abduction?"
>
> "No, someone contacted the Worker – there's been an organised news blackout to stop the public understanding the outrage that Morrison's death has caused. Working people want an apology, an acknowledgement of the management's responsibility for his suicide."
>
> "Do you know who may be behind this abduction?"
>
> "Absolutely not. We're just here to show our opposition to the system that thinks it's acceptable to treat workers in the way Morrison was treated. And to tell them it's not!" Jim raised his fist to emphasise his point.
>
> The newswoman withdrew her microphone and looked back at the camera to complete the item. "Before I hand you back to the studio, I would like to confirm that we've asked both the police and Mr. Morrison's former employers for their responses to this

*breaking news, but, so far, we've heard
nothing from either organisation."*

63

"Christ!" Charlotte didn't know whether to turn-off the TV
or remain watching as she recognised Jack's workplace
and saw the coverage of the demonstration outside. She
listened out for the boys and heard an electric toothbrush
in the upstairs bathroom and a voice complaining about the
time the user of the brush was taking. Happy they couldn't
see or hear the TV she continued to watch and, as soon as
the item was over, turned the TV off. A couple of minutes
later Daniel came down the stairs, dragging his school bag
behind him.

"Do you have anything important at school today?"
she asked, "Any tests?" When he said 'no' she called-up
the stairs to his younger brother and asked him to come
down. "Look, I've decided not to send you to school today,
because I need to talk to you both. I've told you both about
your father having to go away because of his work, but
that's only partly true, I told you that because I didn't want
to worry you and the police asked me to keep everything
secret. So, I need you both to listen to what I'm going to tell
you now – though the police are right, you mustn't worry."
She then told them how their father had been kidnapped.
And when they asked why their father had been taken, she
tried to explain the kidnappers had got the wrong person,
that it was a case of mistaken identity – he hadn't done
what they were saying he'd done. Daniel came across and
hugged her, Tony just burst into tears. "So that's why I'm
not sending you to school today," she told them, "In case
some of the other boys believe what people say about
Daddy." She bent down, put her arm out and pulled Tony
to her.

"You don't believe what they say, do you?" Daniel asked.

"No, of course I don't, your father's not like that. He's kind and he cares for us and for other people. But some people enjoy pointing fingers and saying nasty things; it makes them feel bigger, gives them a feeling of importance. They're like bullies at school."

"But some of the boys heard their parents saying it was as bad as murdering someone, when Daddy sacked that man."

"You've never mentioned this before," Charlotte searched Daniel's face, trying to read what he was thinking.

"Because the teachers told the boys to stop talking about it, although some of them still keep on whispering things at me, asking me what it's like to have a dad who's a murderer and running away in the playground pretending they're scared in case I kill them."

"I'll have another word with your teacher."

"No, don't Mum, because they'll say I've gone to the teacher and told on them. It'll just make things worse." He paused a moment, "Do we have enough money to pay the ransom to get Daddy home?"

"They don't want any money," Charlotte said, "That's not why they've kidnapped him."

"What do they want, I thought all kidnappers did it so they can get money from people?"

"Look, I don't think you'll understand this, but they want your father to feel as unhappy as the man who killed himself."

"Does that mean Daddy will kill himself too?" Tony looked at Charlotte anxiously, and then burst into tears again.

"No, it doesn't. You see Daddy has us and he knows we all love him; the other man's family had died."

"That's why some of the boys' parents say Daddy murdered the man, when he sacked him," Daniel said. "Why did Daddy tell him he couldn't work there anymore?"

"It's difficult," Charlotte said, "But it wasn't your father who decided the man couldn't work there anymore – it was someone else, your father's boss, and he told your father he had to tell the man."

"But why didn't Daddy say 'no'? Get his boss to tell the man."

"Because that's not how things work when you get older." Charlotte knew her answer sounded weak and thought quickly. "I mean, if your teacher tells you to do something, you have to do it."

"But teachers don't tell you to do things that are wrong."

"Well, let's see," Charlotte paused, "If the head teacher told your teacher to do something, they'd have to do it, wouldn't they? And that's the same as your father's boss telling him he has to do something. And if your teacher didn't do it, they'd get into trouble and another teacher would do it instead. So, it would still happen, wouldn't it?"

Her son looked up at her undecided.

"Besides," Charlotte said, "No-one knows if that was the reason the man killed himself, it could have been something else that made him so unhappy."

"Like what?" the boy asked.

"Some grown-up thing maybe. Now go and get changed out of your school clothes, I'm going to take you both to your grandma's for the day. I've got a lot of things I need to do. At least you know now what really happened. Go on, you too," she kissed Tony and gently pushed him back towards the stairs."

Only after they were out of sight did she allow herself to cry, wiping the tears away quickly when she heard them on their way back down again.

64

"I guess you both saw the news this morning, but even if you didn't the TV crew and the mob camped outside the gate demonstrate that Jack Docherty's abduction is now public knowledge." Roger glared across the table.

"The office is buzzing with the news and the factory floor's the same," Geoff shook his head, "It's not good."

"I heard they were offering odds on who would be kidnapped next." Max looked at Geoff and smiled.

"That's not bloody funny, Max," the other man scowled back, "And now they all want to know why they weren't told earlier."

"They weren't told earlier because the police said it might impede their enquiries, that's the easy part of the story; what we have to decide now is what we do in terms of how this reflects on the Company." Max turned to Grimshaw, "I guess we've already discussed this, you know, the need to save costs, the fact we were generous and the fact that John's suicide being due to his redundancy is just speculation. But the area I think we have to discuss is whether to cover the anxiety this will be causing to his family. And, of course, we need to liaise with the police before we do anything."

"Well, if it's going to distract attention from the Company, I think we should mention Jack's family and the pressure this is putting on them," Roger looked across at Geoff for his opinion.

"I agree, Roger," Geoff nodded, "It may also be a useful move within the Company, there still seems to be a negative sentiment running through the workplace, a feeling that this is the Company's fault in some way."

"I can't see why," Roger looked at both the managers in front of him. "For a start, we only had a redundancy programme to protect their jobs and, secondly, had I known more about Morrison's situation I would have taken a somewhat different course. And the fact I was never informed about the potential effect his redundancy might have had indicates a failure in this team."

"I'm sorry Roger, but Jack was Morrison's line manager and he said he'd had a chat with Morrison, and everything seemed ok." Geoff sat back in his chair and crossed his arms defensively. "I have to say that my conscience is entirely clear."

"It's not your conscience I'm interested in," Roger said the words dismissively, "Managers aren't chosen to sit round this table because of their consciences, it's their perceived competence that secures their seat." He emphasised 'perceived' and stared at Geoff as he spoke.

"Has Margaret spoken to Jack's wife?" Max intervened, "Because if she hasn't maybe I could call her and see how she feels about mentioning the family?"

"Is that necessary?" Roger sounded irritable.

"I think so, Roger, we don't want to be accused of being unfeeling to Jack's family as well as to Morrison. We need to be getting people on side at this point. Presenting a cuddlier side to our image, if I may say so."

"No-one's ever accused me of being unsympathetic," Roger sat up straighter, asserting the view he was presenting of himself, "But you can only be sympathetic when the facts are presented properly to you. Have a word with Margaret, Max, and, if she hasn't been in touch, talk to Mrs. Docherty yourself if you feel you have to."

The meeting ended and Geoff and Max got up to leave.

"Max, a quick word please." Roger dismissed Geoff with a nod and Max sat down again. "Look, Max, I just want to say that I don't want Jack to suddenly become a martyr in all this. I'm not sure he's totally blameless; I need to think some more about the situation the Company has been put in because I wasn't briefed properly about Morrison's mental state. Maybe, there's an inference you can place in the messaging we're putting out?"

"I hear what you say, Roger, but I'm not convinced the wider public are discerning enough for that degree of subtlety." He left the room and grimaced to himself as he walked back to his office.

65

Ros had delayed talking to Alison about what Gill had told her following her conversation at the hotel. The extra work they'd had to undertake for the trade show in Jack's absence had made it seem less of a priority, but the news of Jack's abduction had upset her. She liked Jack and knew he wouldn't have fired John if he thought he'd commit suicide as a result. If anyone was to blame it was Grimshaw and she was outraged that Jack and his family were being put through so much pain when it was Grimshaw who'd ordered the redundancy programme in the first place. She needed to catch Alison when she was on her own but Alison had been busy and Ros wanted to avoid anyone over-hearing what was said – although she was still not clear about what she might do with any information that Alison could give her.

Alison was slightly later into the office than usual, and her eyes looked puffy, as though she'd been crying. "I guess you've heard the news," she looked across and dropped her bag into a desk drawer. Ros nodded and said how unfair she thought it all was, but Alison seemed distracted, not listening to what she was saying and then said she had to get on with some urgent work. Ros had thought the news would have the office buzzing, but most of the sales team were out and the atmosphere in the rest of the office seemed subdued. At lunchtime the two of them were on their own and Alison took her lunch and a book into Jack's empty room and started to read, away from her desk. When she'd finished her lunch, Ros walked across, knocked on the door to get Alison's attention, went in and closed the door behind her.

"I've been meaning to talk to you for a few days," Ros began, "It's about something a friend of mine heard when she, was at the Cornford Hotel, the other day," Ros saw the other woman's expression change, she looked wary at hearing the hotel name and her reaction made Ros suspect Alison knew the place.

"I've heard of it, but I don't think I've ever been there," Alison was talking less confidently now, "What makes you ask?"

"Well, whilst Gill was there, running a corporate event, one of the staff started talking about John Morrison's wife."

There was a definite tautening in Alison's face and Ros felt a sudden tension run through the other woman. It was an Alison she hadn't seen before, and she hesitated for a moment before continuing. As she described what Gill had heard about the antipathy Faith had felt towards her husband and then about her affair with the hotel manager, she saw Alison's face begin to crumble and her eyes well-up.

Alison reached for some tissues. "I don't think I can continue talking about this," she said softly, and shook her head in denial, "It's too painful."

"But Jack's been kidnapped because people are holding him responsible for John's death and what Gill heard at the Cornford suggests that John wasn't happily married, like everyone assumes. And, if that's right, what's the real reason for his suicide? And shouldn't people be told?"

"That might help Jack, but it's not going to help anyone else, least of all John." Alison had been holding back her emotions, but now she lost control, the tears running down her face as she turned away and started sobbing.

Ros went round the desk and hugged Alison to comfort her. She felt the convulsive sobs and held her tighter, "But John's dead," Ros said quietly.

"Don't you think I know that!" Alison's voice was raised suddenly, and she lifted her head and looked up at Ros angrily, "For God's sake, Ros, I knew John a lot better than almost any other person on earth. I loved him." Her anger subsided as suddenly as it had arisen, "I'm sorry Ros, I shouldn't have snapped at you like that. John was so laidback, so much fun to be with and I'm devastated now he's gone."

The violence of Alison's initial reaction and what she'd said about loving John left Ros wanting to know more. But she felt unable to ask any further questions, knowing they would be unwelcome. Instead, she gave Alison another hug, walked out of the office and closed the door behind her.

66

Charlotte made herself a cup of tea and stood looking out of the kitchen window whilst she drank it. The garden was peaceful and gave her a chance to reflect. She wondered what Jack was doing, how he was being treated, and then, momentarily, felt guilty about carrying-on with her life whilst he was going through whatever his abductors were doing to him, but she knew it was what Jack would have wanted, for her to stay strong for the boys. She'd had several messages from friends since the news about Jack's abduction had become public, each of them saying how shocked they were and asking how she'd coped since it happened? And, inevitably, why she hadn't called so they could have helped. She'd explained each time that she'd like to have confided in them, but the police had been adamant the news mustn't be leaked, trying to draw out whoever had kidnapped Jack.

Thinking about the boys she picked-up the phone and was about to call her mother and ask how they were when it began ringing.

"Hi, Charlotte, Max Gregory, PR Manager from Jack's Company."

"Hi, Max, I know who you are, what can I do for you?"

"Well, since the news about Jack is public knowledge now, we need to put out some form of messaging to the media and, whilst we don't want to bring more attention to you, we'd like to mention the pressure Jack's abduction has put on his family – and I guess that means you. Obviously, we won't mention the kids."

"Have you spoken to the police about this?"

"Yes, and they're now saying anything that generates sympathy for Jack may be helpful in getting people to come forward and provide possible leads. But, in any case, we'll check whatever we propose issuing with them before it goes out."

"Alright, Max, well let's agree the ground rules first; Jack rated you before he was abducted, and I'll go along with Jack's judgment, but, from my point of view, our kids are paramount – not the company, nor Roger Grimshaw. Ok?"

"I'm with you on that, I promise."

"A promise from a PR man, what's that worth?" there was a silence at the end of the line. "I'm sorry, I was joking, but don't let me down."

"I won't, I like Jack, he's a great guy."

"Well, you won't expect me to argue about that, will you?"

"I guess not." Max smiled at the other end of the 'phone, "All we intend to say is something along the lines of 'abducting a man places enormous strain upon his family and isn't consistent with the stated aims of the abductors, who say they want a more sympathetic society.' How does that sound?"

"Send me a copy of whatever text you agree with the police, and I'll take a look at it and come back to you."

"Right. And how are you coping?"

"I take it this isn't designed to elicit further content for your press release," Charlotte smiled, then realized Max couldn't see she was teasing him, "That was also meant as a joke by the way, thanks for asking. The kids were pretty freaked-out this morning when the news came through, I'd told them Jack was on a business trip, but I've sent them off to my parents for the day. I don't know how I feel; I vacillate between feeling guilty about coping for the boys' sake and feeling totally terrified about what might be happening to Jack." As she spoke, she felt her voice begin to fail, apologised and started to cry.

"I'm sorry," Max waited for her response.

"Oh, it's not your fault, I just worry about Jack. The boys will be ok, I can take care of them, but I don't know how I'll be able to cope if anything bad happens to him."

"Look, is there anything we can do to help?"

"Offer to swap Grimshaw for Jack?"

"Tempting, but despite all his faults, Grimshaw isn't totally bad. He may be a narcissist, but his drive and business acumen are important in helping the Company succeed. On a personal basis, though, I'd offer to swap him for Jack any day. What about the boys, is there anything I can arrange to get them?"

"Just arrange to get them their father back, Max, that's all they need."

"I wish I could, but that's not in my power."

"I know," Charlotte paused for a moment, unsure of controlling her voice, before carrying on speaking. "Look I'm sorry to give you a hard time, Max, I appreciate you calling."

"No problem, I'd like to help if I can. I won't contact you unnecessarily, but don't think twice about calling me if there's anything you need."

"There's a lot of 'I's' in that offer. Does Grimshaw know you've called?"

"He knows."

"Did he tell you to call?"

Max thought for a moment before replying. "He didn't tell me not to, just left it to my discretion. It's one of the traits of a narcissist, they don't always know how to act in some situations."

"That tells me everything I need to know, Max. And thanks for calling." Charlotte ended the call and, when she'd put the 'phone down, burst into tears, angry at what she'd heard.

67

Mike's 'phone rang as he was walking to his car. He looked at the number, saw it was Gill and answered the call.

"Hi, Mike," he could tell she was excited immediately. "I've had some terrific news, one of the companies who attended that thought leadership seminar I organised has just called and wants to run a corporate workshop. And they've asked me to submit some ideas and a potential budget."

"Hey, well done. That's great, sounds like things may be taking off."

"The only thing is the timescale; it's shorter than I would normally like, and I need to have a chat with Misty, that marketing consultant I told you about. Anyway, I called her, and she suggested meeting late afternoon, so I won't be home at the usual time."

"Ok, any idea of when you will be back?"

"Well, I wondered about staying in town afterwards and going for a meal together. If that sounds ok, you could meet me at the wine bar on the High Street around six, after I've finished the meeting with Misty."

When Mike arrived, Gill was talking animatedly to a slightly bohemian-looking woman. Mike guessed she was in her twenties, about the same age as him and Gill, but different from the women he usually came across in business – more flower, than power, he thought – a bit like the women in some old photos he'd seen, taken back in the 1960s. He hesitated about joining them, but Gill waved him over and introduced him. He felt himself staring as he shook the woman's hand and looked back at Gill quickly.

"So, have you come up with anything for this workshop?"

"Yes, we think so, but it's going to require a bit of thinking through, we're playing with 'making assumptions' – you know the dangers of seeing things one way, when the reason for something happening could be completely different."

"We think it lends itself to a number of different approaches," Misty added, "It can be demonstrated by visual images, like the picture in which some people see an old hag and others see a young woman. And it lends itself to team activities – giving people scenarios and asking them to come up with their ideas about what happened and how to proceed. We're going to need some input from a specialist training consultant, but we reckon it will work."

Gill poured the remainder of the wine into their glasses and went to the bar and bought a lager for Mike. She got back in time to hear him asking about Misty's name, put the lager down in front of him and apologised, "You'll have to excuse Mike, he's never grown-up. Still like an inquisitive little kid."

"That's all right, a lot of people ask about my name. No, my real name's Sarah – it was my grandfather who called me 'Misty'."

"What's the connection between 'Sarah" and 'Misty'?" Mike was intrigued.

"There's no connection," Misty smiled, "My Grandfather said I was a dreamer, that my eyes were always misty, and the name stuck. And I still like to dream; I think it's important – if you don't dream, how do you progress? One of my greatest heroes is William Blake, because he was a dreamer. I've never forgotten reading what he said, 'What is now proved was once only imagined'. And to dream is to imagine."

"So, what made you keep the name 'Misty'?"

"I loved my grandfather and using his nickname for me keeps him alive somehow – lets me feel he's still with me."

"That's amazing," Gill felt her skin tingle, "Don't you think so?" She looked at Mike, who nodded. "So do you think his memory helps stimulate your ideas?"

"Sort of. When I think about him it makes me feel different, it's like it generates an electrical sensation and I just feel I'm going to come up with a solution to whatever I'm thinking about. I know it sounds crazy, but it's like having some sort of subconscious reservoir I can tap into." Misty shook her head as she thought about it.

"I just hope they never prove what it is," Gill said, "That would remove the magic. I hope it stays unexplained."

"So do I. If it was explained it would be like having my grand-father die completely – if that makes sense."

They finished their drinks and separated at the door of the bar.

"Let's chat again tomorrow," Gill said as they left, "I'll see if I can find a training consultant and we can start to develop the training aids and costing everything up."

"That'll be good," Misty waved as she turned to walk away.

"Wow, that was all a bit surreal," Mike shook his head.

"So, what did you make of Misty? I could see you were rather taken by her when I introduced you." Gill put her arm through his as they walked along.

"I wasn't taken by her," Mike felt embarrassed, afraid the other woman might have noticed him looking at her. "It was just she wasn't the usual sort of person you work with. The bracelets, the smock."

"Oh, so it wasn't the big brown eyes, the long hair and the beautiful bone structure – although, what's not to like about those? I saw you take them all in."

"Oh, God, I didn't stare at her too long, did I? You don't think she was embarrassed?"

"I imagine she's used to it. Right, where are we going?"

"It depends; what do you want to eat?"

Gill thought for a moment, "I think I'd prefer an Italian meal tonight, with a couple of glasses of smooth red wine."

"You've had half a bottle already; you'll be pissed by the end of the meal."

"That's alright, I've got my knight in shining armour to look after me," she squeezed his arm tighter, "So, what else did you make of Misty?"

"She's verging on the insane from what she said to me."

"I prefer to think she's verging on the genius. It's really easy to work with her. She generates new ideas all the time."

"But dreaming alone isn't enough – think back to your theme for this event, 'assuming things'."

"I think she sells herself short there," Gill said, "She's really adept at understanding what a client is looking for, and very focused in what she produces – assiduous in making sure everything works together. She's good, really good."

"So, dreams first, focus second," Mike paused, "That's beginning to sound like William Blake might have been right – though I'm not sure his contemporaries would have agreed."

"Why? I thought he was seen as a visionary."

"There's a fine line between being a visionary and being insane, and I think he was probably regarded more as insane in his day. I went to see his memorial when I was up in London one time."

"I'm impressed, I didn't know you were a Blake lover."

"I'm not, particularly, but I had some time to spare, and Blake is just one of the people buried in Bunhill Fields. Defoe and Bunyan are buried there and so, I think, is John Wesley's mother. It was a dissenters' graveyard,"

"What's a dissenters' graveyard?"

"It's a graveyard for non-conformists, and it meant they didn't have to use the service in the Common Prayer Book when they were buried."

"Mm, very Misty sounding. Talking about non-conformists, she told me earlier that she'd been going out with one of the protesters who've been organizing the demos about that guy from Ros' company, the one who killed himself. She said he kept arguing with the managers wherever he was working and losing his job. Plus, he was taking money from her purse to go drinking."

"I've never seen the far left as non-conformists, rather the opposite, and there's some speculation that a leftist group is behind the kidnap of that guy, Misty didn't say anything about that, did she?"

"No, all she mentioned was that her ex was helping to organise the demos."

68

Ros was still playing over what had happened at work with Alison, unsure what to make of it. The only thing she was certain about was that questioning Alison further would be a mistake. She heard Sam's key in the front door, the door opened, and Sam came in.

"Hi, good to be home again. I've had an absolute bugger of a day." He took his boots off and carried them through the kitchen to the small lobby by the back door. "How did your day go?"

"Strange. I finally had a conversation with Alison about John and his marriage, I've been putting it off ever since Gill told me they weren't happy, but she went into Jack's office at lunchtime and closed the door, and I guessed it was going to be the best chance I would get."

"So, how did it go? What did she say?"

"She got very upset; said she loved him and was devastated by his death. And you know I always suspected they might have had an affair."

"Sounds as though you were right," Sam smiled, "Do you want one of those ciders? He reached inside the fridge for his usual after work beer. "Just makes you wonder how long it went on, whether they were still an item when his wife and daughter died."

Ros shook her head, "It makes things difficult; I'll need to be careful what I say at work. She reacted badly when I suggested people should know that John's marriage wasn't happy, to take some of the blame off Jack."

"Maybe she's feeling guilty, as well as upset," Sam passed the cider across to her, "And if she was still part of the reason for the problems John and his wife were having, she wouldn't want people looking any deeper into it all. Besides, she's married herself, isn't she?"

"Maybe that was the reason she and John never got together," Ros took a sip of her cider, "Though I got the impression she'd like to have been with John."

69

Jack woke up to the same silence and controlled lighting every time and tried to go to sleep again, to avoid the mindless monotony that would inevitably follow during the rest of the day. Then he reminded himself that he wasn't even sure if it was the day – he'd lost touch completely with time. He'd been vaguely aware of a bell ringing and looked across at the door – a food tray had been pushed through and he looked for some sort of communication from his captors. But there was nothing. He hated them for what they were doing to him and his family, but they were the only people he could communicate with and his only lifeline with the world outside his cell.

"So, you've got nothing to say, today," he shouted as he carried the meal to the table – it was a lunch, although he'd been expecting breakfast after just waking-up. The discrepancy disconcerted him for a moment, but he decided just to enjoy the food and not question the sequence in which it arrived – reasoning that survival was more important than knowing the time, or even which day it was. The food tasted good, and he was enjoying it when the voice interrupted him

"The news is out, everybody knows you've been abducted, as a reminder to others not to treat fellow human beings in the brutal manner you treated John Morrison."

"Well, that's your take on what happened, but you know I don't agree with how you see things."

"But now your kids know. Sat there clutching their mother on TV, crying, because they don't understand how their father could have acted as you did and afraid of what's going to happen next. And your wife apologizing for your actions and asking for you to be released."

'That's a lie. It's bullshit."

"I don't think you're in any position to say that."

"I'm in a bloody great position. I know my wife, what she knows about me and how protective she is of our kids. She'd never allow them to be exposed publicly like that."

"Maybe you should have been watching TV instead of doodling or sleeping."

"Right, I'll just turn it on." Jack picked-up his fork, pointing it like a remote control, walked across to one of the corners of the room and imitated someone trying to turn-on a TV. "Think you better arrange for a replacement TV; this one doesn't appear to be working. You can send it round anytime, I'm always in." He walked back to the table and started eating again.

"Very amusing," the voice said, "But you're just reinforcing the 'cold bastard' impression that led to you being here in the first place. How can you be so flippant with your family in tears on the national news? You're unbelievable."

"No, no," Jack shook his head in denial, "It's you that's unbelievable. I told you, I know my wife and she wouldn't have let them put the lads on display."

"I'm not sure you know your wife that well."

"What's that supposed to mean? Just another attempt at turning a mental knife in your captive's gut – and you say that what you think I did was a form of bullying! God, I recognise you," Jack started writing on the pad and then held it up, it read 'hypocrite'.

"We provided the paper so you could communicate, not for you to abuse us. Maybe it's time to withdraw one of your privileges."

"One of them? What other fucking privilege do I have?"

"You're still alive."

"And so could John have been, except he decided he didn't want to be any longer."

Because you cut off all hope for him."

"No, because something happened that meant he couldn't face the future anymore."

"That's crap."

"How the hell do you know, you didn't even know him. I did, I spoke to him, which is more than you appear to have done."

"What do you know? About John Morrison or your wife?"

"No, you're not going to knock my confidence about either of them. I knew John and, as sure as hell, I know my wife and her dedication to the lads. You're just full of bullshit. I don't even begin to understand what this is all about, but it's not about me telling John he was redundant, it's about something else, something I don't understand."

Jack turned to the table and picked up the small glass phial. "Well John, what's your take on all this? Did you know these people? What's their motivation? What is this all really about?"

"If you hadn't condemned him, he might have had a chance to respond. And how dare you disrespect him like this? Calling a bottle after him and pretending to talk to it."

"I'm not disrespecting him, it's you, who didn't know him, who's disrespecting him, using him for some sort of political statement. John was a human being, a man I knew and liked. A man I spoke and listened to. If the John I knew was here now, he would condemn what you've done."

There was no response, the loudspeakers went dead, and he was on his own in the silence, wondering what to do with the rest of his day. He felt his pulse increasing; his head felt heavier, and the room began to move around him again. He went back to his mattress; worried he might fall and hurt himself. He was aware of a sudden movement, like he'd been the previous time, but now he understood more about what was happening and told himself to stay calm. He heard laughter and cursed the people who were keeping him there and watching, until he realised it was him that was laughing at a vision of a chameleon trying to merge with a rainbow and the colours complaining; red shouting out in anger burning the chameleon's feet; yellow, its voice parched by the desert sand and blue, eerie, echoing around his head. He kept telling himself it was just an hallucination, caused by his isolation and lack of normal sensory stimulations, trying to reassert the reality of the room and the silence. Gradually he re-established control, focusing on Charlotte and the lads, imagining them at home, waiting for him to come back and holding them close when he did.

70

Heather stared at the screen, watching Jack curled-up on the mattress. She shook her head, distressed by what she was seeing. The laughter was particularly disturbing, manic rather than amused, and she felt herself tensing-up whilst it continued. The sudden, extreme change in the man was worrying her, this was the second time she had seen what appeared to be some form of temporary madness. She watched as the man started to regain control, saw the relaxation in his body and began to relax herself.

But it wasn't just the manic behaviour she was unhappy with, the conversation that preceded it was also causing her concern. She'd been impressed by the man's continuing insistence there may have been other reasons for John's suicide and by a developing perception that he was not the hard, unemotional bully he'd been presented as. And she was uncomfortably aware that the only bullying now taking place was by Allan as he tried to make the man understand how John had felt before his suicide. Besides, there was no evidence that the man was likely to do what they wanted and there were other issues to consider, including her concern about how long it would be before someone noticed their visits to the building in which they were holding him. The whole abduction was beginning to look increasingly pointless.

She decided not to say anything for the time being, aware of the probable reaction an intervention would provoke. Her conscience, though, was bothering her and she knew she would have to express her feelings if the temporary bouts of insane behaviour became more frequent. Needing to unburden herself of some of the guilt she was feeling, she called her brother and was relieved when he picked-up the call.

"I've not said anything, Stuart, because I know it will cause trouble, but how do you see this abduction going?"

"How do you mean?"

"Well, I'm not sure we've got the right man locked-up in that room and, even if we have, I'm not sure it's going to turn out as we'd hoped. The more I listen to the man the more I'm convinced he's alright – certainly not some sort of monster who bullied John."

"I know, I'm beginning to feel the same, but I wanted to support Allan, because he saved my life in the desert. Mind you, I've said this pays off everything, my debt's wiped off when this is all finished. There's nothing more to repay."

"But he'll still be a friend?"

"Of course, that's never going to change. We're mates, we've been through a lot together. When you're expecting to die and someone practically carries you back to safety, like he did for me, you never forget it – it's a lifelong thing. Besides, he's your husband."

"It's just that, sometimes, he gets fixated on something and it's impossible to divert him. And this is one of those occasions. But I don't think I can continue much longer without saying something. I don't think the man we've got in the room is going to crack like he's supposed to."

"So, what do you want to do?"

"I'm going to have to speak up, at some point. I couldn't live with myself if I didn't."

"I've been thinking the same. I've been to hell and back with Allan, but he's got this wrong – I understand why, but he's way out of line. We need to make sure he's never identified as being involved – not least because we'd both be dragged down with him – but first we need to persuade him to change his plans."

"So, will you support me when I say it should stop?"

"Of course, but let me know before you confront him so I can be prepared for the fall-out."

"Why are you guys like this?"

"That's an easy question to ask when things are going well, but when the shit hits the fan, you may be glad to have someone like Allan around. In this situation, though, he needs to step back and take another look at what happened and why. And then he needs to come to terms with where we are and the best way forward. And I think he will."

"I hope so. I'll let you know before I say anything."

71

Jack sat by the table, doodling on the pad and thinking about Daniel and Tony, trying to visualise them – Daniel looking-up from whatever he was doing and waving when he got back from work and Tony rushing over and grabbing his hand to take him to see something he'd done at school that day. And, in the background, holding everything together, he was constantly aware of Charlotte's presence and felt himself smiling as she walked across to welcome him home. He made a mental note to show how much he valued her if he ever got out of the hellhole in which he currently sat. The worst thing was the nothingness, the boredom. As he thought about his confinement, he began to recognise the rising signs of a panic attack, the anxiety and increasing heartbeat and he got up and walked around, taking deep breaths and then exhaling slowly and deliberately. It demanded all his attention initially, obliterating any other thoughts, until he began to relax again and could focus on Charlotte and the boys.

"Are you ok, Jack?"

It was a female voice and that surprised him. His captors had only had one voice until now and Jack wondered about the change – what had caused it? He was tempted to respond belligerently, but the speaker sounded sympathetic, concerned, and she'd called him by his name; up until now he'd been nameless, dehumanised. He decided to try a more conciliatory approach than previously.

"No, I'm not ok, how could I be ok locked up in this room? It sends you crazy with nothing to do all day – and I'm not even sure if it's day or night."

"How well did you know John?"

"Oh, God, this isn't the start of some 'good guy, bad guy' exercise, is it? I really don't need this, thank you."

"No, I shouldn't be talking to you at all, it could get me into trouble. Please, just trust me and tell me how well you knew John."

Jack didn't answer immediately, still asking himself whether some game was being played. But the tone of the voice sounded different – sounding as though the person was genuinely asking how he was. On the other hand, how many men had been seduced by a female approach, with the anticipated empathy? He decided to try to find out more about why the change had happened.

"Why are you talking to me now?"

"Because I've been watching you, and I'm not convinced you were responsible for John's death."

When he heard what she'd said, Jack felt like crying – crying because there was someone who was not immediately judging him, someone who was prepared to give him a hearing. Thinking about it, he could see no downside in talking more openly to the person.

"Well, to answer your question, I didn't know John that well in later years. We used to be closer, when I first joined the company, and we played snooker each week. But then John stopped playing and we began to lose that closeness. Then I got promoted and became John's manager, which separated us further – but I still liked him, we still got on. He was one of those guys you couldn't dislike – casual, competent, not a star performer – but never a problem."

"So, why was he chosen for redundancy? Why not someone else?"

"Because firms have to decide on measurable criteria, as far as they can, to be fair to all the people who might be affected. And, based on those criteria, John was one of the people who had to be let go."

"Sounds so innocuous doesn't it, that phrase 'had to be let go'? But in this case, it was followed by John's suicide. Didn't it occur to you that he might kill himself?"

"No, I've already told the guy who's been speaking to me that I talked to John and was surprised by his mood. He seemed so optimistic, so upbeat. When he hanged himself, I was as devastated as the next man. I really didn't see it coming."

"So, why do you think he did it?"

"I don't know." Jack shook his head as he thought about the suicide. "I've no idea, I can't even guess at a reason. There's no way I'd have gone along with making him redundant if I'd even an inkling that he might kill himself. The potential guilt will stay with me forever, though I'm really not sure how I feature in all of this. The only thing I can think of is a delayed reaction to the deaths of his wife and daughter."

"Had you met his wife?"

"Years ago, when we played snooker. We took it in turns to drive to the hall and I used to collect him from his house. And I chatted a few times with her if he wasn't ready to leave."

"Was there anything you particularly remember about her?"

"No. It was a long time ago. She seemed nice enough; I can't remember anything more than that. Why are you asking? I mean, what relevance does it have to John's death?"

"Look, I'm going to have to go, and you mustn't talk to anyone else about this conversation. Ok? I'd like to help you, but I can't if the man you've been talking to until now finds out I've spoken to you."

Jack held out his hands and looked theatrically round the room. "Well, I'm spoilt for choice about who to talk to, as you can see. But, if you really want to help me, a book or something to keep me occupied is the thing I need most."

"I'm not sure, I'll see what can be arranged, but I can't promise anything."

"Thank you," John looked up at one of the cameras as he spoke, "But there is one other thing I need to know, how long have I been here and is it night or day outside?"

"You've been here nearly two weeks and it's late afternoon outside."

"God, it seems a lot longer than that. And it's afternoon, so it's still daylight out there." He paused forming a picture in his head of a daylight scene. "And what about my family, how are my wife and sons?"

"I'm sorry, that's something I can't help you with. I haven't seen any news about them."

"But the man said they'd been on the news."

"That isn't true and it's one of the reasons I'm talking to you. We brought you here to send out a message that it's not alright to treat people without compassion and that's what he was doing to you. Just ignore anything he says about your family – unless I confirm it."

Jack nodded so she could see his agreement.

"Oh, and one other thing," the voice said, "Stop calling that bottle John, it just exacerbates matters, he sees it as demeaning to the guy who killed himself. Promise me you'll do that, and I'll see if I can get you that book"

"Ok," Jack nodded again, "And thanks."

"Don't thank me yet, you're still a long way from getting out of here."

72

Heather picked-up the 'phone, called her brother and told him about her conversation with Jack.

"I think it might be time to talk now, Stuart. We need to find a way out of the whole situation."

"Allan's not going to be happy, particularly when he hears you've spoken to the guy. Do you want me there when you talk to him?"

"No, I just need to know you'll back me up when he talks to you – he's bound to ask if we've already spoken. Besides, I thought I'd approach things on a stage-by-stage basis, try to get him to agree to give Jack some reading material and stop him having these fits he seems to experience – maybe a couple of books he can read. Then, assuming there's still no change in Jack's attitude, I'll talk to him again – see if there's any concession he'll make to sweeten the pill and meet Allan halfway."

"Arrange a sort of negotiation between the two, it's a clever idea, but you know how difficult Allan can be. That's the way we survived back then, by being stubborn, conquering the odds, doing something that seemed impossible – catching our opponents when they weren't expecting us to. "

"Well, in a way that's what the softly, softly approach is all about. He knows I'll always support him, but, on this occasion, that may mean saving him from his own stubbornness and that's going to require a lot of tact. Look, I think he's back, I'd better go." She put the 'phone down and was making herself a mug of tea when her husband walked in.

"Any change, down at the industrial site?" He motioned with his head at the laptop screen.

"He started to have another one of those fits."

"Right," he went to the screen to take a look, "Perhaps it's beginning to work."

"I don't think so; this time he seemed to have learned how to control whatever he was experiencing – to recover himself quicker than he did before."

"It always works eventually, it affects everyone, even if they don't completely crack. We just need to give it more time. You're right, he seems fine now, sitting there staring into space. But we'll see how long it lasts."

"How long do you think we'll need, because to be honest, I don't want to go on like this for much longer? I don't think he'll open that bottle – it was a nice idea, but it doesn't look like he will. And he's meant to be here because he didn't show empathy with a man who subsequently killed himself, but what empathy are we showing him?"

The man frowned and his face became angry. "I don't believe I'm hearing this. We all agreed what we were going to do, and what we wanted to achieve – me, you, your brother. What does Stuart think about it all, I suppose you've spoken to him?"

"Have a word with him yourself, but I think he feels like I do – we don't have the time to crack this man, the sort of time you've had before. You know we support what you're trying to achieve but, when we started all this, we didn't agree to anyone harming him."

"I don't want to harm him – I want to break him." Allan was shouting now and thumped his hand on the kitchen table, the force making the laptop jump in the air. "He's a bastard, a total bastard."

"That's not what we signed-up to, Allan. We never agreed to break him. We always envisaged letting him go."

"So, what do you suggest, open the door and ask him to step out so we can arrange a taxi to take him home?"

"Of course not, but what do we want out of this? A more compassionate society generally, and, more specifically, a recognition that individual circumstances shouldn't be ignored by a system that operates just for profit. Plus, hopefully, the name John Morrison becoming embedded in the public consciousness."

"So, how will just releasing this bastard achieve that?"

"I'm not suggesting we release him yet, but perhaps we could talk to him less aggressively, negotiate with him. Get him to acknowledge that what happened was wrong, that it was a mistake."

"You can't negotiate with a bastard like him – he'll agree with anything just to get free. Then, afterwards, he'll say he was coerced into what happened, deny he meant it."

"Look, I understand how you feel, but why not try to talk to him?"

"And, if I do, will you continue to support me?"

"Yes, providing you allow him a book or something to fill his time – it's inhumane to leave him with nothing to do. I'm convinced that's why he's having these fits; he's got nothing to stimulate him."

"What do you suggest, 'War and Peace'?"

Heather looked-up at him, hoping to see the beginning of a better mood, but he still looked grimly determined. "I think something more readable, perhaps give him a choice of two or three books – maybe one with puzzles to keep him occupied."

"This isn't a bloody library service; we want him to admit his complicity in a man's death."

"He's not going to do that."

"Then he won't get out."

"I'm sorry, but you have to let him go – Stuart and I will continue to support you for the time being, but not for ever. You need to re-think the outcome of all this. We need to get the guy on our side – to persuade him that what we're doing is right. The problem, as far as I can see, is that he wouldn't disagree with us in general terms, but thinks we're mistaken about the cause of John's suicide in this case."

"How do we know he's not just playing us? Besides, even if what you say is true, it was still him that delivered the redundancy message. Everyone involved in the redundancy programme can claim it wasn't their fault, so the only way to change things is to focus on their joint responsibility and make an example of one as a warning to people like him."

73

Max was sitting in his office working on the draft of a release to the trade press when the call came through.

"Hi, Max, Charlotte Docherty here. Can you talk?"

"Just give me a moment, Charlotte," he got up and closed the door, "I can now. How are things?"

"Pretty stressful, which is why I'm calling I suppose – I think my parents and friends must all be fed-up with me calling them, so I thought I'd find a new victim to chat to. Well, that's the real reason for calling out of the way, the official reason for the call is to see whether anyone there has heard anything about Jack?"

"No, nothing here, what about your end? Have you heard anything more from the police?"

"Oh, the liaison officer liaises, but hasn't got anything to actually say – well nothing of any significance. They really don't seem to be getting anywhere. They've reviewed footage from local CCTV cameras to see if they can identify any vehicles acting suspiciously and interviewed people at the snooker hall – but I don't think they've found anything."

"They've been here as well, interviewing some of the staff, but we haven't seen them for the past few days. I think they've been trying to establish if there's anyone who's been particularly vocal about John Morrison's suicide, and who might have links to an organisation that may have kidnapped Jack. The last I heard they still think he must have been identified by someone inside the company as his name was never mentioned externally."

"What do you think?"

"I don't know, Charlotte. I don't see how Jack's name would have been known without someone from here. How they could have recognised him otherwise, so I guess it's a logical starting point? It's still being talked about around the place and there are different opinions about it all, as you'd expect, but their recent absence suggests the police have drawn a blank as far as anyone being involved from here is concerned."

"The last I heard was that they're still investigating whether some left-wing group was involved, and it was the left-wing media that came out with the story. But I've also been pressing them not to make assumptions and widen their enquiries."

"So, who else do you think it might be?" Max was intrigued by what Charlotte was saying.

"Well, John Morrison's next of kin, for example, might want to punish Jack if they believe he was responsible for John's death. So, I've mentioned to the liaison officer how unhappy I am at the apparent lack of progress and said I'd like them to take a fresh look at everything. I'm desperate to get Jack back and someone's got to fight his corner for him. I can't just sit here, looking after the boys and hoping everything will be ok."

"How are the boys doing? Are they going to school?"

"It's difficult to know quite how they are. I sent them off to my parents when the story finally broke, to keep them away from the reporters camped outside the house, but after a couple of days Tony, the younger one, wanted to come back home. The sudden loss of security and stability has affected them both – I think in some ways the anxiety's going to stay with them, the worry that something that changes everything can happen so suddenly. Tony's been particularly clinging, follows me round all the time. Daniel's quieter, stays up in his room a lot. The school have been good, sending work through for them both, more as a distraction, than anything else, I suppose."

"What about you, how are you coping?"

There was a pause before Charlotte answered. "Oh, I alternate between fear and guilt, tears and anger – but most of the time I have to keep my feelings hidden because of the boys. I can only talk to you like this because my parents popped round and took them out for a couple of hours. Tony didn't want to go, but I needed some time to myself."

"Why guilt, I can understand the fear and anger, but why would you feel guilty?" Max was confused.

"Because life goes on, I suppose, and because I'm still managing and Jack's somewhere with God knows what happening to him. It makes me question myself, who I am and whether I should be coping? And I'm angry, not only with the bastards who've kidnapped him, but with the police and myself for not having been able to do anything more to bring him home."

"Hopefully, whoever's kidnapped him is only looking to make a political or moral point rather than punishing Jack."

"I'm sorry, Max, but I'm not a great believer in people acting altruistically, like latter day Robin Hoods. In my experience it's often a front for rather deeper things like feelings of inadequacy, or those emotions I've been feeling, anger or guilt. I mean, how could anyone possibly justify what's happened to Jack if they even begin to think about the damage it's doing to the kids? To me, this is all down to something deeper, dressed-up to appear altruistic."

She put the phone down and immediately felt the loneliness again. The house was silent, and the boys would be another hour or so before they got home, and she had nothing to fill her time. She made herself a cup of tea, sat down at the kitchen table, placed her hands over her head and sat motionless. Then she sat back up and screamed – loud and angrily.

74

Jack heard the bolts on the door flap sliding back and saw a tray pushed through. It contained sandwiches, water and some books. The bolts slid shut again and he went across to investigate, picked-up the tray and carried it back to the table. There were three books, two popular novels and a book of crosswords. He read the backs of the novels, selected the one he thought he'd prefer and put it aside. Then he picked-up the puzzle book, it contained cryptic crosswords that required him to concentrate, and he ran down the questions on the first puzzle as he was eating. The relief he felt at having something to do was immediate and he picked-up the pen and began filling in some of the answers.

"I hope you're enjoying the books," the man's voice came through the loudspeakers. "We've taken into account the pressures on you in the environment in which you're being detained, now, perhaps you can begin to recognise the pressures on the man you helped drive to suicide?"

"I'm sorry, I am grateful for the puzzles and books, but I really don't think I helped drive John Morrison to commit suicide. I know that's what you want me to say," Jack said, "But I don't believe it's a true reflection of what happened."

"So, you're saying we're wrong?"

"Look, I really appreciate the books, it's a great gesture, but, yes, I think that somewhere along the line you've got it wrong."

"We thought that a show of good faith on our part would elicit a similar show on yours, but it looks as though we were wrong – it was a mistake to give you the books."

"No, it wasn't a mistake, I was going crazy without anything to distract me, but it doesn't alter the basic issue, we don't agree on what caused John to kill himself. It's like the prison authorities asking me to confess to a crime I didn't commit so I can be released. And I want to be released, but I don't want to be branded, unfairly, as a criminal. I don't want my kids bullied at school or my wife ostracised when she goes out – all because I took the easy way out of here."

There was a pause, the speakers went dead.

"What he's saying is perfectly reasonable, you can't make him confess to something he didn't do." Heather was angry, pointing at the man on the laptop screen as she spoke. "Just imagine what it would be like for his family if he admitted driving John to kill himself. It would mean losing his job, moving his family away – you know how eager people can be to point fingers and marginalise other people."

"I'm not sure I want to listen to any more of your ideas. 'Treat him more humanely' I believe you said. 'Talk to him, negotiate more'. And when I went along with you and we gave him those books, what did it achieve?" He was shouting now, "Nothing, absolutely nothing."

"So, what are you going to do, Allan? Just keep him here forever, leave him to rot in that bloody room?"

"What's going on," Jack's voice could be heard on the laptop in the background, "The sound has gone. Are you still there?" They could see Jack on the screen, looking-up at the speakers.

Allan looked down at Heather and she saw his features harden. "What would you do?" he asked. "Just forget about what happened to John and let the rest of the world forget as well. In which case, John died for nothing."

"I'd let him go; I can't see him changing his mind now. I don't see what other choice you have."

"We could just forget him, like they used to; turn the room into an oubliette and walk away," he leant over and pushed a button on the laptop keyboard and the screen went dark.

"No!" Jack's voice shouted out through the laptop speaker.

75

When the lights went out Jack was in total blackness and panicked. He couldn't see anything, even his own hand and he was afraid of walking into the table or toilet cubicle or tripping against the mattress and hitting his head on a wall or the floor. He sat down where he was and tried to work out the direction of the mattress so he could reach it and lay down. He felt the panic begin to take him over; the complete silence and darkness were bad enough, but he didn't know what it all meant, whether the lighting had just failed or whether it was a deliberate act on the part of his abductors and, if so, how long they intended leaving him there, abandoned and forgotten.

"What's going on, the lights have all failed." He tried calling out, but there was no response. "For Christ's sake, you can't just leave me here. I can't see or hear anything." He tried breathing deeply and exhaling slowly, but the darkness made everything worse, and he began to feel claustrophobic, imagining the walls closing in on him. He thought he heard a noise, a scuffling sound and worried again about mice or, worse still, rats in the room and listened more intently, turning his head in the direction of the sound, to hear better. But there was just silence again.

He started crawling in the direction he thought the mattress should be but came up against a wall. Turning to his left, reasoning that he must have deviated too far towards the door, he eventually found the mattress, climbed on and lay down. The mattress made him feel more secure, he told himself it was ridiculous to feel as he did but felt it anyway. The real question was how to get out of the room, how to escape from the nightmare he was in. He felt helpless and angry – he'd done nothing wrong, just been singled out as an example by people who didn't appear to bother about families and the effect of their actions on the type of people they purported to represent. At the same time, he realised they would ascribe that impact to him, and not to their own actions. It was just another turn of the screw, another thing for which he was being held responsible.

The mattress started to feel less comforting, so he curled up and lay like a foetus, trying to ignore the lack of sensation.

76

"Now you've gone too far," Heather looked up into her husband's face, "I'm sorry, but I can't support this any longer. Either you agree to let him go, or Stuart and I will let him out, whatever the cost. Do you understand? How could you even think of turning off the lights like that?"

Allan looked fixedly at her, weighing-up her reaction and considering the options left to him. Heather stared back, adamant it was over.

"Ok," he said reluctantly, "But only on the condition we don't tell him now that we're going to release him."

Heather nodded, then walked over and put her arms round him. "I'm sorry, I know what you were trying to do, but it's not turned out as we thought it would. If you want a way out, why don't you ask him to record something we can release to the media, supporting what we're trying to achieve – I'm sure he'll do that. Let me prepare something, we'll pass it into him and, if he agrees, maybe it will influence the public and lead to some of the changes we'd like to see in the future."

"For Christ's sake switch the bloody lights back on," Jack's voice intruded on their discussion.

Heather looked across. Allan stared back for a moment then nodded agreement, and she reached across to the computer keyboard, put her finger on a key and tapped it. The computer screen lit up again, showing Jack on his mattress.

"Oh, God, look at him, curled up like a baby. This isn't right. There may be times when it might be justified to treat someone like this; to save lives or defeat terrorists, but this isn't one of those times. I'll get working on a script and we'll see if he'll read it for us."

77

As soon as she was on her own Heather called her brother, worried by Allan's reaction. Whilst he'd agreed to release Jack after producing a video of him speaking in support of their objectives, she'd felt a coldness when she'd hugged him, a distraction that scared her.

"I've not seen him like this before, Stuart. This has become a personal battle; one he's determined to win. I'm not sure he's going to release Jack so easily; he says he wants to break him. I said what he was doing wasn't right, but I'm afraid he's not listening anymore."

"For a start, I don't think it's a good idea if he begins to believe you're getting too involved, Sis, seeing the guy as a person – that's the last thing he wants. It's easier to handle the situation if he can distance himself and see the other guy as nothing more than a cypher. So, make sure you don't use his name when you talk to Allan."

"I'm not sure he needs to put any more distance between himself and Jack; his reaction was dreadful, it scared me because it was so unfeeling. He just turned the light off, plunged the room into darkness without any warning and talked about forgetting Jack, leaving him there – and that's not what we agreed when this all started."

"What did the guy do?"

"He panicked, screamed out. What would anyone do when they're plunged into darkness and silence and locked in a room they can't escape from?"

"But we still can't be sure about how far he's prepared to go. I know you understand him better than anyone, Sis, and

I take what you're saying seriously, but we still don't know he's changed his mind."

"So, what do you suggest?"

"I'm not sure," Stuart stopped to think for a moment, "If we oppose him, it's likely to make him more determined – he may even start to believe we're turning against him, and that would leave him feeling totally isolated."

"But we can't take the risk he might go too far."

"Then we need to keep a closer watch on him, make sure he doesn't get the opportunity of doing something daft. For a start, make sure you're the one who prepares the guy's food. And we need to find out a bit more about the drug he used to get him here, especially the dosage – it's the same drug he said he'd use to get him out. The only real danger is that he'll overdose the guy – instead of releasing him."

"This is becoming a mess, he seemed so certain he could manipulate Jack before it all started."

"He's driven, always has been, but you can understand why, particularly in these circumstances. Just keep an eye on him and let me know if he does anything that starts to alarm you."

"One thing that really unsettles me is his taunting the guy with this cat idea – he's enthralled by the idea it can be alive and dead at the same time whilst the box is still closed, but he's just using it as a threat. It's bullying, giving him an almost God-like power as it's him who can change whatever's going on it that room and, of course, it's him who finally opens the box. And Jack knows he's powerless to protect himself – it must be terrifying."

"Well, we'll just have to try to ensure we protect him, that nothing takes place to harm him. We can't stop the taunting, but we may be able to stop anything worse happening."

78

Roger checked the time, poured himself a cup of coffee and reached for another slice of toast. There were two pieces left in the rack and he offered the last one to his wife. She looked-up from her book, took the toast, smiled briefly as she did so and carried on reading. Breakfasts, Roger reflected, were rather like their marriage, sedate occasions with the same things to eat most mornings and only occasional lapses into intimacy. They had been different when the children were at home, hurried, noisy and frequently bad-tempered affairs with mislaid schoolbooks, anxieties over things that had happened the previous day or were expected to happen later, and passionate arguments about beliefs and opinions. He sat still for a moment, thinking back, and decided to see Margaret that evening.

"I may be home late tonight, Hilary. Max Gregory was talking about arranging a meal with a client. I'll call you later and confirm what's happening when I've spoken to him."

His wife looked up and said nothing for a moment, just facing him across the table. She seemed undecided at first, thinking about what to say. But then he saw her features harden. "You don't have to make excuses, Roger, I've known about your meetings with Margaret for years. I've never said anything because it's suited me the way things are. We've rubbed along well enough together – and there's no reason we shouldn't continue to in future."

"What!" Roger choked on the piece of toast he was eating. "Don't be so ridiculous."

"Please don't insult me by trying to lie about it, I'm not an idiot. I really don't mind any more, but I think it may be time for us to agree to sleep in separate rooms – I can't see any reason to stay as we are."

"This is crazy," Roger's quiet appreciation of his breakfast was replaced by a feeling of panic.

"I'll move your things into the larger guest room whilst you're at work," Hilary looked down again and turned the page in her book. "As I said, there's no need for anything else to change – I'm happy with the way things are. You've done well, we have a beautiful home, some nice friends we share – and others we don't," she smiled briefly, "So let's just go on with our lives the way we have been, behave like adults and avoid any fuss. You can see Margaret whenever you want, and I can see my friends."

"You spring this on me just before I go to work?" Roger felt angry and insecure. "It's not on. What do you think the children will think, when they come to stay and find we're in separate rooms?"

"We can tell them it's because of your snoring," Hilary remained calm, matter of fact. "I really don't see what all the fuss is about, nothing's going to change except for our sleeping arrangements. Let's face it, you haven't been interested in me for ages."

"We need to talk about this," Roger began to speak, but she cut him short.

"Look you need to get to work, and the cleaner will be here shortly, and we can't talk in front of her. And you're not coming home until later, are you?"

"I only said I might be late coming home. In view of this I'll tell Max to cancel the client dinner if it's still on."

"Whatever, my dear," Hilary smiled, "You really don't need to keep this pretence up, it doesn't matter anymore." She got up and took their plates into the kitchen.

He pushed back his chair and followed her, pausing in the hall to pick-up his case. "I'll get Max to cancel the client meal. We've obviously got a lot we need to talk about. I'm not at all happy with this."

"I wasn't happy when I found out you'd been having an affair with Margaret, but I got over it after a while; I realised there were a lot of plusses about staying married to you, the lifestyle, the less frequent demands you made on me and the freedom I began to feel – and we've always got on. I hope we can make this new arrangement work, for everyone's sake." She followed him as he turned to leave, reached up and touched his cheek briefly with her lips and picked a speck of something off his lapel, before dusting the material down with her fingers.

When he'd gone, she leant back against the front door; a smile on her face, feeling relaxed for the first time in months. Roger on the other hand was shocked by the calmness with which she'd confronted him and the admission that she knew about Margaret. He was angry too, about the reasons she'd given for staying, feeling used and humiliated. He liked Margaret, but she was an undemanding distraction, fun to spend time with sometimes. Hilary was central to his life, his position, the stability he'd come to depend on outside work – and always there to return to, when his past affairs had ended. He wondered whether to tell Margaret that Hilary knew, but if he did, she might expect more from him and he decided against confiding in her. Better to keep things as they were, casual without any commitment and uncomplicated as far as his relationship with the children was concerned.

Margaret knew something was wrong when she saw him approaching his office. She picked-up her notepad and followed him in, closing the door after her. "What's the matter?" she asked, "You don't look very happy this morning."

"I'm fine, just a bit of a row at home."

"Can I get you a cup of coffee?"

"Please," Roger nodded.

"Do you want to talk about it later?"

"I'm sorry Margaret, but I've got to go home early this evening, something's come up. Do you mind if I take a rain check?"

She shook her head and smiled. "I'll get that coffee."

79

Richie switched on his computer and opened the Worker's page to look at the morning news. There was a picture of a pale-faced, unshaven man beneath a headline 'Kidnapped Manager Slams Redundancy Decision'. He clicked on the link and played the short video.

Jack was sitting at a table and looking up at a camera. The little that could be seen of the room was bare, giving no clues about the building he was being held in. His hair was unwashed and untidy, and he looked tired. His voice, when he started speaking, sounded flat, lacking expression.

>*"Hi, I'm Jack Docherty, and I'm being held because I was the sales director who told John Morrison he was redundant before he later committed suicide. If I'd known John's true mental state, I would not have continued with the redundancy and would have recommended he receive support from the company until he was able to come to terms with the loss of his wife and daughter earlier in the year.*
>
>*But I didn't appreciate how he was feeling and, as a businessman, rather than a mental health professional, can only conclude I must have misread the signs during my discussions with him.*
>
>*I truly regret and apologise for anything I did, which may have helped lead to John's suicide, although I recognise this is a totally inadequate*

response as far as John or any surviving members of his family are concerned.

Having had time to look back, with the benefit of hindsight, I now believe the system that my abductors wish to see implemented, requiring a fuller professional assessment of workers who may be at risk, should be introduced by law, before any more people suffer in the way that John did. And, because this system results from the anger generated by John's dismissal and suicide, I believe it should be known as 'John's Law', in commemoration of John Morrison.

Our present laws regarding redundancy have been shown to be inadequate and it's time for them to be changed, protecting workers in the same way as health and safety legislation.

Once again, I would like to express my sorrow at John's death and my regret for any part I may have played in it."

The man looked down and the video cut out. Richie called Jim immediately and found he hadn't read the Worker's online edition that morning. "The Worker's obviously got an inside track on this kidnapping, Jim, you sure there's not something you want to share with me about who's holding this guy?"

"I'm sure – I'd have told you if I knew anything. Give me a moment and I'll take a look." He played the video, whilst Richie waited for his reaction. "Hey, it's pretty good stuff, sounds as though he's come to realise that what they did to Morrison was wrong, This John's Law sounds like a great idea."

"I'm sorry, Jim, I still reckon he's a bastard – he must have known that what he was doing could push the guy over the edge. I just hope whoever's holding him makes him feel like the guy he helped to kill. Understand how fucking cruel the whole capitalist system is."

"Well, I guess we can help with that, Richie. Sounds to me that we need to organise a fresh demo outside the company again. We can show people the video on our 'phones, draw the parallel with the guy who killed himself. And, this time, perhaps target the top man. We can find out who he is and call for his resignation."

"I'm up for it, I'll get in touch with some of our people and get things organised. So, you've no idea how the Worker got hold of this?"

"No, but great they did, otherwise I don't think anyone would have got to see it."

80

Charlotte heard the 'phone ring and rushed to pick it up. It was the police liaison officer.

"Hi, I don't know whether you've been looking at online news, but there's a video of Jack. The mainline media are holding-off; it's come through the Worker again. I guess you'll want to watch it but suggest you don't show the boys."

"Why? What's wrong with Jack?"

"Nothing's wrong, although he does look tired, a bit untidy – might be upsetting for them. Not like the father they know and love. But he's ok, chooses his words carefully."

"Did you get any clues about who's holding him or where?" Charlotte was anxious for more information.

"Sorry, the film's grainy and focuses on his face, rather than his surroundings. Nothing we can home in on, though it rather backs our theory that some left-wing group is involved in view of the Worker's continuing involvement. But the Inspector has agreed to interview John Morrison's next of kin again, like you've been pressing us to do."

When the call ended, Charlotte checked the link she'd been sent and watched the video. Jack was paler and scruffier than she'd ever seen him – hair tousled, looking as if it hadn't been washed, and his face unshaven. She listened carefully to what he was saying, and then played the video again, in case it gave any clue to where he was or who had taken him – but there was nothing she could pick up on. She stopped the video and burst into tears. When she'd recovered from her initial shock, she called Max.

"Hi, there's a video online with Jack talking about that guys' death and his abduction." She sent him the link and waited while he watched it. "So, what do you think?"

"He doesn't look as though he's shaved in a while, but, otherwise, he seems ok. And there's nothing to give away his surroundings – these guys look as though they're professionals."

"But how will Grimshaw view it?"

"I'm not sure," Max wanted to say what he really felt, but realised the pressure Charlotte was already under, "I think he'd preferred to have avoided the video. Are the police agreeing to its release to the mainstream media channels?"

"No, I think they're trying to control any release of information and avoid me and the boys experiencing even more stress."

"Good, but would you object to me sharing it with Grimshaw?"

"How can I, it's public knowledge and I don't think Jack says anything controversial, does he?"

"Not as far as I can see; he sounds remarkably balanced after what's happened to him, but Grimshaw is hyper-sensitive at the moment."

"Well, it's already out there and I guess we can't put it back in the closet. Besides, it was Grimshaw who initiated the redundancy programme."

"It's not quite that simple, Grimshaw sees the programme as necessary for the rest of the workers. In his eyes, he's the one with the vision to save their jobs, make sure they can stay working. And, in some ways, you have to agree with that conclusion, hard-nosed as it may be."

"So, Jack's a martyr for the rest of the workers, along with John Morrison. But Grimshaw escapes scot-free?"

"It's wrong, I know, but that's how Grimshaw is likely to see things panning out. I have to say, he's been distancing himself from the whole issue since Jack's abduction."

"What?" Charlotte was astounded, "So it wasn't Grimshaw and the programme that were responsible, it was the way Jack implemented it?"

"Yes, I'm sorry, but Grimshaw's a survivor, his reaction is predictable from where I sit. Totally unfair, I know."

"Unfair isn't the word I'd use, exploitative, self-exonerating or delusional are all descriptions that seem more appropriate. What goes on in this man's mind?"

"I can only guess at the answer to that question."

"But doesn't he even begin to accept responsibility for his part in Jack's abduction?"

"Probably not. As far as Grimshaw's concerned he did what was required for the business and if it went wrong, it was the way his instructions were implemented."

"That's scary," Charlotte said

81

Max ran through the video clip again, noting carefully what Jack had said and decided it was essentially the way Jack had presented things at the management meetings after John Morrison's suicide. The part that concerned him was the suggestion that maybe there should be a requirement to assess the possible impact that redundancy might have on a person where unusual personal circumstances existed – it sounded too close to an admittance that John Morrison's situation hadn't been taken sufficiently into account and Grimshaw would be angered by that. But he knew he had to alert Grimshaw to the video's existence and put a call through to him.

"Hi, Roger, I don't know whether you're aware, but there's a video of Jack circulating on social media, talking about Morrison and his suicide."

"No, I didn't know. Have you got a copy?"

"I'll send you through the link and maybe we can talk about it later, when you've had a chance to watch it – it's short and poor old Jack looks pretty rough, I guess he's not being held in very good conditions."

A short while later, Max received a call from Margaret saying Grimshaw wanted to see him. When he arrived, Geoff was already there. Roger got up, walked over to the table and sat down, his face agitated.

"How dare Jack agree to make a video like that? It puts the company in a very poor light. Practically blames us for Morrison's death."

"I agree," Geoff said, "It's reprehensible in my opinion."

"But what did he actually say, that makes you feel this way?" Max looked at both other men sat at the table. "He said pretty much what he said in this room when we discussed it last. The only added message is agreeing it might be prudent to require additional enquiries when making someone redundant if it's known there are exceptional circumstances. And let's remember he's been abducted, is being held prisoner somewhere, and the video may have been edited."

"He didn't need to agree to make a bloody video at all," Roger spat the words out and Geoff nodded in agreement.

"But we have no idea who's abducted him, the conditions he's being kept in – although his appearance suggests they're basic – or if it was just part of a negotiation to release him. We've got no idea what pressures he's been put under." Max was incredulous at the reaction he was hearing. "The way I see I, Jack has taken a hit for the company."

"I'm sorry Max, but I'd suggest it was the other way round – the company's been hit by the way Jack mishandled the situation we entrusted him to manage." Roger sat there shaking his head, lips stubbornly compressed together.

"So, what would you have done, Geoff, if Jack had come to you and said he was worried that John Morrison might kill himself – assuming he actually felt that way?" Max turned to Geoff and waited for his answer.

"I'd have told Roger immediately and suggested we may have to re-think the situation."

"In what way, Geoff? Would you have suggested that someone else was made redundant instead of Morrison, someone who'd been assessed as more likely to benefit the company going forward? Or would you have suggested keeping him on longer, deferring the changes in the sales team for a while and then firing him later?"

"We could have looked at any of those options, if we'd known more about Morrison's mental state. But we didn't, Jack didn't say anything." Geoff appeared uncomfortable, defensive, his face beginning to flush as he felt the heat from Max's questioning and worried about what Roger might be thinking.

"Maybe he didn't say anything because he didn't believe there was anything to tell, because Morrison didn't appear suicidal?" Max was going to say more but was disturbed by shouting outside.

"What the hell is going on?" Roger's face was angry, and he pushed back his chair to look out of the window. As he did so, Margaret knocked on the door and came in, looking concerned.

"There's another demonstration outside Roger, and it appears to be targeting you this time, instead of the Company."

Roger rushed to the window and looked out on a crowd of protesters, many of them holding-up posters with his face and slogans written across it.

"This is outrageous, how the hell did they get my name and photo? Call the police, Margaret. And, Geoff, I'd like to find out who on our staff is colluding with these idiots and fire them."

Geoff started to pick up his papers from the table, but Max waved at him to stay where he was. "Look Roger, we don't know that anyone in the Company is feeding these guys information, they can get your name and photo very easily online. And if we start a witch-hunt here, we'll risk creating something else for the press to latch on to – particularly if someone from our staff is talking to them."

"Look at that bloody poster," Roger was pointing down at the small crowd outside the gates, "They've written 'Capitalist killer' across my face."

"Well, at least the TV crew doesn't appear to be there this time," Max said, "So you're not going to have your face plastered all over the local news."

"And they're holding their bloody phones in the air; what are they doing, taking photos?"

"Max looked out at the crowd again. "I think they're showing the clip of Jack you saw this morning."

"I want those posters of me taken down, how dare they use my photo without my permission. I'll sue the bastards if we can identify any of them," Roger was irate. "And where are the bloody police when they're needed?"

"I'm sorry, Roger," Max was beginning to secretly enjoy his boss's irritation, "But I think breach of copyright is generally a civil offence unless it's done for commercial purposes and not one the police will get involved in."

"Well, this is damaging the business." Roger was florid faced as he watched the protesters below, "And imagine what it's doing for my image amongst the workforce and to staff morale. Those people down there are bloody criminals!"

82

Ros hurried out of work and went to fetch her car, which she'd parked nearby. She'd heard about the video of Jack earlier and demonstrators tried to show it to her, but she waved them away, stared down at the pavement and walked determinedly on. Whilst opinions had been split about the redundancy programme and John's suicide, colleagues she'd spoken to seemed averse to watching the video. Alison had been particularly adamant about not watching it, but then she'd disappeared, and Ros had found her in the women's loo with her phone looking distressed. She reached her car, got in and drove back home.

"I asked Alison whether she had watched it?" she said to Sam when she got in, "She just shook her head and started crying."

"I'll get it online and we can take a look."

"No, Sam, I don't want to see it," Ros shook her head, "It doesn't feel right to watch Jack like that."

"But we are talking about a guy who sacked another guy despite the other guy's family being killed a couple of months earlier in a car crash."

"You don't know Jack like I do," Ros was annoyed by Sam's approach, "He's not the sort of person he's being made out to be and I'm not prepared to sit in judgment on someone I know is a good person. This is all beginning to feel like Old Salem, a Witch Trial based on supposition. I know Jack wouldn't have made John redundant if he'd thought there was any chance of him killing himself."

"I'm sorry, but that's just an assumption, based on what you think of Jack Docherty – and there's no proof you've judged him correctly."

"But at least it's based on some knowledge of the man. Remember, I've worked with him for a couple of years now, and I don't recognise the picture people are drawing."

"Don't recognise, or won't recognise?"

"Don't recognise."

83

When Max and Geoff left, Roger was still feeling agitated and the idea of going home and receiving nothing but blandishments from Hilary did not appeal to him. So, he called Margaret and asked her to come in. When she appeared, he motioned her to shut the door and asked her if she was able to meet up that evening. She hesitated slightly and said she had to go home first but agreed to meet later at one of Roger's favourite restaurants. Then Roger called home and said he'd be late back – this time not feeling the need to make any excuses. Hilary took the news unemotionally and said she might be in bed. Her reaction only annoyed him more.

When it was time to leave, some of the demonstrators were still there and, as he walked towards his car, one of them saw him and shouted to the others pointing in his direction. He unlocked his car, got in and reversed out of his parking space and drove towards the front gate. He waved to the Security Guard, who opened the gate, but as he tried to drive out a man with red hair leapt in front of his car holding up a phone in front of the windscreen. Roger was outraged and kept moving slowly forward, forcing the man back. Then he revved hard, alarming the man who responded by leaping aside, afraid of being injured.

As the man leapt out of the way, his phone slipped out of his hand and fell under the car. Roger continued moving slowly forward and was unaware as the rear wheels ran over it. Other people closed in on the car, attempting to stop him leaving. He slowed, careful not to hit any of them, but still moving forward. The man whose phone had been crushed appeared alongside Roger's car and started kicking the door, raising his foot and striking it with his heel. Roger was enraged and stopped the car, making sure the doors were locked. He picked-up his mobile, called 999, and reported he was under attack and criminal damage was being done to his vehicle. The call handler promised a police vehicle would be diverted immediately. The man kept on shouting at Roger through the window, his face flushed and angry. Roger didn't look at him and wasn't sure what he was screaming, just sat and waited and then heard a siren approaching. When they became aware of the siren, the people around Roger's car started moving back onto the pavement.

The police parked and the two officers walked across to Roger's car. He tried to open the door, but the kicking had dented it and he could only open it with some difficulty. As he got out, some of the demonstrators started shouting 'killer' and the rest took up the chant.

"What's going on, Sir?" the police officer asked.

"I'd have thought that was bloody obvious," Roger was outraged. "This is not a peaceful protest, look at the damage they've done to my car."

"Can you identify who did it?" the officer looked around him.

Roger saw the red-haired man trying to hide at the back of the crowd and pointed him out. The second police officer went over to talk to the man, but the crowd closed together frustrating his efforts.

"Stand aside or I'll arrest you for preventing an officer in the pursuit of his duty," the officer motioned them to move, and they did reluctantly, remonstrating in support of the man and blaming Roger for what had happened. "And what's your name, Sir?" the officer asked.

"Richie."

"Well Richie, we're going to have to arrest you for causing damage to this vehicle," the officer pointed to Roger's car.

"He's a fucking killer!" Richie stabbed his finger in Roger's direction.

"I'm not sure that's your judgement to make," the officer said, 'What's your full name, please?"

Richie gave him his full name and then shouted, "He tried to kill me, run me over and then he ran over my phone."

"That's right," a few voices from the crowd shouted out, "Tried to run him over."

"And what do you say to that?" the officer asked Roger.

"Total bloody rubbish," Roger said, "If you'd been here earlier, when you should have been, you'd have seen the whole thing. This man stood in the road, trying to intimidate me, and when I managed to keep the car moving, dropped his phone and my back wheels apparently drove over it. He was blocking my exit and shouting. You heard them shouting only a few minutes ago; trying to intimidate me and stop me leaving."

"Is this true?" the officer asked Richie.

"Yeah, but we've got a right to protest. This guy's responsible for a guy committing suicide – he needs to be brought to justice."

"I'm sorry, but I think we need to question you down the station. You may have a right to protest but not to harass private individuals or cause criminal damage," the officer turned to Roger, "And I think it would be helpful if you came down too."

"But I've got a meeting," Roger could see Margaret turning up at the restaurant on her own and waiting for him. "And I'm the victim here. Ask our Security Guard."

The police officer went across and spoke to the guard, who Roger could see nodding as he was questioned.

The officer returned and nodded to Roger. "Ok Sir, the guard confirms your version of events, but we'll still need to talk to you. We'll send you a reference number and maybe we can interview you tomorrow. And you'll need to get an estimate of the damage." He turned to Richie, "You'll need to accompany me now, I'm arresting you on a charge of causing criminal damage."

"You're fucking arresting me for denting his car and he goes free after causing someone to kill himself? What kind of fucking justice is that?" Richie was incensed.

"Hold your hands out, please," the policeman took out his handcuffs and placed them on Richie's wrists.

Some of the demonstrators began to protest, but the officer led Richie to the police car and pressed his head down as he pushed him onto the back seat.

84

Roger took the opportunity to drive away and set off towards the restaurant where he arrived late and found Margaret seated at the table he'd reserved.

"I was beginning to think you'd changed your mind again," Margaret took a sip from the glass of white wine she'd ordered. "You look upset, what's happened."

Roger told her about the protest turning violent, the damage to his vehicle and the police intervention. She reached across the table and placed her hand on his. "Things haven't been that good for you recently, have they? You were upset earlier when I suggested meeting-up, what was that about?"

He shook his head, called the waiter and asked for a drink. "Nothing, just a bit of an argument with Hilary."

Margaret paused for a moment, watching him. "It wasn't about us, was it? She hasn't found out?"

It was tempting to confide in her, but he didn't want to change the way things were between them. At the same time, he felt a pressing need to share the hollowness his conversation with Hilary had left him with. He shook his head and said nothing. As the waiter brought his drink to the table, the restaurant door opened and Max walked in with another man, looked over and smiled in acknowledgement.

"Oh, God, that's really made my day," Roger shook his head again, but in disbelief this time, "Now Max has come in."

"Has he seen us?"

"Yes, he's just smiled and nodded. They've sat him towards the back of the room. You couldn't make it up," Roger put his drink back down on the table and ran his hand across the top of his head, "I had no idea he knew this restaurant – I must be paying him too bloody much."

"Perhaps the man he's with brought him here?"

"However he got here, it's embarrassing. God knows what he'll make of seeing us together." Roger picked his glass up and took another drink.

"Well, if we just sit here looking embarrassed, he'll know," Margaret reached for her bag, "The only way to raise any doubt in his mind is to brazen it out. I'll go to the ladies' room and say 'hi' to him on the way there."

"What else are you going to say?"

"Don't look so worried, it only makes you look guilty. If he looks across smile and acknowledge him." She got up from the table, turned round and walked towards the back of the room.

He saw her stop at Max's table, be introduced to the other man and start to talk to them both. Then she moved on to the ladies and emerged a few minutes later and walked back.

"That man with him is very charming. Very well turned-out and wearing an elegant after-shave. He just smells of money." She thought for a moment, "Max isn't gay, is he?"

"How the hell do I know?" Roger shook his head, "I've never even considered Max's sexuality, just know he's not married. But that's not important; what the hell did you say to them?"

"I told them what a lovely treat this was, and that you'd been planning to bring Hilary, but she'd felt unwell and suggested you brought me here instead to recognise the work I do. So, I think we'd better leave earlier than normal as you'll obviously want to get home early with your wife unwell, won't you?" She smiled at him and dropped her voice. "And it means we can spend more time at my place."

Roger sat back in admiration, "How the hell did you think up that story?"

"I've had a lot of practice – I had to keep up the pretence with my ex-husband for a couple of years after all. Cheers!" She raised her glass to him and grinned.

They called the waiter over and ordered their meals and when they'd finished Roger paid the bill and they got up to leave. Margaret waved at Max on the way out and Roger forced himself to smile and nodded.

"Don't forget to say that Hilary's better tomorrow, if Max asks you. Just a headache – headaches always stop the conversation going any further, everyone gets them at some time."

"It's beginning to worry me how good you are at this!"

"I told you, I've had a lot of practice. I'm surprised you're not better at it yourself after all the time we've been seeing each other." They reached her house and Margaret opened the front door and pulled him in. "Still, there is something you are good at." She threw down her bag, kicked-off her shoes and hung her jacket over the post at the bottom of the stairs.

He wasn't aware of falling asleep and, when he woke up later the room was totally dark. Roger panicked, looked at his watch and saw it was nearly eleven o'clock. Margaret was asleep next to him, breathing softly. Despite what Hilary had said to him previously, Roger felt guilty and wanted to get home. He turned over and shook Margaret gently. She didn't want to wake up and went back to sleep almost immediately she'd opened her eyes, so he shook her again.

"Oh my God, we fell asleep. What time is it?"

Roger told her, got out of bed and started to dress.

"What are you going to tell Hilary? You're not usually this late home."

"I don't know, but I'll think of something." He lied, knowing Hilary wouldn't care but wanting to keep up the pretence with Margaret, grabbed his jacket and keys and left.

When he got back, the house was dark, and he couldn't decide whether he was relieved or upset that Hilary hadn't cared enough to wait up. He closed the front door quietly behind him and listened for any sign Hilary might still be awake, but he couldn't hear anything and went to the kitchen to get a glass of water. He saw the note on the table as soon as he turned the light on; it was propped-up against a half empty wine bottle. *'Have gone to stay with Mandy, will be back tomorrow, Hilary.'* The note angered and upset him; it was so impassive. He'd been able to depend on Hilary being there for over thirty years, but now he realised there was no way back, she'd been very clinical when she'd talked to him, still his friend, but she had other friends. He wondered who they were.

When he got to the top of the stairs, he went to their old room, turned on the lights and looked at the bed. It stood there with just the single pillow where Hilary slept. It occurred to him to move his own pillow back in and spend the night there again, it felt so familiar compared with his new room, but, at the same time he knew Hilary would see it as an irritating intrusion and realised he might find it upsetting without her there. So, he turned the light off and walked back along the landing to what had once been their son's room. The bed had the covers pulled back, just as he had left it that morning. He put the water glass down next to his book and looked around at the unfamiliar objects that surrounded him. He removed his suit, took the hanger from the handle of the wardrobe door and hung his suit on it. When he opened the wardrobe he saw his clothes, all neatly hanging there. And he felt totally alone.

85

Jack thought he was in the kitchen with Charlotte and someone else – he wasn't sure who the other person was, and he was looking down. And he could see strands of blood, extruding through the pores in the skin on his legs, waving sinuously, like strands of fine red plastic filament. And, as he watched similar blood strands started emerging, extruding through the third person's skin, the person whose face he couldn't see. The strands on both their legs became longer, still waving. Charlotte stood apart watching as the strands increased until one of his touched the floor and burst leaving a smear of liquid blood as his leg movements jerked it away from its point of contact. More blood smears appeared, this time on the third person's skin and still Charlotte stood and watched, her eyes anxious and her mouth open in a silent scream. He dabbed at the smears with his foot, trying to remove them from the floor, but the blood only spread further.

Then the floor seemed to recede, and the image faded. And when he opened his eyes, he was on the same, familiar mattress, in the same, familiar room. His pulse was racing, and he could hear his heart beating, the sound seemingly amplified by the pillow where it was wedged beneath his neck. The dream disturbed and mystified him; disturbing because of its vividness and mystifying because he had never seen anything like it before, either in a previous dream or in real life. He wondered who the third person was and re-visited the image briefly, but he still couldn't see their face. And why had Charlotte just stood there, and hadn't bled?

Gradually, as the dream faded, his heartbeat slowed and the panic he'd felt subsided. He felt sweaty, and hot where he'd been lying down and rolled onto his other side, still slightly drowsy and his eyes closed. When he opened them again, he glanced across at the door, but there was no food tray there and so he remained where he was drowsing and in his half-awake moments still trying to make sense of everything – what had happened to him, how Charlotte and the boys were coping, why he'd had the dream.

86

Jim looked at the phone but didn't recognise the number. He let it go to answerphone, heard Richie's voice and picked-up.

"So, the pigs let you go, then, Richie?"

"Yeah, but the bastards have charged me with criminal damage to that bastard's car."

"Sorry I didn't pick-up immediately, but I didn't recognise the number."

"That's what's pissed me off so much, he ran over my phone. I'm going to have to buy a new one. I've just borrowed this one to make the call."

"Bad news mate, but, looking on the brighter side, I think we have some legal friends who will act in your defence, without you having to pay."

"Well, thank Christ for that, 'cos I've just lost my job as well! I was late in today after being kept late by the pigs and my bloody boss fired me – said it was happening too often. Talk about kicking a bloke when he's down. Bastard. I told him to fucking watch out after the revolution, 'cos he'd be on the list of capitalist stooges."

"Tough, brother. I feel for you."

Yeah, well feeling for me's not going to pay the rent, especially now Misty's buggered-off. And I'm pissed-off with the attitude of the bastards down at the dole office – they treat you like a criminal, just because you need a bit of help."

"Look, I've got some contacts who may be willing to help, I'll see what I can do."

"I'd appreciate that – any chance of a temporary loan for a new 'phone?"

Jim shook his head at the other end of the call, "Sorry mate, my card's maxed out."

87

The early news included a short report that a video of the man who'd been kidnapped had been circulated on social media; together with a statement that the mainstream television channels were refusing to feature it because it might cause distress. Gill was watching the news, as she did most evenings and called Ros at the end of the bulletin. "Hi, I've just seen the reports about the video on the news, what have you heard at work?"

"No more than you've heard, probably," the whole thing is distressing as far as I'm concerned. I don't buy all this nonsense about him being a killer. Sam's downloaded the video, but I won't watch it."

"Why not?"

"Because I don't think Jack instigated John's suicide and I don't want to see what they've done to him – Sam said he looked pretty unkempt."

"Well, I can't argue with that, but that's not the main reason I called; I've had some good news, I've got a new job for a management workshop, and I'm meeting up with Misty, a new marketing partner, tomorrow afternoon in the wine-bar in the High Street. We'll have finished talking around five thirty and I thought you could join us for something to eat afterwards. Make it into a social occasion. It's nice in there and the food's ok."

....

When Ros reached the bar, she saw Gill sitting with a casually dressed woman at one of the low tables by the front window. A wine bottle in a bucket had been placed on the table and a spare glass and chair were waiting for her. Gill introduced her, reached across and poured out a large wine into the empty glass.

"I'm not too early, am I?" Ros felt slightly embarrassed at possibly interrupting their business conversation.

"No," Gill poured some more wine into Misty's glass and the remainder of the bottle into her own, then waved to one of the barmen and held up the empty bottle. "We've pretty much sorted things out. Just need to get some of the material ready for sign-off by the clients."

"That's nice." Ros tried the wine, twirled the glass stem between her fingers and stared momentarily at the cool, clear liquid inside, nodding appreciatively as she did so. "So, what's the theme of this workshop?"

"Well, the company wants to improve the decision-making skills of its managers and we don't believe enough research is undertaken by many companies before they spend money on trying to establish a brand or launch a new product. So, we've chosen 'making assumptions' as the theme."

"So many decisions are taken by people who 'know their market'," Misty used her fingers to indicate the inverted commas, "But, often it's only a perception, based on something they've heard from the salesforce, or a senior manager's favourite idea. It can work, some people understand things intuitively, but it's not the best way of reaching a decision."

"And that can also be the case in non-marketing areas of a company," Gill interjected, "People suppose or assume based on what they think is fact or strong evidence, when it's nothing of the sort."

"Bit like they've done with Jack, our sales manager, holding him responsible and kidnapping him because a guy called John Morrison killed himself, a few weeks after being made redundant."

"Yes," Misty nodded, "Gill told me you worked for him. And, coincidentally, I went out for a few months with one of the people who've been organizing the protests outside your factory. In fact, your bosses' kidnapping was one of the situations that gave us the idea for the workshop."

"Jack wouldn't have made anyone redundant if he thought it would drive them to suicide." Ros paused and took another sip from her glass. "It's all a case of 'no smoke without fire', people linking possibly unrelated events and, in this case, coming up with the wrong answer."

"But there are other assumptions being made as well," Misty leaned forward, "For instance, because of the left-wing protests and the leaks about the kidnap and the video being revealed by the Worker, there's an assumption that it's a left-wing group that's holding him. But, if that's true they'd need to be a lot better organised than my ex and his mates – organising a protest isn't too difficult, you just mobilise the normal people, get them to make some banners and meet-up at the agreed place. But this would have required far more planning and attention to detail."

88

The phone rang and Heather picked-up the call. It was Sergeant George wanting to make an appointment for a further interview. Shocked, she passed the phone across to Allan who asked why they were being interviewed again? Were they suspects? Did they need a solicitor present? The sergeant was vague about the reason for a new interview and said they were re-visiting their previous interviews for additional information but couldn't be more specific before they met.

……………………

"I'm not convinced this is going to produce any real results" Bracken turned to George as they drew up outside the Morrison's house and prepared to get out of the car, "But we've got no other leads for the time being and we're under pressure from the guys at the top, who're also under pressure from the media and Docherty's family."

"Enquiries amongst anyone who's got contacts in local leftist groups haven't produced anything, it's totally dead on that side," George reached behind him and pulled his jacket off the back seat, "I'd have put money on them being involved with the way the abductors have presented the kidnapping and released it through the left-wing press."

"Maybe that's the way the abductors wanted us to see things," Bracken opened her door and got out of the vehicle. "Maybe we've been deliberately misled and, if we have, the guy we're seeing here has the type of background to pull a stunt like that – and the motive."

They walked up the drive and rang the bell.

"Thank you for seeing us again," Bracken smiled at Allan, as he opened the door and stood aside to let her and George enter.

"It's not because we want to see you," Allan didn't smile back before following them into the lounge, "It feels more like persecution after what's been a very upsetting family tragedy. So, let's cut to the chase, what is it you want to know now?"

"May we sit down first, please?" Bracken pointed at the sofa and, when Allan nodded, she and Sergeant George sat down together.

Heather came into the room, looking very nervous, nodded at them in acknowledgement, and sat in the same chair she had used previously. Allan sat on the arm of her chair, next to her. Neither spoke, both waiting silently for Bracken to begin asking her questions.

"I recall you telling us you were a security consultant when we last interviewed you. Could you tell me where you work from, please?"

"Why is that important to your enquiries, inspector?" Allan guessed the reason for her question but wanted it to appear that he didn't understand.

"Please just answer the question, sir."

"I work from home."

"So, you have an office here?"

"I believe this is my home, Inspector."

Bracken ignored the sarcasm and continued with her questions. "So, do you have any other premises? A storage facility, perhaps?"

"No, I only provide consultancy. I have an office upstairs and that's perfectly adequate for my needs. You're welcome to come up and look."

"That won't be necessary, thank you, sir." There was a touch of irritation in Bracken's voice. "Do you know the snooker hall in London Road?"

Allan was ready for the question, expecting her to try to catch him off-guard. "Sorry, I don't play snooker, and I don't know of a London Road locally."

"I didn't say it was here," Bracken said, "The London Road I'm referring to is in Camford."

"Even if I played snooker, which I don't, there must be several closer places to play than Camford. It's nearly two hours away – as I realise you must know having just driven here." He shook his head dismissively. "Why are you mentioning this place? I'm afraid you're going to need to spell it out, what's it got to do with me?"

Bracken sat and appraised his response but couldn't read his expression. 'Not the sort of person you'd want to play poker against,' she told herself. She tried another change of direction. "Do you manage any sites for clients?"

"No, I only provide advice and assess the adequacy of existing security or test the comprehensiveness of new systems."

"So, you don't have continuing access to any of your clients' sites?" George took up the questioning.

"No, sorry sergeant, there's no need for me to have that type of access." Allan shook his head and put on a mystified expression, "Why are you asking me these questions?"

"And you don't rent any storage space, a garage or something?"

"I think you'll understand that with just the two of us living here, we have perfectly adequate storage space for anything we're likely to want to store. I assume you saw the garage when you came up the drive." Allan pointed in the direction of the double garage attached to the house. "If you're so concerned about whether I might be storing something I shouldn't be, I'm perfectly happy to show you round."

"Thank you for the offer," Bracken said, "But, again, it won't be necessary for the time being."

"Look, Inspector, I really don't see the point of this interview, or why you're harassing us like this. Is there anything else you want to know before you go?"

Bracken looked at her sergeant and then back to Allan. "I think that will do for today, sir, we trust you'll make yourself available if we have any more enquiries." She got up to leave.

"So, are you telling me that you two police officers have come all the way here just to ask a few questions you could have asked on the phone or via a computer app? Isn't that rather a waste of police time and money – unless of course you're now treating my wife and I as suspects. When will you allow us to grieve?" Allan showed the two officers to the door and shut it as soon as they stepped outside, without waiting to see them down the drive

"I'd award you an Oscar for your performance today," Heather said, "I just hope to God they never find out it's us who're holding Docherty. You needn't have antagonised them quite like that."

"Relax, they're not going to find out. We've been careful – they've got nothing to go on – they're just fishing. We'd better checkup what's going on with Docherty." He went back to his office, retrieved his hidden laptop and connected with the surveillance cameras again.

89

Jack lounged along the mattress reading one of the books he'd been given. He reached the end of a chapter, put the book down and rolled over onto his back, staring at the ceiling. He kept going over what he'd said in the video, worried in case anything might be misunderstood or have been edited to sound differently by his captors. He hadn't wanted to make the recording, but the books had been a lifeline, stopping him going completely insane in a vacuum of mental stimulation, and they'd begun a bargaining process between him and his captors. He'd made the video in the hope that it might help him obtain an earlier release, although once it had been publicised it left him without anything to negotiate with. The small bottle still sat on the table, but he no longer picked it up or referred to it – and he still had no intention of drinking what was in it.

He decided to do another crossword puzzle, stood up, walked across to the table and flicked through the book until he found a new one. The first few clues were difficult, and he sat there, letting his mind wander about the words, hoping it would come up with a solution. When he still couldn't come up with an answer he moved to the next clue. When he couldn't answer that he threw the book down and just lay there.

At first, he'd found the puzzles easier, but in the last couple of periods of waking (he didn't refer to them as days because he didn't know how much time he'd been awake) he'd found it more difficult to solve them. And, as he lay there, he wondered how Charlotte had reacted to the video. At least she would have some reassurance that he was alive, although he knew he must look a mess and hoped the lads hadn't seen it and been upset. He tried to visualise her, standing in the kitchen cooking or out in the summer sun, reading in the garden, a large straw hat with a floppy brim shielding her face. But the longer he'd been incarcerated in the room, with its bare walls and the silence, the more difficult it was to form mental images – the starkness of his prison kept intruding, dragging his attention back to his current situation.

"Having difficulty with the crossword?" The man's voice had a slightly mocking tone and Jack didn't respond immediately. "Perhaps I can help you?"

"Ok, thanks," Jack decided it might be to his advantage to be compliant and read the first clue out, giving the man the number of letters in each word.

"That wasn't quite the type of help I was suggesting," the voice replied, "I thought it might be useful if I helped you practice, build your mental capabilities back up again – being isolated appears to have affected your ability to think and solve problems."

"So why not just let me go? I've made the video and you know I'm not going to drink what's in that bottle," Jack pointed at the table.

"I'm sorry, I thought the point of keeping you here was to get you to acknowledge your part in ending someone's life and help to make sure it doesn't happen again."

"I thought I'd done that in the video, which you've no doubt released, so what's the point of keeping me here still?"

"Well, if the video's the best you can do, it sounds like we've got some time to fill – a lot of time. So, why not fill it by amusing ourselves?"

"I'm not a masochist, so I'm not sure your idea of amusement will be the same as mine."

"Oh, very droll. Well, just try it, you may be surprised."

Jack sat still and said nothing, knowing he was powerless to stop his captor doing whatever he planned to do.

"You'll need the pad and pencil," the voice said, "I can see it on the table."

"All seeing, all hearing, all powerful – it must be difficult not to get a God complex." Jack continued sitting on his mattress.

"You're not helping yourself behaving like this," the voice said, "Do yourself a favour and go and get the pad and pencil."

"What's in it for me if I do? What sort of favour will I get?"

"More puzzles when you finish the book you've got?"

"Try, we'll send you home, and you've got a deal."

"But if you continue with your present attitude, life could get tough – like it was at the beginning. No more books, nothing to do. Perhaps nothing to look forward to."

Jack shook his head, got up and sat down at the table with the pad and pencil in front of him.

"That's better. Now, let's have a practice at solving cryptic clues. Write down what I say so I don't have to keep repeating it."

Jack held the pad and pencil in the air and then put the pad back on the table.

"First clue across. 'A Germanic refusal sounds like this creature's chances'. One word, three letters."

Jack wrote the clue down, "Too easy," he shouted. A refusal in German is 'nein', sounds like 'nine' when you say it, and a cat has nine lives or chances. So, the answer's 'cat'."

"Very good." The voice was patronizing. "Let's try the first clue down; 'Terms of the reward.' Three words – four letters, two letters and five letters." "

"What reward?" Jack shouted, "What reward are you talking about?"

"Oh, now you're disappointing me. Think for a while and find the connection. I'll come back to you." The loudspeaker went dead.

Jack didn't want to play anymore but was equally anxious not to allow his tormentor to win. So, what reward was the voice talking about? The books? The puzzles? Jack thought hard but still couldn't identify a connection. He began to feel stressed, concerned how long it would be before the voice came back to torment him. But however hard he thought, he couldn't come up with an answer.

"Oh, come on," he shouted, "If this was a crossword, there would be other letters from other words that would give me a clue."

"That's true," the voice spoke to him again, "So, the clue is the letter 'a' in 'cat' transects the third letter in the first word."

Jack wrote 'cat' on the pad and then the spaces for the second clue, but it was still no clearer. The 'a' in 'cat' crossed the third letter in the first word of the second answer, but what was the word? He went back and re-read the clue. 'Think for a while', the voice came back to him 'and find the connection'. So, what was the connection between 'cat' and 'terms of the reward'? And then he saw a mental picture of a poster he'd come across on a family walk, a poster nailed to a post with the face of a dog and the word 'lost' above with a reward below. But it still didn't make sense – besides he'd always joked about the posters people put up, claiming they looked like those wild west posters offering a reward 'dead or alive'. And that was the answer, staring him in the face, a cat, dead or alive? They were back to Schrödinger's cat again and whether it was alive or dead in the box.

Jack waved the paper at a camera, "It's bloody Schrödinger's cat. Does this mean you're going to let me out?"

"It might, the voice said, but when we open the door what are likely to be the terms on which you're released? Will you be dead or alive?"

90

Jack lay awake, waiting to hear the bolts on the door panel being slid across and planning to try to prevent the panel shutting again, giving him some leverage to try to force the door open. When he heard the bolts being withdrawn, he jumped up from his mattress and rushed over, but he was too late. The tray was pushed through quickly, and he heard the first bolt sliding across again as he arrived. He wanted to try to kick the panel open, before both bolts were across but the tray was in the way. And, whilst he hesitated, the second bolt slid into place. So, he bent down, picked-up the tray and noticed there were pages containing newspaper items, placed under his meal. He'd been expecting dinner, but it appeared to be lunch, a sandwich removed from its packaging on a paper plate. He assumed they'd removed the packaging to hide the sell-by date as usual, but the items from the papers had dates at the top.

The dates were different, the coverage from the Worker being a day earlier than the second story. Both were about his abduction, issued a couple of weeks after he'd been kidnapped, but he realised the dates didn't tell him anything as he couldn't work out how long ago they'd been published. The Worker article was condemnatory about the redundancy and his role in it, the second item gave more details about how he'd disappeared after an evening at the snooker hall and mentioned the distress caused to his family. There were also a couple of extracts with coverage of the protests that had taken place outside the company and a quote from Max explaining the company's view of the situation. The police were making extensive investigations, apparently, but admitted they'd made no progress to date.

The items from the Worker were particularly interesting. It wasn't a paper that was as easily accessible as the papers containing the other items and it suggested that his captors shared the same political views – although he was becoming increasingly aware of the mind games they were using against him.

"So, why have you sent me this now?" he shouted.

But this time there was just silence. The voice didn't answer, and he took a bite of the sandwich. It tasted good, bacon lettuce and tomato – not bad, he told himself, for prison food, but was it the right meal, at the right time? He had no way of knowing, thought again about eating with his family and finally swallowed the rest of the sandwich. But now it no longer tasted as good.

91

Mike saw the smile on Gill's face as she walked in. "So, I'm going to make an assumption here – the presentation to the clients went well."

"They loved the concept and Misty produced some fabulous supporting material – really superb. So, on this occasion your assumption was correct. Now all we need is a good post-workshop response and get a series of similar workshops, either with this client or a new one."

"That's great, I'll be able to retire soon and become a man who lunches."

"Dream on, I'm not having you and Sam down at the pub every day, drinking at my expense. But, as I said a couple of days back, maybe we can start thinking about the future, getting our own place. You've been working for a few months now and my accounts are beginning to look ok, so it may be time to start looking."

"So, you're not looking to get rid of me just yet?"

"Not just yet!" she smiled. "It hasn't been that long since we met. How much of a Cinderella moment was that?"

Mike thought back and nodded. "I was the Cinderella; redundant, worrying how I was ever going to get another job. Then, outside my front door, I heard someone sweeping the stairs and as I'd nothing else to do and the woman lived upstairs and I fancied her, I offered to finish the job while she went to work."

"Oh, that's nice, so you only offered to help because you fancied me! I'm not sure I fancied you back, it was more your cleaning capabilities that attracted me. But ever since we moved in together you've seemed less and less keen on demonstrating them."

"I like to think of the other areas I've improved in, like my culinary expertise. And, talking about that, I took the opportunity of gathering a few delicacies for this evening's meal on the way home."

"And tonight, we have? Tripe and onions again?"

"Tonight, we have," he paused in a mock effort to stimulate interest, "Bobotie!"

"What?"

"Ba-boor-tea, I think it's pronounced, it's like a South African Moussaka, but hotter."

"Where on earth did you find that?"

"I was listening to the car radio on my way to see a customer, and they were talking about it. It sounded good so I thought we could try it. Mind you, as you've noticed, it meant, regrettably, that I didn't have time to get the cleaner out when I'd finished my day job. But sometimes you can't fit in everything you want to." He smiled and then ducked to avoid the cushion she picked-up and threw at him. "And before you start throwing anything else at your chef du jour, I'd like to add that I also acquired a couple of bottles of South African wine."

"Splashing out a bit, aren't we?"

"Well, I had some good news today as well, I'm getting that bonus they talked about at the end of the month, so I thought I'd invest a little of it in advance, on an exotic meal. Come on, I've got to start preparing things, the wine's in the fridge. I'll pour you a glass in the kitchen."

"By the way, talking about moving, how do you fancy driving me and Misty to see an empty industrial building on Saturday? It's in Wrighton, there's an old industrial estate they're looking to demolish; the clients are based near there and think it would be perfect for the workshop, a bit like Hashima, that deserted Japanese island they use in films when they need somewhere run-down and abandoned."

"Hang on a minute, that's a bit of a mental leap – besides, I'm not sure where my chauffeur's cap is. And Wrighton's a couple of hours away."

"We could turn it into a bit of a day out and have lunch after we've seen it." Gill smiled, "I'll treat you on the firm!"

"But what's so great about an empty factory? Aren't there more attractive and interesting places to visit?"

"Probably, but the client has specifically asked us to use the place because it is so bare – they like the ambience, the high ceiling and the space. Anyway, that's one of the reasons for going up, to see whether the idea works and what it will cost."

"OK, but aren't we supposed to be seeing Sam and Ros in the evening?"

"That's no problem, it's no more than two hours' drive each way and, say a couple of hours lunch and an hour looking round the place, we can get back here in plenty of time."

92

Heather was surprised to see the car parked outside the building adjacent to the one they were keeping Jack in. It looked new and she wondered what it was doing on a run-down industrial estate that was due for demolition. She drove past and stopped her own vehicle further along the road than usual, grateful it looked older and less out of place than the one she'd just seen. The new vehicle meant there were people around and it raised the question of how she could get the meal and other items into Jack without risking the occupants emerging and seeing her. She sat still for a few minutes and then decided to drive away and return later.

Inside the building Mike was looking doubtfully around at the high dirty windows and messy walls. And there was rubbish left on the floor. Gill and Misty had gone to look at the toilets and kitchen facilities and he met them on their way back to the main factory space. They appeared to be happy with what they'd seen, but the toilets looked filthy, and the kitchen was primitive. It was nothing like the type of premises he'd ever seen used for a corporate event and he couldn't understand their obvious excitement. They both seemed to be making copious notes and, at one point, Misty started spinning around with her arms outstretched and her notepad leaves flapping.

"Isn't it fantastic?" Gill asked and, when he just stood there slightly open-mouthed, shook her head and asked what was bothering him?

"But it's so run down, no wonder they're going to demolish it. How on earth do you think you can dress this up for a corporate event?"

"Easily. We'll bring the seating and staging in, a large screen for the videos and visual displays, and install lighting that will focus attention on the speakers and stage and make the surrounding area disappear. And we'll complete it all with panelling to hide the audio-visual equipment and run things – it will look terrific."

"But what about the toilets, they're awful, and the kitchen equipment is non-existent?"

"Well, we'll be bringing a buffet in from outside caterers, and we only need the ability to heat water for drinks. And the building lends itself to simpler times, trestle tables with white cloths for serving from and smaller tables for people to eat or sit at, unless we decide to go more communal and sit people all together at two or three long tables – to stop them becoming isolated."

"As for the loos, that's easy," Misty said. "We can get them cleaned, change the seats, that can be done cheaply enough and fit them out with modern soap dispensers and paper towels – get them looking more like hotel loos."

"You're both crazy," Mike was in denial, shaking his head as he looked around him, "You can't tart up a place like this."

"It doesn't have to last more than a day. And think about a theatre, how bare and grubby it can look between shows and then, suddenly, it's transformed into a place of magic. And that's basically what we're doing for this event, setting up a piece of theatre." Gill looked at Misty for support.

"She's right," Misty nodded, "Wait till you see the visual mock-ups, the whole place will look totally different."

Gill and Misty began to take photos of the main space and the kitchen and toilets, and Mike went outside to wait. The whole area was run down. There was no sign of any activity and he sat against the wing of his car just enjoying the sun. He'd been sitting there for a few minutes when a small red car drove past and then, just when he was beginning to feel slightly impatient and was thinking about going back in to see how much longer it was before they could leave, it drove past again and stopped further down the street. Mike waited for the driver to get out of the car, but she remained seated for a while. Then, finally, she got out but seemed unsure what to do. She appeared to make up her mind, opened the boot, took out a bag and walked towards the adjacent building.

"Hi, what are you doing?" Gill and Misty had finally finished their assessment of the factory unit and Gill called across to Mike as she locked-up.

"Just sitting here, enjoying the sun and waiting to go for lunch. So, have you finished here?"

"Yes, the only issue is security. It's risky to leave a lot of expensive equipment around in a place like this – although there doesn't appear to be any damage to the building, and it's been unoccupied for nearly a year."

"Well, there are people around," Mike pointed up the street, "A woman got out of that car over there a few minutes ago."

As he spoke the woman appeared again and walked back towards her vehicle. Gill waved, and started to walk towards the woman who, again, appeared unsure what to do.

The woman stopped, put something in the boot of her car and then shut the lid. "Excuse me, please," Gill called out as she approached the woman, "I wonder if you can help me? We're hoping to hold an event here and wondered whether there's much vandalism in the area."

"That's the reason I'm here," the woman said, "Making sure our place is ok – we've still got some stuff stored here. Nothing very valuable, but we'll be moving it shortly, they're going to demolish all these buildings. What sort of event are you planning?"

"It's a corporate event, our clients want to use the old factory back there," Gill pointed to where Mike and Misty were standing, "They love the atmosphere in the old buildings. But we'd need to leave some equipment over night."

"Well, it's not really something I can help you with," the woman said. "What we've been storing isn't worth much, but we like to keep an eye on the place, and we haven't had any trouble so far. But, having said that, you could move your equipment in and find someone breaks in that night. When are you thinking of having the event?"

"Within the next couple of months, we're still in the early stages of organizing it."

"Right. Well as I said, we've been lucky with our stuff here, but it is pretty deserted, particularly at night, and the days will be getting shorter." She went to get back in her car, but turned to Gill as she did so, "I'm sorry, but I really can't help you."

Gill thanked the woman, who climbed into the driver's seat, started the engine and drove away. "I think we'll need to budget for some security," she said, as she reached Mike and Misty, "We can't risk anything happening to the gear."

"That woman seemed very uncomfortable," Misty said, "What do you think she was doing here?"

"She said she was checking a building they've been using to store some of their equipment or goods, but she did seem a bit uneasy."

"Probably just nervous with three of us suddenly turning up when she wasn't expecting to see anyone," Mike looked at his watch, "Anyway we need to find somewhere for lunch, it's later than we planned."

93

Mike dropped Gill and Misty off at Misty's flat to chat about their ideas, reminding Gill they were meeting Ros and Sam later. As they climbed the stairs, Gill wondered what the flat would be like, what it might tell her about Misty and the woman she shared it with. It was in an old building, with a large bay window in the lounge, looking out onto a main road, and a long corridor that led to the kitchen at the back. She followed Misty to the kitchen, said 'yes' to a cup of coffee and then followed her back to the lounge. The décor was much as she had guessed it might be, with throws and cushions covering what she suspected was a somewhat worn settee, heavy, floor-length curtains and a lot of objects scattered around the available surfaces.

"Sit down," Misty nodded at the sofa and sat herself down in the solitary armchair. She placed her own coffee next to a Chinese looking lamp on a small bedside cupboard that was being used as a side-table. Gill put her coffee on a low wooden stool by the side of the sofa and picked-up an intricate wooden puzzle.

"I haven't seen one of these for years."

"I like puzzles, but I haven't played with that one recently. I sometimes play with the maze next to it when I'm trying to come up with an idea. It stops me thinking too hard – ideas come better when I set my mind free and wait for an answer to emerge."

"Well, it seems to work for you, so why knock it?"

"I know Mike thinks I'm mad when I talk about my grandfather still being there and inspiring me, but it's true, although I understand why Mike and other people react the way they do."

Gill felt embarrassed by Misty's sincerity, but still tried to deny how she knew Mike probably viewed her. "Mike's just a cynic and likes to joke around. The everyday, the mundane, it's a backcloth he tries to enrich by flinging fun across it, like splashes of paint."

"The problem is that I understand Mike's view of the world, it's one I share with him, but I keep getting these feelings that intrude upon the rational part of me and, in some ways, become more real than reality."

"In what way?" Gill asked.

"It's difficult to explain; I feel things, feel them strongly sometimes, but I know I've never really experienced them. For instance, I cry when I hear some music – I've no idea why it makes me cry and I know I'm going to cry before I play it."

"We all cry when we hear sad music or see a sad film, that's normal."

"But I don't feel sad, more wistful. Sometimes I can explain why I feel like I do. For instance, certain songs remind me of people who've gone, but were an important part of my early life – and I wish they were still here. I suppose it's a form of sadness, but it's also a feeling of ecstasy. And it's the same with some songs that have nothing attached to them, except, somehow, a sense of belonging."

"I'm not sure I follow what you're saying," Gill was hesitant; what Misty was saying was obviously important to her and she didn't want to seem dismissive, like Misty believed Mike had been.

"Well, when I hear certain folk songs, I have vague backdrops come into my mind, like I'm reliving a previous life's memories – but I don't believe in previous lives or any future ones. We come into being and then we cease to be, so why do I feel a part of the past so strongly? I can't explain where the ideas come from, they're just drawn up from a subconscious well. And I get feelings about things, intuition I suppose you'd call it. Like earlier today, when we went to see that empty factory, it gave me goosebumps."

"I can't say I'd have liked being there on my own, but empty places do that to you, it's one of the reasons the clients want to hold the workshop there, because of the atmosphere, the high ceilings, the dead space, it makes it easier to concentrate the audience's attention, focus it on the stage without any distraction. A bit like sitting in a church and listening to a preacher and questioning how you've acted previously and how you intend to change."

"That's not it," Misty was shaking her head in denial, "I was feeling there was something going on, something nearby. It made me think of that guy from Ros' work, the one they kidnapped, it seemed such an ideal place to hold someone prisoner. And then, when we spoke to the woman, I didn't believe what she told us was her reason for being there."

"But what made you feel like that, connect two such disconnected events?"

"I don't know; the idea just came into my head. But even as I talk to you about it now, I know it's ridiculous, that something just spooked me."

Gill didn't know how to respond and decided to change the subject. "We're all driven by emotions. I wonder sometimes whether we put too much emphasis on our rational side, things we've been taught about, or trained to do – things that inhibit the underlying instincts that drive us. They always say we should trust our instincts more. And you combine the logic and the creativity better than anyone I've met – you seem to understand the issue immediately and your ideas are always so focused."

Misty shook her head, "But I definitely felt something earlier."

"Well, you could mention it to the police, but that would mean them saturating the area with forensics and possibly having to move the workshop."

"I don't think that would happen. Can you imagine the police reaction if I went and told them I'd had this intuition about the kidnapping – they'd be more likely to lock me up than listen to me?"

"Well, we can always take another look around the place when we go back – put your mind at rest."

Misty took another mouthful of coffee and nodded. "Please don't tell Mike we've had this conversation; I know he thinks I'm crazy and I'd hate to make it difficult for us to work together."

"That's not going to happen, Mike's not like that. But tell me about you and your ex, I'm interested – I don't quite see you as a left-wing activist."

"Well, I do support a lot of their ideas about unfairness, I suppose it was what attracted me to Richie in the first place. But I soon realised he was just venting his anger because he feels victimised all the time – although he brings a lot of it on himself by the way he behaves. I don't think Richie will ever really come to terms with life, that's why he has these drinking bouts."

"I don't think I could deal with someone who drinks too much, although I have to admit that I've been known to escape reality with a few too many drinks on occasions."

Gill took another sip of her coffee, "Beats killing myself. I may have a hangover when I wake up the next morning, but at least I wake up."

"That's not all of it, though. He was also taking money from my purse – to fund his boozing. I caught him when I got back from work after he'd been sitting on his backside all day plotting the fall of capitalism. Besides, the whole movement is ruthlessly mechanistic in pursuit of its beliefs. That's not me, I haven't got that sureness about whether I'm right or wrong, I just want to get on with my life without hurting anyone."

Gill finished her coffee, looked at her watch and realised she needed to rush. She picked-up her mug to take to the kitchen before she went; "Look, I've got to go, I'll call you in the morning. Oh, and don't worry about Mike – I think he's got a soft spot for you."

94

Mike and Gill got to the bar early, and she chose a seat whilst he ordered lagers for himself and Sam and a bottle of pinot gris for Gill and Ros. He carried the wine bucket and the two empty glasses to the table and went back for the lagers. Ros and Sam walked in as he was coming back from the bar, spotted Gill and went across. He said 'hi' as he joined them and passed one of the lagers to Sam – then sat down opposite, whilst Gill filled the two wine glasses.

"I like this bar," Ros looked round, "It's not as scruffy as the one you two guys go to."

"Well, that's a good start," Sam took a mouthful of lager, "She starts by slagging-off our favourite bar, Mike. Are we going to be targeted like this all evening?"

"She's right, though," Gill supported her friend, "That bar you go to is filthy, it's a good job they don't have carpet on the floor, the amount of beer you see spilled. Sleazy is the only way I can think of describing it."

"Friendly, traditional, lots of banter are a few of the ways I'd describe it," Mike shook his head, "And after that place we went to earlier today, I don't think you're in any position to point any fingers."

"Don't listen to him, Ros, I asked him to drive me and Misty to a prospective venue – and he didn't think much of it."

"So, Gill and her mysterious friend …" Mike began, but Gill interrupted.

"Her name's Misty, but Mike keeps calling her mysterious because he thinks she's a bit off the wall."

"A bit off the wall is an understatement," Mike took another mouthful of lager and put his glass back down, "She calls herself Misty to keep in touch with her dead grandfather who helps her dream-up new ideas from the ether. He must have spent the industrial revolution in a factory after what I saw today."

"It's safe to say that Mike wasn't impressed with the location, but it's what the client wants and it's very atmospheric."

"A bit like Misty," Sam said.

"Exactly, Sam," Mike nodded, "Although it's worrying that you've already picked up on what she's like. She's not beaming out messages to you as well, is she? Bit like that film, 'Play Misty for me'. By the way, Gill, what was her flat like when you went there?"

"What do you think it was like?"

"Untidy, cushions, ornaments everywhere and Indian throws over the furniture."

"Mmm, not bad, pretty close in fact."

"Well, it wasn't difficult to imagine." Mike grinned at Sam.

"Enough, I'm not going to sit here listening to you two guys goof on about Misty all evening, she's really talented and she's got some great ideas. Ros can tell you; she's met her."

Ros nodded, "Ignore them, Gill they're just trying to wind you up."

"So, as we're driving back," Mike continued, "She starts saying what a great sort of place this old industrial estate would be to keep somebody captive in – like your boss, Ros, the one they kidnapped."

"Perhaps she heard something from her grandad?" Sam suggested.

"You haven't even met the woman," Ros slapped his arm. "Just behave."

"It's alright, him and Mike are just feeding off each other. It's the way she links improbable ideas together that makes us such a good team." Gill refilled her glass. "She thinks so differently from most people, whilst I follow up on the day-to-day practicalities and make sure everything happens like it's meant to."

"Joking aside, I like her, she's good company." Mike took another mouthful of lager, "And good-looking too, in a kind of Bohemian way."

Gill looked across at Ros and smiled, "Mike couldn't take his eyes off her the first time they met. Anyway, I'm hoping to work a lot more with her in the future."

"Poor Jack," Ros finished her glass of wine and put it back on the table. "It's been over two weeks since he disappeared, I just hope he's still alright. Here we are, all sat round a table enjoying a drink and God knows where he is – his wife must be going mental."

95

As Heather drove home, she was distracted about what she'd heard. There were going to be people in an adjacent building, and she was anxious about having been seen in case it was ever discovered where Jack had been kept. In her own mind she was quite clear he had to be released, for their sakes as well as his own. He had said consistently he wouldn't drink the liquid in the bottle, which had been their original intention, to simulate a suicide, and now there was going to be a large event held just yards from where he was being kept. The risk was no longer worth taking. She called Stuart and told him what had happened, and he agreed she should raise the issue of bringing the abduction to a close again but wasn't sure what reaction she'd get.

Back home Allan listened carefully to what she had to say, but she couldn't read how he was thinking. He poured himself a drink, went out into the garden and just stood there, shaking his head and taking sips of whisky as he thought things through. When he came back in, he looked defeated. She went across and gave him a hug, her face pressed close against his chest, understanding the hurt he was feeling. This time, as she held him, she began to feel him relax, and he placed his free hand on her hair and stroked it. When he stopped, she pulled away and looked-up at him.

"So, what do you think?"

"I think we have to get the bastard out of there."

"Are you sure?"

"You're worried, Stuart agrees with you and there doesn't seem any chance he'll drink the drug by choice. It makes me feel sick, having to give up on what we set out to achieve. Every fibre in me says I'd rather kill the bastard than let him go."

"No, we have achieved something. There have been the demonstrations and the video we circulated has received a lot of support. It didn't work out as we'd hoped it would, but the name John Morrison and his death has left its mark on the public consciousness – it's had an impact. He won't be forgotten."

"So, when do you want to get him out?"

"Let's not leave it too long. The longer we keep him, the more of a risk we run."

"When are they holding this event in the other building?"

"The woman said it would be within the next couple of months."

"So, we've got some time still."

"But why do we need more time? We've already agreed we're not going to achieve anything by keeping him there, just increase the risk of something happening and getting ourselves caught. And for what?"

"For John," the response was strong, and the man's face looked more determined.

"No," she shook her head, "This isn't about him anymore, this is about you. It's about beating that man in there. No, it's more than that; it's about what you said before, you want to break him. For what? Ask yourself; what good will breaking him do."

He didn't reply, just stood staring out at the garden.

"And if they find us, what about Stuart and me? Do you want to take us down with you? So, we're all locked in cells and our whole lives ruined? And will you blame that on this whole redundancy business, because I won't – I'll blame you for being so bloody stubborn."

He waited, before responding. "Alright, we'll get him out whilst we're still ahead. There's no point in letting the bastard ruin our lives as well. I'll call Stuart."

96

Stuart messaged his sister later that evening 'Allan finally agreed to end it. Making plans to get guy out in next couple of days. Sounds as though you convinced him finally.'

She messaged back, 'Call you tomorrow when I'm on my own, still worried about what he plans to do.'

"So, why are you still worried, Sis?" Stuart asked when she called him. "He's talking about clearing the room out, taking the guy back to near where we grabbed him and leaving him in a park or on some open land, so we won't have as much chance of being seen."

"I'm still worried about him hurting the guy – or worse." Heather felt ridiculous as she said the words and hesitated before continuing, "Look I've never asked Allan this, never thought it was appropriate or wanted to know, but did he ever kill anyone when you and he were in the forces?"

There was a silence at the end of the 'phone before Stuart responded. "You can ask me almost anything Sis, but not that. That's for him to tell you – if he chooses to."

"Why, what difference would it make now?"

"It could change the way you see him if I said he had."

"So, is that a way of telling me he did, Stuart? I need to know because I don't want anything to happen to Jack." She waited anxiously for Stuart's reaction.

"Ok, look I know we've done some tough things in the past, but back then, it was our job. The circumstances now are completely different. Besides, you'll be there when he puts the drug in the guy's drink – just let him know you're watching, although I think you're worrying unnecessarily."

"I wish I felt as sure as you do that it's going to be alright."

"What makes you think it isn't?"

"I don't know Stuart, it's just his mood over the past few days, the guy's really got under his skin, really riled him. I feel he hates him; hates the fact he hasn't been able to make him act as he wanted him to. It frustrates him."

"I know what you mean, Sis, he's used to controlling people and circumstances, it's what we were trained to do. But if he's told you he's going to let the guy go…"

"That's just it, he hasn't! He's just talked about getting him out of the room, not about letting him go"

"But isn't that the same thing?"

"I'm not sure, maybe he's just choosing his words very carefully."

97

The bell rang and Jack sat up, looked at the door and was surprised as he saw it closing. The tray had been passed through as usual, but instead of the breakfast he'd been expecting, it appeared to be a dinner. He couldn't decide whether he'd forgotten a meal or whether it was just another mind game to confuse him. He picked the tray up and took it back to the table to investigate. It looked like moussaka and smelt good. Despite a slight hesitation about the apparent timing of the meal, he felt hungry and began to eat, savouring the richness of the tomatoes and the spiciness of the meat after the blandness of the meals he'd been given previously. He guessed it may have been prepared earlier and then re-heated – not one of the usual frozen meals his captors had been serving.

"Be better with a glass of red wine." He shouted, wondering whether his abductors were listening. He waited but there was no immediate response.

"Miaou might be a more appropriate response!" The man's voice came over the loudspeaker.

"Why, Miaou?" Jack asked.

"Cat's go 'Miaou'.

"So?"

"I'm disappointed in you," the voice sounded dismissive, "I can't believe you've forgotten Mr. Schrödinger's cat already."

"What's that got to do with anything?" Jack shouted back.

"Oh, now you're really upsetting me. I can't believe I so over-estimated your mental capabilities. Perhaps you were just an unwitting tool in John Morrison's death – didn't understand the consequences of carrying out your instructions. Perhaps, I gave you more credit than you deserve. And, if so, I apologise for having detained you; perhaps you were as much a victim as John Morrison."

"For fuck's sake, I know the theory of the cat – how it can be alive and dead at the same time, until the box is opened. But what's that to do with me, now, in this bloody room?"

"You seem to have forgotten part of Schrödinger's premise, that there was something else placed in the box with the cat, something potentially fatal – and that's what led to the discussion about whether it was still alive or dead. Whether the other thing in the box had been released and killed the cat or not."

Jack started to feel anxious.

"'Cat got your tongue' as they say?" the voice asked.

"Is the box being opened?"

"Now that's better, a degree of comprehension at last. Perhaps my earlier comments about your mental capability were a little premature."

"And what will be found when the box is open? Will I be alive?"

"If you're not, it won't matter to you. If you are, tell people what it's like to be as alone as you've been – as alone as John Morrison was when he decided to hang himself."

"So, that's why you gave me the moussaka, so you could put something in it without me knowing what I was eating."

"You might have known there could be a sting in the tail, the same as you might have known the possible outcome of telling John Morrison he was redundant."

"So, what have you done? What have you given me?"

"How do you feel?"

"What do you mean? How can I feel anything but anxious?"

"But rather like Schrödinger's cat, it's unimportant to you – ultimately it's just an intellectual exercise."

"How can my existence be just a mental exercise?"

"As I said a little earlier, if you die, it's no longer relevant, but, if you don't and you're released from the room, your previous world will be restored. So, looked at in one way, you can only win in the situation."

"That's a bloody tortured logic."

"How do you feel?"

"Fucking angry!"

"Why so angry?"

"Because you feel you've got the right to put me and my family through all this. What the hell do you think gives you that right?"

"That's something you'll never learn – hopefully."

"So, will I still be alive to learn."

"The box isn't open yet."

"When will it be open?" Jack shouted, "When will I get to see my family again?"

The voice didn't answer him this time and Jack could almost feel the silence in the room. The helplessness he felt began to overwhelm him; whatever they'd planned was going to happen, he'd eaten or drunk whatever it was they'd given him. But then he thought back over his time in the room, the mental games his captors had played and realised this could be just another game. He felt a brief sense of hope, which was replaced almost immediately by the dread of being incarcerated in the room for longer. An impending sense of doom seized him, and he pushed away the chair and made for the door, intent only on escaping. Using his shoulder, he tried to force it open, but it remained solidly secure and, as he pushed against it again, he began to feel his strength sapping away. He staggered slightly, confused as the room began to spin and fatigue enveloped him. So, was this it? He asked himself the question but was becoming so tired the answer no longer seemed to matter. The mattress was behind him, and he tried to get back to it, wanting to rest, but it was too far away.

98

"Right, we need to get him out. Here, cover his face," Allan handed Stuart a hood, "The sooner we get rid of the evidence the better. I'll put his shoes back on – we don't want to leave anything that can connect us with the abduction. "Ok?" he checked the hood was in place.

"What about the table and chair, and the mattress?"

"We can put the table on its side and the chair between the legs, then put the mattress in place and wedge it in – it'll stop things moving about on the drive." They each took one side of the table and carried it through the door and out into a small office space; it was bare except for the microwave oven they'd used to cook Jack's food and the door they'd replaced with the reinforced door they'd fitted. "We can put the microwave and books in the cab with us," Allan dropped his end of the table, opened the door and they carried it outside and put it in the van. Right, we'll get the chair and the oven next and then we can get the mattress in place."

They put the other items in the van and checked round the room and the office space to make sure there was nothing else left behind.

"He didn't leave any clues did he, like writing some message on a wall?" Stuart checked the closet and took a quick look round. "There's still the cameras and lights to take down, and we need to put the old door back in place; guess we could do that now, whilst we've got the van?" he ticked-off the items on his mental checklist

"I suppose it won't take that long, just a question of undoing a few screws and putting it back on its hinges. And he's not going anywhere." Allan nodded at Jack's body, still lying on the floor. "We'll leave checking the place out for a final time until we come back for the other stuff. They unhung the door, took it out to the van and re-fitted the old one. Right, let's get him out," Allan picked-up Jack's shoulders, "You take the legs."

"Bloody dead weight," Stuart said, "Bloody glad I don't work in an undertakers."

"It's not far to the van; and you've carried a lot more, a lot further, in the past."

"Yeah, but I was younger and fitter then, and I was carrying it on my back. The medics dealt with the bodies."

They moved outside and placed Jack's shoulders onto the mattress. Working together, they manouevred him into the van.

"Do you think we might've got the wrong man?" Stuart looked down at Jack's body lying on the mattress. "I didn't get the impression that this guy was the bastard we'd imagined."

"Maybe, but it's a lesson to the other bastards out there who mess with people's lives. That's the important thing and if what we did saves just one other life, the ends will have justified the means."

"How's his family going to react when he's found? It must have been tough for them wondering what was happening to him over the past weeks."

"If he was worried about his family, he shouldn't have done what he did. He didn't give a damn about his family or anybody else, so why should we?"

Stuart looked at the determination on the other man's face and decided to let things drop.

"What shall I do with the sleeping bag and pillow?"

"We'll dump them separately, put them in a bag and leave them at the tip – they'll be taken away to be burned within a couple of days. We'll chop and burn the table and chair, back home."

"And the mattress?"

"We'll find a place to leave that on the way back – after we've got rid of him. Come on, we'd better get moving, it's a couple of hours drive."

99

The journey was spent largely in silence. Both men felt tense, alert, watching out for any sign of the police, knowing the van might be searched if they were stopped, and a body found in the back.

"Might take a bit of explaining," Stuart turned to his friend, "I'll be pleased when he's out of here and we've just got the furniture to dispose of. So where do you plan on leaving him?"

"Somewhere there aren't cameras. Dropping him back in his own town will let the police make the easy assumption he's been held locally – and it fits in with all the demos. Then we'll dump the rest of the stuff that may have DNA clues miles away and the demolition guys will do the rest when they knock the building down."

"Let's dump him as quickly as we can, eh? We'll be in the town soon and there's more chance of police being about or being caught on camera. Have you got any ideas?"

"I looked up a map before we left and there's a park on the road in. Parks will be deserted at this time of the evening – although the downside is that it won't be too long before he's found."

"Stumbled over by some illicit lovers maybe," Stuart managed a nervous laugh, "Here's a good place, darling. Oops, what's that, it's a body!"

Allan pulled over as they approached the outskirts and Stuart picked-up a tin of grease they'd brought with them, took it outside and smeared it on the number plates in case they were tracked by cameras going into the town.

"We'll wipe it off again as soon as we get back out of the town," Allan pulled away immediately, "The less evidence we leave of being here, the better.".

They checked their Sat Nav and drove towards the park Allan had chosen, watching out for cameras. When they reached it, they found an area with easy access, stopped, checked again to make sure there wasn't any surveillance and, happy they weren't being filmed, pulled Jack out of the back of the van.

Allan pointed to a park shelter a hundred yards away. "Let's leave him over there. Then we'll get the hell out of here and get back home." They checked the road and, seeing no cars around, hurried across to the shelter. "Drop him down on the bench and take the hood off." Stuart did as Allan said and as soon as they'd left Jack on the bench, they ran back to the van and pulled away. They stopped again outside the town, wiped the grease off the number plate and dumped the mattress an hour later in a small wood.

When they reached Wrighton; Allan dropped-off Stuart and drove the short way home. By the time he got back, his mood had darkened, and he looked down at Heather dejectedly, his face grim and defeated. "So, we failed. John's death is almost forgotten just a few weeks later."

"I'm sorry, Allan," Heather placed her hand on her husband's arm to comfort him, "But I'm not sure we got the right man, and to be honest, I'm not even sure that John's death was due to his redundancy."

"Well, if his redundancy wasn't the cause of John's suicide, what was? That's one of the things that pisses me off most, that bastard looking up at the cameras and telling me I didn't know my brother. Can you imagine how I felt when he said that to me?"

"But was he right? Did we know him anymore? Think about it, how often did we see or speak to him?"

"How often did he contact us? It can't all be one way; besides, you have to be careful not to be intrusive. He would have contacted us if he needed support. He knew we'd be there for him."

"I'm not sure, Allan, I think that guy may have had a point. I know John was your brother and you loved him but, if you look back over the past few years, our whole relationship had become little more than an exchange of Christmas and Birthday cards."

"That's life nowadays," Allan shook his head as he thought back to how it had been when they were younger, "Families don't keep in touch the way they used to. People don't just pop round to see their friends or relatives anymore, they're generally too far away for that sort of thing. But when something important happened we were there for him, like when Keira and Faith died."

"You mean we went to their funerals and offered a few comforting words. I can't remember us being able to do much more than that – other than inviting him to come and stay if he wanted to. And you did call him more often after they died." She paused, "Thinking back, though, I don't remember hearing much about Faith at their funerals, it seemed to be all about Keira as far as John was concerned. Perhaps he and Faith were no longer happy together."

"So, what are you saying?"

"I'm saying we weren't part of his life. Not in the way we might have been. We didn't have any real idea about anything that was happening to John. We didn't meet-up as families, visit each other's homes. We weren't close."

"Well, that was down to his bloody wife; all she seemed to want to do was control him, isolate him from his friends and family. And John was too easy-going with her, too weak to fight back."

"Perhaps we should have made more effort when he was alive, rather than just punishing some poor sod for his suicide after he was dead. Let's face it; we didn't really know John anymore. And, yes, it may have been down to Faith wanting to keep him to herself – or, maybe, if they were unhappy, it was a way of her punishing him, isolating him from the people he loved and knew. Without talking to John, and we can't do that now, how could we ever know?"

"So, I failed, as a brother."

'No," Heather shook her head, realising his misery, "I wasn't saying that."

"But you're right," Allan remembered the remoteness he'd felt whenever he had spoken to his brother in recent years, "I failed to be there when he needed me, and then let him down when he was dead."

"No, it's not as simple as that. You've punished one man for what happened to John, don't start punishing yourself as well." She reached up and held his face between her hands. "Even if you'd been closer, you don't know there's anything you could have done. Remember what the man said, John's suicide surprised him, that he thought John seemed to be seeing a new future ahead. Whatever changed must have changed suddenly and you couldn't be there every hour of the day. Don't beat yourself up any more than you already have."

"I failed him."

"No, you can't protect everybody all the time. However much you may have wanted to be, you couldn't be your brother's keeper." Heather reached-up and kissed him. "Pour yourself a drink and when you've calmed down, come up to bed."

100

The first sensation Jack was aware of was the hard surface on which he was laying and the coolness of the air. He opened his eyes and reacted with a start as he saw a man's face looking down at him. It was a rough, red face with several-day-old grey stubble and rheumy eyes, made visible by the bright moonlight. The owner of the face, surprised by Jack's reaction, moved back, and Jack raised himself from the seat anxious not to remain lying down and vulnerable. In front of him stood an untidy figure, wearing a dark overcoat tied with string and a pair of dirty trousers above a pair of shabby looking trainers. As soon as he sat up Jack winced, his head throbbing painfully because of the sudden movement, and he saw the man step further away from him.

"Where am I?"

The man said nothing just peered more closely at Jack, who repeated the question.

"Park," the man's voice sounded slurred, and he shook slightly as he stood there.

"Did you see who brought me here?"

The man shook his head.

"Have I been here long?"

"Dunno, came 'ere 'cos ah sleep 'ere when ah can't get into the 'ostel."

"So, where is this park?" Jack was still feeling confused and couldn't recognise his surroundings. "What's the name of the town?"

The man mumbled the town's name and Jack realised he must be near home, but he still wasn't sure which part of the town he was in, so he got up from the seat, felt himself stagger slightly and held onto the shelter to keep his balance. And, as he stood there the relief at being free overcame him; he swallowed, his throat seeming to swell and his mouth trembling uncontrollably. Then the sobbing started, racking his body as the tears ran down his face. He shut his eyes and breathed deeply, feeling the tension beginning to drain from him. When he opened his eyes again, the other man was no longer standing where he'd been previously; he looked round and found him sat along the seat that Jack had woken on, clearly claiming it as his own.

"What's your name?"

"Jonah, they call me Jonah," the man muttered.

"Well, Jonah, I don't think I've ever been as pleased to see another human face in my life."

Jonah sensed there might be an opportunity to benefit from the situation and held out his hand. "Spare a few pence, mister, for breakfast in the morning?"

"Sorry, Jonah, I'm as broke as you are, I've got nothing – no wallet, no watch, no keys, nothing." He patted his pockets showing the other man he had nothing in them. "And I don't even know what day it is."

The man mumbled something that Jack couldn't catch, put his bag behind him on the seat and supported his head on his arm preparing to go to sleep. Anxious to get a clearer idea of exactly where he was, Jack walked away from the shelter and towards the road he could see nearby. When he reached the road, he recognised he was in a place on the other side of town from his home, near the area dominated by the University buildings and decided to try to walk into the centre to either reach the police station or find someone who would help him. Without any money or a 'phone he couldn't call a taxi, and he was impatient to contact Charlotte and let her know he was ok. His head still hurt, and he couldn't remember what had happened before he woke up in the shelter, how he'd come to be there.

So, at least he knew where he was and that it was night-time, but he didn't know the actual time or even which day it was. The roads were deserted, there were no cars about, and no other people – but he knew that would change as the night progressed. He tried to catch a sight of himself in the windows of the houses he passed, but it was impossible in the dark. His beard had grown and felt softer now than it had been, and he guessed his hair must look wild despite his attempts to wash it in the small washbasin and style it without a mirror to check it in. 'Probably look a bit like Jonah' he thought and made a mental note to approach anyone he saw carefully and avoid alarming them. As he approached the river, he passed the station and found a clock – the time was 12.41, so it would still be a few more hours before the town started coming back to life. And he guessed it couldn't be a Friday or Saturday night as there would still be people enjoying themselves on the street. As he walked, he experienced a growing euphoria, as uncontrollable as some of the panic attacks he'd felt during his captivity, but far more welcome. He was out and he'd be home as soon as he could find someone to help him.

The sound of a car made him turn round and he stepped off the kerb trying to catch the driver's attention. The car slowed and he could see 'POLICE' written across the front. He stepped back on the pavement and waited for someone to get out.

A policeman emerged from the passenger side, carrying his hat in his hand and raising it to his head. "Good evening, Sir, and what can we do for you?"

Jack was aware the policeman was looking at him critically, trying to decide what sort of person he was talking to, and introduced himself immediately. "Hi, my name's Jack Docherty, I was abducted, kept somewhere in a room. I don't know how long ago it all happened; I don't even know what day it is."

The man stared, appraising him and then turned to his colleague who had got out of the car as a back-up. "He says he's that guy who was abducted – Docherty, Jack Docherty." He turned back to Jack. "So, how did you get here?"

"I don't know, no idea," he shook his head, "I woke up in the shelter in the park – with some homeless guy standing over me."

The two officers looked at each other and then motioned Jack across to the car. The driver walked away and got back in, whilst the other officer turned round and opened the rear door. "Jump in, we'll take you to the station."

101

The phone was ringing, intruding on Charlotte's dream. She rolled over and checked the time on her bedside clock. It was the middle of the night, and she picked the 'phone up, apprehensive about what she might be about to hear.

"Hello."

"Hi, Charlotte? It's me, Jack."

"Jack!" The line went quiet and then, when she'd recovered from the shock, the questions came. "Oh my God I thought I'd never hear your voice again. Where are you? Are you ok?"

"I'm fine, look a bit of a wreck though. Anyway, I'm down at the police station, I'll be back in a couple of hours when the police have had a chance to debrief me. Are the lads ok?"

"They'll be a lot better when they see you. They've been at my parents for a few days, but they're home again now."

"Look, I must go, the quicker I do the debrief, the quicker I'll be home. They've called the inspector who's been handling the case and she'll be here shortly."

When Bracken arrived, she looked as though she'd just got out of bed, which Jack assumed she had, and asked to interview him in a small room equipped with recording equipment. "So, what can you tell me about the night you were abducted?"

"Not very much," Jack said, "I remember being at the snooker club and being in good form that night, winning both games, and ordering a drink, but after that I can't remember anything until I woke up in the room they kept me in. I think they must have drugged me."

"And what was that room like, describe it to me," Bracken sat back in her chair and waited for his reply.

"Again, there isn't much I can tell you," Jack was apologetic, "It was just a large, high-ceilinged room, an industrial building I'd guess, with a toilet, a table and chair, and a mattress. And the lighting was always low, bright enough to read and move around, but not bright enough to keep me awake. Nothing that would identify the room except for the four video cameras and speakers high up on the walls."

"So, you don't know how long it took them to drive you there?"

"No, sorry," Jack shook his head, "The first thing I remember is waking-up there with a bad headache."

"So, were there any memorable conversations you had with your captors. Anything that would give us a clue to their motives or identity?"

Jack recalled some of the conversations he'd had and described some of the bizarre experiences his incarceration had caused. The only things he could recall that might offer a clue to his abductors' motives or identity were the continued references to using him as an example to other people, the male and female voices, and the obsession with Schrödinger's cat.

"What do you recall about your release?" Bracken asked.

"Nothing," Jack shook his head, "I think they must have used some sort of drug to make me unconscious – the same one they used when they abducted me. It's the only way I can explain the amnesia I suffered about both events."

Bracken asked a few more questions but realised she was unlikely to learn any more during the interview and arranged for Jack to be taken home.

....

"So where do we go from here?" George asked when he got in the following morning.

Bracken shook her head at her sergeant, "I don't know, we've got so little to go on. Docherty can't give us any clues and we haven't been able to uncover anything in our other investigations. I guess the best chance we have is locating the place Docherty was kept and forensics finding something, but we've no idea where to start looking. Let's look at the CCTV cameras in the area around the park where they dropped Docherty off."

102

When the police car stopped outside the house, Charlotte hurried to open the front door. The Jack she saw in front of her was unfamiliar, his appearance neglected with wild hair and a patchy beard, and he'd lost weight.

"It is me," Jack stood there a moment, "Can I come in?"

Charlotte nodded and then started to cry.

"I thought you'd be pleased to get me home." He put his arms round her and gave her a hug. "Instead of which, you burst into tears."

"God, you smell as well." Charlotte pulled away from him; "You need a shower – and a shave before the boys see you. They'll wonder who you are otherwise."

"Any chance of a decent cup of tea?"

"I'll make one while you have your shower. And try to be quiet, the boys are asleep."

He went upstairs, stood in the doorways of each of their rooms and listened to them breathing. Then he carried on to his own bedroom. It all looked the same as when he'd left, and he felt the relief flooding through him. He was home, it was over. Taking his clothes off he threw them on the floor and stepped into the shower. It felt wonderful, the water beating down on his skin and beginning to wash the past few weeks away. And the creamy soapiness of the shampoo was luxurious after the cold water he'd had to use from the sink in the cubicle. He cleaned his teeth, his mouth tingling when he'd finished, shaved his emerging beard with some difficulty and went downstairs.

"I'm ready for that tea now, they gave me a mug at the police station, but it was awful, tepid and tasteless." He sat down at the kitchen table and stretched, his legs out in front of him, his arms reaching up towards the ceiling.

"So, where did they keep you?"

"In a room. It looked like the inside of an industrial unit, with high ceilings, bare walls and no windows. And no noise – that was probably the worst thing of all."

"But what did you do all the time? It must have driven you crazy, just stuck in a room with nothing to occupy your mind?"

"I think that was the whole idea, to make me feel the emptiness they believed John must have felt before he hung himself. And, after a few days, they gave me a small bottle, with liquid in it and said that if I drank it, it would release me from the room."

"But you didn't drink it?"

"No, I didn't want to admit defeat, to let them win, and I wasn't sure if they actually wanted me to commit suicide, like John had. So, I refused."

"But what kept you going? Why didn't you begin to feel the same as John had?"

"Because I never felt tired enough of life that I gave up wanting to live. Because, in a funny way I felt guilty for putting you and the boys through whatever you were experiencing and wanted to get back and make things all right. Besides, I was angry at whoever had kidnapped me and, if I'm honest," he smiled, "Because I'm afraid of dying."

"And have you no idea who abducted you?"

"No, I never saw them and I've no idea where they were keeping me either. There are just blanks in time; between being abducted and finding myself locked in the room and between being in the room and waking up in the park – and I've no way of knowing how long those blanks lasted. And, whilst I was in the room, I didn't know whether it was day or night, or how long I'd been there."

"But what did they say to you? Didn't that give you any clues about who or what they were?"

"No, the police asked me about that; I get the impression they think it might have been some left-wing group, but there was nothing to suggest that's true. No political catchwords or slogans, it all felt much more personal; they kept impressing on me my individual responsibility for what had happened to John. It was almost religious, about confession and repentance and, ultimately, putting myself in the same place John had been."

"But you didn't go there?"

"No, I didn't." Jack reached across and put his hand over hers.

"Do you want a sleep?"

"No", he looked at the clock on the kitchen wall, "I'm not tired, my body clock feels all over the place, and it will be light soon. You sleep if you want to, I think I'll sit here and enjoy the dawn – I haven't seen daylight since I was kidnapped."

"Let's go into the conservatory, we can sit on the couch and watch the sky get light – it's so good to have you back," she gave him a hug, "But we need to keep our ears open, the lads have been disturbed by everything that's happened and they've been waking-up more frequently than usual."

They sat on the sofa, Charlotte leaning against him. He heard her breathing change and realised she was sleeping. And to the East, the sky started brightening, the red sky beneath the clouds turning blue and the sun climbing over the hills in the distance. He breathed easily and slowly, unlike he had with the panic attacks he'd felt in the room, but flashes of the room, the bareness and silence, appeared randomly, disturbing the stillness. And that, he guessed, had been part of the issue, the silence and bareness had been oppressive, making it difficult for him to relax, the absence of stimuli had been stultifying, numbing him of any desire to do anything. And, as he sat there, thinking about his experience, he began to understand what John must have felt – although he still couldn't reconcile the feeling with the conversations they'd had in the weeks before.

"Mummy, mummy, where are you?" He heard Tony calling, steps along the landing and then more cries of 'mummy', but this time more hysterical.

"Hey, wake up, Tony's calling for you," he shook Charlotte gently, "Better you go and see him first, he's expecting you."

She got up, went into the hall and called up to let their younger son know she was there. Then he heard her start to climb the stairs and the familiar creaking sound as she reached the landing with the loose floorboard. Tony was still crying, but he heard her talking to him and then going along to Daniel's bedroom and waking him. Daniel was still complaining as they came back along the landing – it was too early, and he wanted to go back to bed. He was still complaining when they got back down to the hall but stopped when his mother said there was someone who wanted to see them.

Jack stood up as they entered the lounge, waiting for them to realise he was there. Tony was the first to react, shouting 'Daddy' and rushing over to be picked-up and cuddled, but Daniel held back, looked-up at his mother and shook his head.

"It's alright Daniel, Daddy's come back."

Daniel began to cry, "But will they take him away again?"

"Why would someone take him away again?" Charlotte asked.

"Because of what he did, making that man kill himself?"

Charlotte looked over at Jack and then knelt down and looked Daniel in the face. "Your father didn't make that man kill himself, we don't know why the man did what he did, but it wasn't your Daddy's fault."

"They said it was his fault at school."

"I know they did, but they were wrong, and whoever told the other boys that was wrong as well. And the people who kidnapped your father were wrong. Your Daddy is a good man – that's why I love him."

Jack gave Tony across to Charlotte and went and knelt in front of his elder son as she'd done. He spoke softly, "I'm sorry I haven't been here, and you've had to manage on your own, it must have been difficult, particularly with other boys saying nasty things about me. But it's not true what they've been saying, the man and I were friends once and I would never have done anything to hurt him." He held out his arms and gave his son a hug. "No school for either of you today, we all need to get to know each other again." He moved back and stood up again. "Now, I don't know about anybody else, but I'm hungry. Shall we all have breakfast together?"

Daniel smiled for the first time and nodded.

103

Sam put on the local morning news and started to make a cup of tea, listening vaguely for any item of interest.

> *'The man who was abducted, following the suicide of an employee he'd made redundant, has been released. Police say he was found walking through the*

town centre in the early hours of this morning after being drugged and left sleeping in a local park. The man is now back with his family and has not been harmed physically by his abductors.

According to police sources, the kidnapped man has been held in a sound and light-proofed room since his abduction over two weeks ago. He had no idea, when found, of how long he'd been imprisoned or who his kidnappers were, although he has revealed that at least two kidnappers were involved, a man and a woman. The police are appealing for any information about the identity of the kidnappers and for any witnesses to either the original abduction or the return of the man to the local park.'

"Hey Ros, they've found your boss." Sam called out to Ros, in the other room, "He's ok, back home."

"Really? Thank God." She hurried into the kitchen and listened to the rest of the bulletin, "That's fantastic news, I'm so relieved for Jack – and his family must be over the moon that he's back. There's no news about who kidnapped him, though; the police don't seem to have any leads and what they did to him sounds awful. Can you imagine being kept in total isolation, not knowing where you are, what day it is or what's going to happen to you – it's horrendous?" Ros' voice faltered for a moment, "I can't imagine John Morrison approving of doing something like that to anyone in his name – he was far too nice a guy. I guess it may be a few days before we see Jack back at work, though."

"I wonder what sort of reception he's going to get," Sam started to drink his tea, "From what you've heard there seems to be some suggestion it was his fault the guy killed himself; that he handled the whole redundancy thing badly."

104

Margaret had just got herself and Roger a first cup of morning coffee when her 'phone rang. She picked-up the call and recognised Jack's voice immediately.

"It's great to hear from you again, Jack. I saw on the news that you'd been released. How are you feeling? Are you alright?"

Jack assured her he was, thanked her for her concern and asked to talk to Roger. He picked-up a slight hesitation before Margaret apologised and said Roger wasn't available, but she would get him to call later.

"I'm so glad you're ok," she ended the call and then looked-up at Roger who was standing beside her desk.

"You better get Geoff and Max to come and see me, I need to check with them about the best way of handling this. The way Jack handled Morrison's redundancy has caused a lot of issues for the Company."

Geoff arrived first and sat down. When Max arrived, Roger asked him to shut the door. Max did as he'd been instructed, and Roger joined them both at the table.

"So, as you've probably heard, Jack has been released by whoever kidnapped him and he called the office this morning. I didn't take the call as we need to decide how to handle his return."

"In what way?" Max was confused. "Don't we just welcome him back when he's had enough time to recover from whatever ordeal he's been put through? It must have been traumatic for him."

"I understand that Max, but it's also been a traumatic time for the Company. I've called you in because Geoff and I have been discussing whether to conduct a disciplinary hearing when he gets back, based on the insensitive way in which he implemented Morrison's redundancy and the damage it's caused to the Company's reputation."

"I'm sorry, is this some kind of a joke?"

"Far from it, Max. I'm surprised you should even suggest that."

"And are you going along with this?" Max turned and faced Geoff.

"I can see Roger's point," Geoff flushed slightly, "The company's received a lot of bad publicity and we've had several demonstrations outside the gates. We've never had anything like that before when people have been made redundant."

"But Jack just did what he was told to."

"Jack should have used more judgement. Disciplining him will show a sympathetic corporate face, demonstrating publicly, that we care about our employees and giving the lie to those bloody lunatics who've been protesting outside." Roger pointed at the window as he spoke, stabbing his finger towards the front gates. "As I've said before, Jack should have made a case for treating Morrison differently from the rest, but he didn't. All he needed to do was discuss it with Geoff and me. So, can you prepare a story along these lines for the media, Max?"

"I can prepare the story, but I can't be part of it – from where I sit it just looks as though we're abandoning Jack. Making him into some sort of sacrificial lamb."

"But didn't Jack just abandon us?" Roger closed his notebook and stood up, "We didn't have the chance to show Morrison any compassion."

"Jack didn't abandon the company, he was kidnapped and, from the sound of it, subjected to some inhumane conditions. And you do realise that disciplining Jack amounts to a corporate admission of responsibility for John Morrison's suicide? Jack was acting for the company, so, if he's responsible, the company's also responsible."

Roger sat down again and looked across at Geoff but got no reaction.

"And, looked at another way it could just confirm the Company's lack of feeling for its workers, getting one employee to fire another one and then publicly crucifying him after he does. Besides, up until now, we've been publicly defending the redundancy programme and made no mention of any mismanagement. This will just give the media another opportunity to criticise what the company did – we'll have a reputation for being both ruthless and inept."

"What do you think, Geoff?" Roger pressed the other man for an answer.

"And for the record, we still don't know whether the redundancy was responsible for John's suicide." Max interrupted before Geoff could answer.

"So, what are you suggesting we do, if we're asked for a comment, Max?"

"Say we're pleased Jack has been released unharmed but, at the same time, condemn this type of illegal action against individuals by political or other groups. And, perhaps, point out once again that the reason for John's suicide has never been established."

"But what about disciplinary action for the damage Jack's actions have done to the Company's name?"

"On that basis you could take action against Geoff as well. You knew about John's family being killed, didn't you Geoff? You're in charge of human resources, why didn't you intervene and suggest John was given more time to get over his loss? Come to that, why did you allow him to be included in the redundancy programme in the first place?

Why wasn't a corporate decision taken to exclude him from the programme?"

"But I wasn't Morrison's line manager."

"You're a corporate manager and just as responsible for ensuring the Company's reputation isn't compromised. Jack must have talked to you about John's situation, I can't imagine he didn't."

Geoff sat still, not answering.

"I think we've spent enough time on this. I can see where you're coming from, Max, but I'm not happy. I'll get Margaret to call Jack and tell him to come back when he's ready and you can go ahead and prepare a press statement along the lines you've mentioned." Roger closed his file and stood up again, "And, by the way, I don't want either of you talking to Jack about this meeting."

105

Charlotte looked up from her magazine and saw Jack had put his book down. Instead of reading, he was sitting and staring out through the glass doors at the back garden. She'd noticed he'd been quieter since he'd been back home, his face passive, showing nothing about what he was thinking. She wasn't sure whether there was something worrying him or whether he was just reflecting on the time he'd spent in isolation.

"You know you weren't responsible for John Morrison's death," Charlotte tried to second-guess his thoughts, reached over and placed her hand on his arm. "It wasn't your decision and, anyway, you talked to him about how he felt, and you said at the time that he seemed quite upbeat about the future – despite what had happened to his wife and daughter."

"Yes, I was surprised at his reaction, and I still find it odd. He seemed to think it was an opportunity to re-start his life, take things in a new direction. But, although I tell myself I wasn't the reason for his suicide, it's difficult to feel totally innocent. There's still a nagging doubt in my mind, a question about how things might have been different if he'd still been able to keep working."

"That's impossible to know, because it didn't happen. There's no point in torturing yourself about it."

"I'm not torturing myself, but I don't suppose I'll ever be able to exonerate myself totally. It would be good if I could. But that's not what I was thinking about when I was looking out of the window."

"What was it then?"

"I was just thinking how wonderful it is to be free. Hearing the birds so excited on the feeders, looking at all the different colours of the plants, imagining the smell of the roses and knowing I can go out there and enjoy them if I want to."

"So, why didn't John Morrison feel the same?"

"Who knows? I can sit here and appreciate it all because I have you, the kids and a degree of security. And I can enjoy my freedom, rather than being afraid of it. Whilst those little birds out there look so pretty, there's fighting going on for the food when you look closer and they're forever on the look-out for enemies, like the hawk that sometimes comes down and tries to grab one of them. Maybe, John just became exhausted, gave up because he didn't feel it was worth fighting any more to prolong what, for him, had become an existence, rather than a life."

106

Misty grabbed some groceries for the weekend and walked out of the supermarket towards the bus station. The weekend wasn't looking very exciting, the friend with whom she was sharing the flat had gone away and being single, since she'd split from Richie, she guessed it would probably involve nothing much more than a good book, more wine than was healthy for her and, at some point, a long lounge in the bath.

"Hey, Misty," she heard someone calling her name, and when she looked round saw Gill and Ros. "Do you fancy a drink? We're celebrating the end of the week."

"That will be great. Good to see you two again. Where are we going?"

"Usual place, wine bar in the High Street."

They reached the bar, found themselves a table and ordered a bottle of wine. There was a loud clunk of bottles as Misty put her bag down.

"Sounds as though you've already got supplies in for the weekend," Gill indicated the bag.

"Yes, my friend has gone away, so I thought I'd cook myself a good meal tonight and wash it down with a bottle of red whilst I put my feet-up and watch TV."

"Nice to have the luxury," Ros said, Sam will be wanting to do something, go somewhere – a bottle of wine and a long wallow in a bath sounds wonderful."

"How are things at work?" Misty moved aside as the barman brought across their wine and poured each of them a glass, "Has that guy they kidnapped come back yet?"

"No, not yet, I've heard he's coming back sometime next week – he's had a few days off to recover. He's spoken to Alison, my boss, and she says he seems ok."

"He must be an exceptionally strong person, staying sane in a room without any sounds or anything to do for over two weeks. It's amazing."

"He is Misty – plus he's a nice guy," Ros took a sip of her wine and nodded her appreciation.

"I hate to say it, but the description of the room in which he'd been kept would fit the buildings on that estate where we're holding the workshop. Maybe, your intuition wasn't playing tricks on you, Misty?" Gill thought back, visualising the old industrial units, but then told herself there must be dozens of similar sites up and down the country.

"I guess that's immaterial now, the guy's out and safe, and that's all that really matters. The important thing for us is to make sure the workshop goes well, although, I must admit I'm still tempted to take a look at the building that woman was visiting when we go up again – just to satisfy my curiousity."

"It's not long now," Gill shook her head, "I think we've got everything ready, but I always get so nervous, there's so much can go wrong on the day. The presentations are all ready, but the audio-visual equipment is always a worry – without it the whole day can be ruined."

"Well, I suppose we ought to be going, the men will be wondering where we are and your meal isn't going to improve sitting in that bag," Ros nodded at Misty's bag.

"And the wine is asking to be allowed to breath," Misty smiled at the other women, "And thanks for the drink, it's made a good start to what might have been a long weekend."

"Do you want a lift home?" Gill asked, "My car's in the car park by the bus station, I'm giving Ros a lift back, so you're welcome to jump in."

Misty nodded. "Thanks, that'll save me having to carry this bag at the other end."

"Our weekend isn't going to be exactly scintillating, we're taking Mike's mother out to lunch on Sunday. Don't get me wrong, she's great, but I think Mike sometimes tries to over-compensate for his dad not being there. I need to pop in to see her on the way to the car, I'll introduce you if she's free, she works in a shop near the car park entrance."

"What happened with Mike's Dad?" Misty asked, "Did he and Mike's mother separate?"

"No, his dad died two or three years back – before we met. I think it affected Mike quite a bit. I know he's a grown man, but the responsibility he felt for his mother and the loss of someone he was close to left him with an underlying sense of inadequacy. Then, to make matters worse, he was made redundant. And, ever since, he always worries in case something goes wrong and he won't be able to cope."

"I know Sam was very concerned when Mike lost his job," Ros added, "And then you two got together, he got his new job and he's been so much better since. I think both of the guys worry about losing everything and finding themselves on the streets, like Jonah."

"Who's Jonah?" Misty shook her head, "I haven't heard his name before, except like in the bible."

Gill pointed in the direction they were going, "You may be lucky and meet him in a minute or two. He sometimes pops in to see Mike's mother and scrounge some fags, although I'm not sure if he'll be disappointed now – she gave up smoking a few weeks back."

They turned the corner with the car park ahead and Gill excused herself and went ahead into the small shop to make sure the arrangements for lunch were still ok. She came out again with Mike's mother and was introducing her to Misty when Jonah shuffled up.

Misty took in the ragged coat tied with string and the red vinyl shopping bag that he carried his cans of booze in, but she said nothing.

Jonah ignored the younger women and spoke directly to Mike's mother, asking her for a cigarette.

"Now you know I've given-up, Jonah."

"But your young man 'was 'ere last time and 'e bought some fer me." Jonah looked at each of the three younger women as appealingly as he could.

"Now, you can't keep coming here, begging people to buy you cigarettes," Mike's mother waved a finger at Jonah as she spoke, admonishing him.

"What on earth was Mike doing buying him cigarettes?" Gill looked surprised at what she'd just heard.

"Don't worry yourself," Mike's mother leapt to his defence, "He doesn't normally go round buying Jonah cigarettes, but as I've given up and didn't have any, I think he just felt sorry for the old boy."

Gill paused a moment, then took out her purse, "Go on, let's buy him another packet of whatever Mike bought him." She handed Mike's mother some money, took the packet from her when she came back out of the shop and held it out to Jonah.

Jonah took the packet immediately, opened it and put a cigarette in his mouth. "Need a light."

Mike's mother turned back, reached across the shop counter for a packet of matches and lit the cigarette. He inhaled deeply, a smile appearing momentarily on his face. Then he looked round at the younger women. "Can yer spare a few coins fer something to eat?"

"Behave yourself, Jonah," Mike's mother waved him back, "And don't puff that smoke out around me – it's hard enough giving up smoking without you coming here and reminding me what I'm missing. Here, you'd better take these too." She handed him the matches.

Jonah tipped his hand with the cigarette up to his forehead in a gesture of thanks.

"Poor old sod, he's a nightmare, but I'd miss him if he wasn't around." Mike's mother looked after him as he walked away and then turned to Misty. "Always asking for money for food, but he just wants it to buy booze."

"What does he drink?"

"That strong cider usually – it's the cheapest way of getting what he needs."

Misty shook her head and then smiled at the others. "Well let's give him a special treat this weekend." She called 'Jonah' after the ragged figure, but the figure kept walking without looking back. "Just give me a moment, he can't have heard me." Reaching in her bag she pulled out one of the bottles of wine, "I know I shouldn't, but it won't harm him to have a treat occasionally."

She put her bag down and hurried after Jonah, tapping his shoulder when she caught up. He turned to face her, and she pushed the bottle towards him. He took another puff on his cigarette and seemed confused by what she was doing.

"Here, you wanted money for food, try this instead."

Jonah's mouth opened, but only smoke came out. He put his bag down, took the bottle and placed it inside. Then he picked-up the bag, held his hand up to his forehead again and grinned. "Thanks," he mumbled, anxious to get away and open the bottle, "You ain't …"

"No, I haven't," Misty smiled, "That's all you're getting."

107

The Priest reached out, raised the heavy black metal latch and pushed open the large wooden door. He loved visiting his church, wandering through the graveyard, looking up at the tall steeple and imagining the priests who had preceded him. Men who had walked up the same pathway over the centuries since the church had been built and passed through the same arched entrance and into the same flint-walled porch with the sundial above. Priests with very different names: Saxon and Norman names in the beginning – and a different faith before the foundation of the Protestant Church and the denial of the Pope's authority. Times when the priest could look down from the pulpit at a packed congregation, the choir and the musicians filling the chancel. Times when parishioners walked miles to attend on cold winter days, wrapped-up in their heaviest clothes, their shoes covered in mud and feet sodden by the rain. Easter times when the spring days were warmer, but still chilled, and parishioners could regain their hope, looking forward to the rebirth of nature and the warm days ahead. Hot summer days when they would arrive perspiring in their Sunday best, and autumn days, when they could drag their feet through fallen brown and orange leaves as they walked along. And, throughout the seasons, all converging on a common destination, bound together by their faith and fear of their God.

In those days priests had been superior, powerful, arbiters of the faith, reading and interpreting the Bible for people who couldn't read themselves. Now his role was to educate, his Sunday sermons prompting parishioners to think about their faith in their everyday lives, or to act as their counselor when they were experiencing difficulties or questioning their beliefs. He didn't regret the changes in his role, although the lack of parishioners and empty pews at services, despite all his efforts, sometimes tested his own faith. Today, as he entered, he saw the Church was not empty; the woman was there again. And, instead of just nodding and acknowledging him, she turned, got up from the pew, walked over and said she was finally ready to talk if he had the time to listen.

"Of course, if you're sure you're ready."

"I am sure."

"So, what is it you want to talk about?"

"It's a sort of confession."

The priest paused before responding, "Before you start telling me anything, you must understand I can't give you absolution, in the Anglican Church we believe that only God can do that. And, unlike a Roman priest, I'm not bound by an Oath of Secrecy, although you have my assurance that I won't repeat anything you say, if it doesn't require me to share it."

"Do you mean like doing something criminal?"

"Exactly."

"I've not done anything criminal," the woman shook her head, emphasizing what she was saying, "My problem is a moral one."

"Well, that is something I may be able to help with" the priest smiled, "But, I've noticed you're wearing a wedding ring," he pointed at her hand, "Is there any reason you can't confide in your husband? Or perhaps you're widowed?"

"I'm married." The woman looked down at the floor, "And there are two issues, neither of which he can help me with. In fact, unknowingly, he's part of the problem."

"I see," the Priest looked towards the vestry, but then hesitated. "Look, the Rectory's only a short walk, why don't we go there to talk? If we use the Vestry someone might come into the church and overhear us. Is that ok with you? My study is far more secure."

The woman nodded and followed him out of the church and back down the pathway. The rectory was an old, detached house, and the priest opened the front door, which was unlocked and led into a small hall. He reached for the handle of the door to his study, and stood aside to let her go in.

"It's a bit austere, I always feel, but it's the best place to talk." he motioned her to sit in one of the two armchairs standing in front of a bookcase, with a low table for coffee or papers between them. His desk and office chair were under the window, but he ignored them and sat in the armchair opposite her, leaning back and making himself comfortable. "Please try to relax and, when you're ready tell me what's been bringing you to the church these past weeks?"

She waited before speaking, trying to decide where to begin.

"Take your time," the priest held his hand up urging her not to hurry, "Before you start, would you like to tell me your name? You don't have to if you'd rather not."

"My name?" she hesitated for a moment," My name's Alison and I worked with both the men involved in what's happened. And being married is the reason for the dilemma I've been facing."

"Start at the beginning," the priest said, "When did it all start."

"Oh, that was some years ago," Alison thought back, "When I began an affair with a man called John Morrison. You may have heard the name?"

'Isn't he the man who was made redundant and whose subsequent suicide led to another man being abducted?"

"Yes, but I'm not sure the redundancy had much to do with it all. In fact, being totally honest, I don't think it had anything to do with John's suicide."

"What about his wife's and daughter's deaths a couple of months earlier? Do you think they may have been the reason for his suicide?"

"John was very upset by his daughter's death, yes, but not necessarily by the death of his wife. You see, I'm not sure they had any real feelings left for each other. They'd drifted apart, were living virtually separate lives – that's how we, John and I, found ourselves together. I wasn't happy in my marriage, but I don't think he realised that at first; he was just drawn to me because we were friends and he'd learned to trust me. Obviously, being unhappy myself, I'd recognised how unhappy he'd become and when I offered sympathy, he told me about the issues he and his wife were facing. They'd married early, childhood sweethearts, and, although the marriage had lasted, it was no longer working for either of them. To compensate for the gradual alienation she'd felt, she seems to have thrown all her love and effort into their daughter. Like many men, he felt neglected. It's a corny old story, but that doesn't stop it being true."

"So, when did this all happen?"

"Oh, this is going back years, ten years or more. Anyway, it all started at an office party, one Christmas, like so many things do. We'd had too much to drink and we were both lonely. And we'd grown closer as we'd confided in each other over the preceding months. It was an affair in waiting, just needing a spark to ignite the passion."

"What happened afterwards?"

"Well, we started seeing each other whenever we could. John used to play snooker every week with Jack, the man who told him he was redundant and who was kidnapped afterwards. John was a colleague of Jack's at the time, but Jack later became his boss. After we started seeing each other he gave up playing snooker and used to meet me instead. We used to laugh about him never forgetting his snooker cue when we met."

"When did the affair end?"

"Not until a couple of years back. I was younger than John and, when it started, I'd been trying for some time to have children with my husband, but it never happened. John already had his daughter, Keira, the girl who was driving when the car crashed and killed her and her mother. I wanted John to leave his wife and live with me. I guess I thought there might be more chance of conceiving if I tried with John instead of my husband; although, I don't want to pretend it was just about having children. I loved John for himself, but he wouldn't leave his wife because of Keira; I always thought he loved her more than anything else in life. Oh, he loved me too; I knew that, but not enough to risk losing her. I begged him to leave for years, but he wouldn't and, finally, the knowledge that I wasn't enough for him began to eat away at our relationship. It drifted on, but more because it was better than either of us had with our respective partners and it was comfortable. By the time of Keira's crash, it had ended – finished a couple of years previously. But the loss of Keira and the death of his wife changed everything as far as John was concerned. He was alone and had nothing more to lose and he began to pester me to leave my husband and go and live with him."

"Why didn't you go? Were you happier with your marriage by then?"

"I wasn't happier, but living with my husband was no longer so demanding, we'd drifted into a sort of married friendship. And though I didn't love him like I'd loved John, I didn't want to hurt him after so many years together."

"The passion had died."

"Yes, I suppose that's a good way of looking at it. I was settled, contented with my lot – however mundane it had become. But the passion had been reincarnated in John; he needed me, and I began to be afraid that my husband would find out about the affair, so I asked John to stop contacting me – although it was difficult because we still had to work together."

"Was this before or after he was made redundant?"

"Before. When I heard he'd lost his job, I called and met up with him. He was full of ideas about what we could do together, the redundancy payment was generous, and he was talking about travelling, selling our houses and starting again somewhere different. But I couldn't do that, I was willing to help him, to be his friend, maybe even to be his lover sometimes, but not to force my husband to give up his home and re-start life at his age."

"The opposite situation to the one when you wanted him to leave, but he refused because of the effect it would have on someone he loved."

"Yes, ironic isn't it."

"And then John was made redundant."

"Yes. Roger Grimshaw, the boss, imposed a cost-saving programme and a major part of it fell on Sales. And that's where Jack became involved. And then John committed suicide. The rest is history; the demonstrations, Jack's abduction and, thank God, his release."

"Was Jack unfair when he chose John for redundancy?"

"No, he was scrupulous in applying the rules, you wouldn't expect anything less from him. I've worked with Jack for years and he's a good man, always fair. In fact, I know he was worried about John when it happened. He realised this was a blow on top of the loss of his wife and Keira and asked if there was anything he could do to help. But John said 'no'; he was still trying to get me to leave my husband and buy-in to his romantic plans. But people didn't know about that, that's not what the media reported. They wrote about a man devastated by the loss of his wife and daughter and then losing his job."

"Well, I guess hearing the details rather detracts from the story; it waters down the drama, destroys the simplicity of the situation, makes it harder to make judgments." The priest sighed and ran his hand through his hair.

"And people do like being judgmental. I guess it brightens up their everyday existence," Alison said, "Makes them feel less insignificant, but it's not an attractive trait."

"I suppose it sometimes makes people feel worthier," the priest nodded, "Disguises their own feelings of guilt. But then, you have to feel sorry that this may be all they really feel able to be a part of, in a life that's otherwise dry and empty. That's why I became a priest; I believe that faith can inspire people, rescue them – although it can also be destructive. My job is to encourage the inspiration and combat the destructiveness. No fire and brimstone sermons on Sundays! Are you a believer?"

Alison shook her head.

"Me neither sometimes – but don't shout that around! There are occasions when even priests have doubts. So, what made you come to the church?"

"It's quiet and it makes me feel connected in some way. My family has lived in this part of the country for several generations – my grandmother used to come here after my grandfather died. I feel more at peace somehow when I'm here."

The priest smiled. "Not believing isn't a problem, my church is open to everyone. Carry on with your story."

"After the suicide some of the staff started blaming Jack for everything."

"They didn't blame the top man, the man who had initiated the redundancy programme?"

"No, I think that because Jack is such a nice guy, they felt they could blame him safely, but Grimshaw is scary, he can be hard, and that makes people afraid of him. They know what to expect if they cross him. And then the press started taking an interest and the whispering at work got even louder. But Max, the PR manager made sure that no names were released to the press, so it couldn't be the media that identified Jack as the person who'd actually fired John."

"So, you think it must be someone on the inside who identified him to his abductors – whoever they were."

"I suppose so, and that makes it more difficult. The police started interviewing people at work, to see if they could identify anyone who felt strongly enough to accuse Jack – but those investigations didn't get anywhere as far as I know."

"And you don't have any suspicions?"

"No," Alison shook her head, "Jack himself has no idea who abducted him, or where he was kept. They think the abductors used some kind of date-rape drug on him because he's no clear memory of how he was kidnapped and how he came to be released. But I just feel so guilty about it all."

"And that's why you come here?"

"Yes, it becomes unbearable at times. It's difficult to forgive myself for not telling the truth, about what really happened with John."

"Are you saying you feel responsible for what happened to the two men?"

"In some ways, although I think it was Keira's death that was mainly responsible for John's suicide. He turned to me again because her death had left him feeling such emptiness. But that placed me in an impossible position – upsetting John or upsetting my husband. The way I saw it, John had had the chance of being with me when I wanted him to leave home. Then John hung himself and if I'd revealed why, Jack may not have been kidnapped, but my husband would have found out about our affair and been just as devastated. It may have been a convenient excuse to hide behind, but I kept telling myself that Jack would be released eventually."

"Jack and his family being hurt temporarily, perhaps, or the final part of your husband's life ruined irrevocably? It's a difficult decision to make, and it wasn't you who created the situation that posed it. Ultimately, from what you've told me, it was a combination of events: Keira's death, John's devastation, your loyalty to your husband and the misguided beliefs everyone had about the actual cause of John's suicide and the desire amongst some of them to avenge him. Plus, of course, the political campaign against the way companies behave. So, what are you going to do now, I take it you still don't want anyone else to know what you've told me?"

Alison shook her head. "That's where I need your help. Even though Jack is safely home I'm sure he'll still feel the bad guy, responsible in some way for John's death. But, if he knew the whole story, how much Keira's death had weighed upon John and how John had seen his redundancy as an opportunity, not a tragedy, it would help him come to terms with himself. So, I'd like someone to talk to Jack and I've got no one else I can ask. The only condition is that Jack can't know it was me who was involved, I can't risk hurting my husband – avoiding him knowing about the affair was how this all started."

108

Roger looked-up from his computer, saw Max standing in the doorway of the office and waved him in. "Hi, Max, sit down," he motioned to a chair, "What can I do for you?"

Max sat down and placed his folder on the edge of Roger's desk. And then, before he could speak, Roger started talking again.

"Thank God all this business about Morrison and Jack is over. I've been meaning to have a chat with you, to say 'thank you' for your part in the way we managed it all."

"Well, thanks for that, Roger," the 'we' irritated Max, but he didn't respond. "Actually, that's the reason I've come in to see you."

Roger smiled briefly, trying to anticipate what Max had come to see him about.

"What I'd really like," Max paused and took an envelope out of the folder he was carrying, "Is to leave with your blessing, please Roger. The last few weeks have made me sit back and think about where I want to go with my life and I've decided it's time to move on, there's no more for me to do here. So, I'd like you to accept my resignation."

"But what about the programme you've put together for the rest of the year?"

"Obviously, I'll work out my notice period whilst you appoint my successor, assuming you decide you need to appoint one," he allowed himself a mental smile at the subtle dig at the irritating 'we', "But I need to move on and whoever takes over my role can manage the programme. I'm taking up a new role with a financial institution –

that's what I was concluding the night I met up with you and Margaret in the restaurant. It's exciting, I'm going to take a month off to organise my affairs and then I'm off to Singapore!"

Roger sat still, not knowing what to say – he knew how difficult it would be to replace Max, like it would be to replace Hilary, but he recovered quickly, stood up and held out his hand. "Congratulations, Max, you've done a great job here; I'm glad we've been able to help you showcase your talent, and this sounds like a terrific opportunity." When Max had left the room, he sat down again at his desk, holding his head in his hands.

"What's wrong?" Margaret had come in and was surprised to find him, sitting there, looking defeated.

"Max has just handed in his resignation – just when things were getting back to normal. I feel tired, very tired."

109

Jack picked-up the 'phone when it rang and asked who was calling. The man identified himself as the priest from a nearby Parish and said he needed to talk about John Morrison.

"I'm sorry, but I've nothing to say about John or his suicide, it's something that's caused a lot of pain to me and my family." Jack started to end the call, but the man interrupted him.

"No, please, just give me a moment, because what I've been asked to tell you may help alleviate that pain – it's something you should hear. The person who confided in me was insistent I speak to you, to put your conscience at ease."

Jack hesitated, unsure whether the call was some sort of hoax.

"I realise this must be rather sudden," the man continued, "But I really think that hearing what I've been asked to say will help you and your family put the matter behind you. And I think it's something we should discuss face-to-face. I'd be happy to talk to you and your wife, if you'd both like to come to see me."

"So, why are you hesitating?" Charlotte asked when he told her about the call. "He's asked you to go to the Rectory, so you know it's not a hoax and he seems quite insistent it will help us lay John's ghost, so to speak." She winced, jokingly, and then apologised for what she'd said, eyes raised heavenwards.

"I really don't know whether I want to go back over the same old ground." Jack shook his head as he spoke. "What else is there to be said that hasn't been said already? I'm tired of it all. And by the way," he reached out and placed his hands on her cheeks, smiling as he spoke to her, "It doesn't seem quite right, joking about John's death."

"I'm sorry, but I've got a feeling that this could be helpful." She stared up at him. "Why would someone insist on a priest contacting us, if it wasn't important?" She took his hands off her face and walked away, before turning round and teasing him. "It's like some form of divine intervention!"

He heard her running up the stairs after she'd ducked out of the room, giggling happily for the first time since he'd returned.

110

"You're sure you're ok about doing this?" Charlotte asked.

Jack nodded, waited for another car to cross the narrow bridge over the river, and then drove into the Rectory drive and parked. They walked together to the door and rang the bell. A woman with a smiley face opened it and ushered them in.

"You must be the Dochertys; nice to meet you. Trevor's in the garden, he likes to go there to think. Please," she opened a door into what appeared to be a study, "Take a seat, I'll let him know you're here."

The priest came in, introduced himself and asked if they'd like a cup of coffee or tea. When they declined, he shut the study door and thanked them for coming.

"Before you start," Jack said, "Can you give us a little more information about your source? How reliable are they? How closely were they involved in all of this?"

"I believe they're in the best position of anyone to know the truth behind John Morrison's death. But, before I start, how is Jack handling things following his release?" He looked at Charlotte as he asked the question, "I'm asking you to get the straightest answer possible as you know him better than anyone."

Charlotte glanced at Jack before responding. "Well, I think he's coping well. It must have been hell being locked up in a room on his own for over two weeks, but I think he's showed remarkable resilience."

"And what about blame, does he blame himself for his colleague's death?"

"I think he feels there were some confusing signals from John, in the time between his redundancy and suicide, but I'm not sure he blames himself – I think it would be more accurate to say he can't totally absolve himself from blame."

Trevor turned to Jack. "Is that how you see it?"

"Yes, I guess the best analogy is to compare it to a car accident where you know the other person was responsible, but you can't help asking yourself if there was something you could have done differently to avoid it."

"So, how long did you know John?"

"About twenty years I guess, ever since I joined the same company. He was older than me and had been there a couple of years already."

"And did you know him well?"

"Yes, we became quite good friends. We both enjoyed a game of snooker and played together every week at the local hall. But after a few years he seemed to lose interest and stopped going. We still got on well but weren't quite as close, and then I got promoted – John was never very ambitious."

"And how did he react, when you said he was being made redundant?"

"Well, obviously, after the loss of his wife and daughter I was very worried, but when I spoke to him about it, he said it was possibly the best thing that could have happened – the redundancy money would enable him to plan a new life and put the deaths behind him. I thought it was a bit of a strange reaction, but he seemed committed to the idea of moving away and starting over again."

"So, have you any idea why he stopped coming to the snooker hall with you?"

"As I said, I think he just lost interest."

"No, that wasn't the real reason," Trevor shook his head, "But what I'm going to tell you is in confidence and I'd like you both to give me your word not to reveal it to anyone else. And I realise that maintaining that confidence will be difficult for both of you, after you've heard what I've got to say." He paused and smiled at them, "I'm not sure whether you are believers, but, on this occasion, your reward has to be in heaven and not on earth."

Jack and Charlotte looked at each other and nodded their confirmation.

"Thank you," Trevor decided to begin with an assurance. "I think after you hear what I'm going to tell you, you can leave with the knowledge you weren't responsible for John's suicide. People have rushed to judgment without knowing the real facts. At the time of his wife's death, John was not in love with her – he hadn't been for a number of years. And the reason for giving up his snooker evenings was that he was having an affair. His wife still believed he was going out with you; he'd leave the house with his cue but go to meet a woman instead. She wanted him to leave his wife, but he wouldn't because he didn't want to lose his daughter. Then, after the accident he tried to persuade his former lover to leave home and move away with him, using the redundancy money to help finance their new life. But it was too late for her, and she turned him down. It was her refusal that compounded his feelings of loss after his daughter's death and possibly helped lead to his suicide."

Charlotte looked across at her husband, but Jack just sat still, his mouth slightly open as he tried to put together the pieces of what he'd heard.

"So, your kidnap and the protests were all based on a false premise, people adding two and two and coming up with any number other than four. People using John's death for their own purposes, which is why, even if you were tempted to say anything it would probably be pointless. The same people wouldn't want to listen – they'd be more likely to accuse you of trying to excuse your part in it all by blackening the name of a man who can no longer reply."

"Thank you," Charlotte responded on Jack's behalf.

"I hope that helps you come to terms with everything, Jack." The priest leaned forward in his chair.

"Yes," Jack still seemed confused by what he'd heard as he got up to leave. "Yes, it does, thank you."

111

Jim paused before making the call but told himself it was the right thing to do. Richie was a good guy and more capable than people gave him credit for. The issue, as far as Jim could see, was the type of organization Richie had been working for previously in his career and how his socialist beliefs were so at odds with the way companies conducted themselves. Until private businesses were in the hands of the people, Richie needed to work for a non-profit organization, one that obtained funds from different bodies, including private companies. He could imagine Richie's pleasure at taking money from the capitalists and using it for a socially desirable cause. It was a marriage made in heaven.

He made the call and reflected again on the solidarity at the heart of their socialist comrades. It's what set them apart from the capitalists, their organization and dedication to achieving a socialist future – instead of the constant warring to making more money and dominate everyone else. The lack of vision and constant competition would be the downfall of capitalism – as Marx had said, the last capitalist to hang would be the one who sold the rope. Jim played briefly with the idea, and then picked-up the phone – they needed loyal foot soldiers to achieve the revolution, foot soldiers like Richie. He heard the ringing tone a couple of times before Richie picked-up.

"Hi, it's Jim, I've got something you may be interested in – it's a great opportunity to make sure you're ok. I've been told there's a job going in a Charity, raising money in support of disadvantaged kids. One of the Councillors mentioned it to me. Could solve your money problems going forward."

"I guess it depends on what it pays," Richie sounded interested but hesitant. "Do Charities pay that much? And what would I have to do?"

"Well, it's not badly paid and it's for a great cause. And the best bit is that it's siphoning-off money from capitalist companies that want to pretend they care about social issues."

"That bit sounds good – exploiting the exploiters. But I've never done anything like that before. Why would they choose me for the job?"

"Don't angst, mate, we've got influence on the selection committee – comrades of ours. And the spotlight you helped to create about the guy who committed suicide and the bastard who sacked him has attracted some favourable attention amongst the party's top guys."

'Yeah, but it was the kidnapping that made it big news and the Worker earned the credit for digging out that story. The only good thing is that while we may not have had anything to do with his kidnapping, our demos may have persuaded someone else to do it."

"Hey, don't doubt yourself or the party, mate, whether the guy deserved to be kidnapped or not, it highlighted an important issue – struck a blow for the working class."

" I know, the ends justify the means and all that."

"Exactly. You know what Marx said: 'We have no compassion, and we ask no compassion from you'. This is a war, a war to free the working class. And that's why you should go for this job, help give working class kids similar opportunities to privileged kids – and the pay's not bad either. All you have to do is convince the panel you're committed and can help raise funds."

"It sounds good, Jim, I've got to admit I don't feel fucking comfortable doing what I've been doing so far and ripping-off people for some rich bastard or businessman. How do I get to apply?"

"I'll send you a link. If you want to chat about what to put on the form, give me a call. Give me a call anyway and come over for a drink. It'll be great to see you. This could be a new start – the job's made for you."

112

After the corporate day was over, Misty decided to look at the building from which she'd seen the woman returning to her car on her previous visit. Still intrigued by the strong feelings she'd experienced when she'd last visited the location, she was determined to investigate further. She spoke to Gill, who was making the final arrangements for the vacating of the factory they'd been using, and walked towards the building she'd seen the woman emerge from. It was one of the smaller buildings on the site with windowless walls forming most of the ground floor, a small retail space at the front, and offices above. She guessed it may have been used as a bakery or some similar business.

As she approached, she'd expected to feel some sort of excitement, a subconscious thrill but, instead, she felt nothing. She walked across to one of the windows and peered through, her hand held above her eyes to remove any glare from the glass and see more clearly. There was nothing that would suggest any recent use, a tiled floor, a bare counter and some racking. No sign of any activity. The door into the remainder of the ground floor was open and, as far as she could see, there was just an empty, dark space behind. Disappointed, she made her way back to the building they'd been using for the event and met Gill coming out.

"Well, what did you find?" Gill asked.

"Nothing, the building was empty." Misty shook her head, "I guess I just fell into the same mistake we've been warning about all day, that it's easy to make assumptions, and easy for one's intuition to be misguided."

113

A few weeks later the wrecking gangs and bulldozers moved into the old estate. Allan was passing and stopped to watch. They'd been meticulously careful, clearing the room in which they'd kept Docherty of everything that was left, but he still felt relief as the demolition took place. With the building gone there'd be no evidence to find, just a pile of rubble. When he got home and told Heather she placed her hands together as though she was praying, closed her eyes and, for the first time in weeks, began to relax.

"That's great news, I should have trusted you more; it's worked out like you said it would. By the way, Susan called earlier, she said she needed to come round and show us something she's found amongst some of John's papers. I asked when she wanted to come, and she said to call her when you got back in. Said it was urgent but wouldn't tell me anymore over the phone."

When Susan arrived, she was carrying a shopping bag. Heather ushered her into the lounge and, when she'd sat down, she took out a child's small toy case.

"I recognise that," Allan pointed at the case, "That's John's treasure case, from when he was a boy, the one in which he stored all his most precious things. He kept his old penknife from the cubs in it, his exam results and other things that marked important points in his life."

Susan nodded, grim-faced. "I don't think you're going to like this Allan, but he also kept something far more recent in it, I think we've probably found the reason John committed suicide. I was going through the papers I brought back from his house and looked in his case, like we used to when he was young, and I found this." She reached inside, took out an opened envelope addressed to John, and passed it across to her brother.

Allan looked at the envelope but didn't take it from her at first, "What's in it?"

"You need to read it, it's a letter from Faith."

Allan was reluctant to take the envelope, but she waved it at him urging him to take it. It's postmarked a few days before he killed himself."

"I gather it's not good," Allan accepted the envelope and started to take out the sheets of paper inside, but the look on his sister's face made him stop, and he stared across at her for some indication of the gravity of the contents.

"It's worse than not good," Susan's lip begun to quiver, "It's far worse than that, it's evil."

As Allan unfolded the letter Susan began to cry. Heather put her arm round her, staring across at her husband and trying to read his expression as he started to read.

'Dear John,

If you read this letter, I will be dead, because it contains a secret I would never divulge otherwise. If you'd died before me, I'd have told Keira what I'm now telling you. I want you both to know the truth.

Ours hasn't been a happy marriage, but I realise you know that as well as I do. When we met and first married, I had such dreams and believed you would help me make them come true. Dreams of a better life, of achievement, of being looked-up to, but those dreams faded when it became clear you didn't share them. For you it was more important to enjoy an easy life and be liked by other people.

And people did like you, you had such charm. If you'd applied yourself to your career nothing could have stopped you, with all the natural advantages you had. But you didn't.

I worked in those early years, to help us get a start in life. After a while, I got a job at the Cornford Hotel and I met a very different man from you, tougher, more ambitious, a man who showed all those attributes you lacked. We began an affair and, mentally, I was preparing to leave you. Then I fell pregnant – I knew the baby wasn't yours because we hadn't slept together for a while. But after I went on maternity leave, the man started seeing other women and I felt betrayed. And then the man was sacked when a maid complained about him assaulting her in one of the bedrooms.

I still intended to leave you, but having a young baby meant I needed your support. Keira brought us together temporarily and I prayed you would show more ambition, to succeed – for her if you weren't prepared to succeed for me. I loved Keira unreservedly and you made a superb father. But she was my baby not yours. And then, one day, I realised she loved the man she called 'daddy' even more than she loved me, her birth mother.

You have no idea how difficult I found that, to be jealous of my own daughter and her relationship with the husband who had let me down as surely as her real father had. As she grew up, I knew that if I tried to leave, she would choose you, rather than me, and I couldn't have borne that, which is the only reason I stayed with you all this time.

But now I'm no longer here, to feel the disappointment of losing her, I hope you will have the courage to tell her the truth, that the 'father' she loves is an impostor, a man who denied both *her and her mother the good things we might all have enjoyed in life if he hadn't wasted the God-given advantages he enjoyed.*

I resent what you did, taking my daughter away from me with that easy-going charm. How dare you have made her love you in the way you did, displacing me in her affections. So, for once in your life act like a real man, stop living the lie you have lived all these years and tell her the truth – that you're not her father. Tell her it was me that conceived and loved her and continued to love her throughout her life.

You stopped me having the life I wanted, but now it's you who will have to face up to failure. Whether she decides to stay your 'daughter' or not, things will be bound to change when you tell her the truth. Even your charm may not be enough to keep her. As for me, I'm beyond hurting and hope to God she rejects you.'

When he'd finished reading, Allan passed the letter across to Heather without saying anything and watched as she read it. "That's brutal," she said as she finished and handed it back, "She must have really hated him to leave a letter like that."

"I suppose she never thought that she and Keira would both die at the same time," Susan had composed herself, "But it's still evil, John couldn't possibly have deserved that, he was far too generous a person. And the hardest thing is that he had no way back, no way of making any sense of his life anymore with both Keira and Faith dead."

"Where did the letter come from?" Allan looked at the sender's address on the back and recognised the name of one of Faith's cousins. He pointed at the name and asked Susan if she'd contacted them.

Susan nodded, "She said Faith gave her the letter some years back and asked her to send it if she died before John. She had no idea what was inside. The woman's a widow, she's been staying with her daughter in Australia and didn't hear about Faith's death until she got back. That's why it was so late arriving."

"But why would John keep the letter, especially in his 'treasure' case?" Heather was confused, "It must have blown his world apart."

"Perhaps he couldn't get rid of it yet, needed to read it over again to come to terms with it. Or maybe, he knew we would be likely to look in his case, it was special, he and I used to play with it all the time when we were kids." Susan held the case closely. "He may not have wanted anyone else to know, it could be intended as a type of suicide note, just for us to find and understand why he did what he did – he didn't leave any other explanation."

Allan stood up and walked across to the window, looking out at the garden, remembering what they had done to Docherty in John's name and the tensions it had caused between him and Heather. "I hope Faith rots in hell. She killed John as surely as if she'd kicked the stool away herself." He spat the words out and ripped the letter in two, "Nobody else must ever see this."

ALSO FEATURING JONAH

JONAH AND FRIENDS

Jonah is homeless and wanders the streets. Grateful and grumpy in turn, smiling when people give him money and scowling when they brush him aside. He's an observer, a looker-on, and sometimes a trigger for other events. Some of these stories are about him, in others he's just a passer-by - there fleetingly, as the people around him live out their own stories. Welcome to the world of Jonah and his 'friends'.

THE RETURN

It's the start of a nightmare when Laura's former boyfriend discovers she has a new relationship. Darren insists that it's him who decides when their relationship is over, despite Laura ending it when he went to prison. He threatens to punish Andy, her new man, unless Laura agrees to a humiliating proposition. When she refuses, Laura and Andy find themselves facing Darren alone, except for a small number of close friends and, ultimately, the Marsh brothers - two men more frightening than Darren himself.

ABOUT ROBERT COULSDON

As a child, I wanted to be a hero, like the ones on tv or in films. And so, I made up stories. At first, the stories were mental fantasies, waking dreams in the daytime or imagined adventures at night. But, as soon as I'd learned how to spell and print words, I started to write.

I suppose it was a way of experiencing something more exciting than school and, later, more exciting than work. Something to take me away from the mundane, everyday world, but I never seemed to have the time or discipline to finish anything other than short stories, which is when Jonah came into my life.

I started life in South London, a boy playing on the streets, surrounded by a large family who all lived within walking distance of each other. Then I moved away, to the country and played in woods and made camps, exhilarated by the excitement and freedom. Since then, I've lived in many places, in the UK and abroad, some exciting, some not.

Now, I live by the sea in Southern England and, with fewer distractions, I've found more time to write, and more time to spend with Jonah, sharing the streets and the lives of him and the people who inhabit his world.

www.ingramcontent.com/pod-product-compliance
Lightning Source LLC
Chambersburg PA
CBHW071129200626

46817CB00018B/2487